Hester Burton

Ian Serraillier

Ursula Williams.

Leon Garfield.

James Reeves

Eilis Dillon

Trease

Noel Streatfeild

William Mayne

Mary Treadgold.

AUTHORS' CHOICE

AUTHORS' CHOICE

STORIES CHOSEN BY

GILLIAN AVERY	HESTER BURTON
PAULINE CLARKE	EILÍS DILLON
LEON GARFIELD	ALAN GARNER
JANET McNEILL	WILLIAM MAYNE
JAMES REEVES	IAN SERRAILLIER
NOEL STREATFEILD	ROSEMARY SUTCLIFF
MARY TREADGOLD	GEOFFREY TREASE
ELFRIDA VIPONT	BARBARA WILLARD

URSULA MORAY WILLIAMS

ILLUSTRATED BY KRYSTYNA TURSKA

HAMISH HAMILTON
LONDON

This anthology first published in Great Britain 1970
by Hamish Hamilton Children's Books Ltd
90 Great Russell Street London WC1
© in this collection
Hamish Hamilton Children's Books Ltd 1970
Printed in Great Britain by
Western Printing Services Ltd, Bristol
SBN 241 01830 7

Acknowledgements

The Publishers are indebted to the following for the use of copyright material: The Society of Authors, London, as the literary representatives of Katherine Mansfield, and Alfred A. Knopf Inc., Publishers, New York, for permission to include *The Doll's House* from THE SELECTED STORIES OF KATHERINE MANSFIELD, copyright 1923 by Alfred A. Knopf Inc. and renewed 1951 by John Middleton Murry; A. D. Peters & Co. Ltd., London, and Harold Matson Company, Inc., New York, for permission to include *The Fog Horn* from THE GOLDEN APPLES OF THE SUN by Ray Bradbury, copyright 1951 by The Curtis Publishing Company; A. D. Peters & Co. Ltd., London, and Alfred A. Knopf Inc., New York, for permission to include *First Confession* from TRAVELLER'S SAMPLES by Frank O'Connor; David Higham Associates, London, and A. Watkins, Inc., New York, for permission to include *The Tower* by Marghanita Laski; Ernest Benn Ltd., London, and Henry Z. Walck, Inc., New York, for permission to include *The Fillyjonk Who Believed in Disasters* from TALES FROM MOOMIN VALLEY by Tove Jansson; Thomas Nelson & Sons Ltd., London, for permission to include *The Tale of the Silver Saucer and the Transparent Apple* from OLD PETER'S RUSSIAN TALES by Arthur Ransome; George G. Harrap & Co. Ltd., London, and Harold Matson Company, Inc., New York, for permission to include *Spit Nolan* from THE GOALKEEPER'S REVENGE by Bill Naughton; A. M. Heath & Co. Ltd., London, and the Estate of the late Elizabeth Enright for permission to include *A Christmas Tree for Lydia* by Elizabeth Enright; Mrs. George Bambridge, Macmillan & Company, London, and Doubleday & Company, Inc., New York, for permission to include *The Maltese Cat* from THE DAY'S WORK by Rudyard Kipling and *The Miracle of Purun Bhagat* from THE SECOND JUNGLE BOOK by Rudyard Kipling; David Higham Associates, London, for permission to include *The Glass Peacock* from THE LITTLE BOOKROOM by Eleanor Farjeon; Jonathan Cape, Ltd., London, and Doubleday & Company, Inc., New York, for permission to include *All You've Ever Wanted* by Joan Aiken; The Bodley Head Ltd., London, for permission to include *Its Walls Were As of Jasper* from DREAM DAYS by Kenneth Grahame.

The Publishers also acknowledge the following editions from which

v

ACKNOWLEDGEMENTS

out of copyright material was obtained: THE BODLEY HEAD SAKI
from which *The Lull* by Saki was taken; FAIRY TALES AND LEGENDS
BY HANS ANDERSEN, illustrated by Rex Whistler and published by The
Bodley Head, from which *The Emperor's New Clothes* was taken; an
edition of Jane Austen's minor works selected from the definitive text of
Professor R. W. Chapman, published by The Oxford University Press,
from which *The History of England* was taken.

The Publishers acknowledge with thanks the help of the authors who
have co-operated in the preparation of this volume by supplying introductory notes and biographical details; the latter can be found at the
end of the book from page 207 onwards.

Contents

THE DOLL'S HOUSE   *Katherine Mansfield*   1
Chosen by Gillian Avery

THE FOG HORN   *Ray Bradbury*   11
Chosen by Hester Burton

THE LULL   *Saki*   23
Chosen by Pauline Clarke

FIRST CONFESSION   *Frank O'Connor*   31
Chosen by Eilís Dillon

HISTORY OF ENGLAND   *Jane Austen*   41
Chosen by Leon Garfield

THE TOWER   *Marghanita Laski*   53
Chosen by Alan Garner

THE EMPEROR'S NEW CLOTHES   *Hans Andersen*   63
Chosen by Janet McNeill

THE FILLYJONK WHO BELIEVED
IN DISASTERS   *Tove Jansson*   71
Chosen by William Mayne

THE TALE OF THE SILVER
SAUCER AND THE TRANS-
PARENT APPLE   *Arthur Ransome*   87
Chosen by James Reeves

SPIT NOLAN   *Bill Naughton*   101
Chosen by Ian Serraillier

A CHRISTMAS TREE FOR LYDIA   *Elizabeth Enright*   111
Chosen by Noel Streatfeild

THE MIRACLE OF PURUN BHAGAT   *Rudyard Kipling*   123
Chosen by Rosemary Sutcliff

THE GLASS PEACOCK   *Eleanor Farjeon*   139
Chosen by Mary Treadgold

ALL YOU'VE EVER WANTED   *Joan Aiken*   149
Chosen by Geoffrey Trease

OUR FIELD   *Mrs. Ewing*   159
Chosen by Elfrida Vipont

vii

CONTENTS

THE MALTESE CAT   *Rudyard Kipling*   171
  Chosen by Barbara Willard

ITS WALLS WERE AS OF JASPER   *Kenneth Grahame*   193
  Chosen by Ursula Moray Williams

THE CHOOSERS   207

THE CHOSEN AUTHORS   215

The Doll's House

BY KATHERINE MANSFIELD
CHOSEN BY GILLIAN AVERY

The Doll's House was written in 1921, two years before Katherine Mansfield's death from consumption at the early age of 34. In her Journal that year she made brief notes on the stories that she planned for a new volume, and under the title of *At Karori* there appeared the following: "The little lamp. I seen it. And then they were silent." These are, little altered, the closing words of the story which was ultimately published as *The Doll's House*, and they bring a touch of happiness to a sad and moving tale.

When I first read *The Doll's House* seventeen years ago I felt both guilt and shame. I could see aspects of myself in three sets of the characters. I recognised one aspect in the wretched Kelvey children, because I remembered that there had been a time when, as a small girl, I would have accepted any humiliation, any insult, just to be liked. The same longing to be liked and to stand well with the other children at school would have made me, I guiltily suspected, side with the crowd who in the story despise and torment the Kelveys. My better self might have told me that they were base and cruel, but I doubt whether I would have dared to say so aloud. And finally, I knew how fatally easy it was to behave like Aunt Beryl in the concluding paragraphs—to kick out savagely at something or somebody just because one has been kicked oneself.

Katherine Mansfield was a master of the short-story form. In these two or three thousand words she conveys, chiefly by the use of conversation, the characters of the three little Burnell girls, their young aunt, and the outcast Kelvey children, and also the character of the community in which they live. The setting is New Zealand, where the author spent her childhood.

GILLIAN AVERY

WHEN dear old Mrs. Hay went back to town after staying with the Burnells she sent the children a doll's house. It was so big that the carter and Pat carried it into the courtyard, and there it stayed, propped up on two wooden boxes beside the feed-room door. No harm could come to it; it was summer. And perhaps the smell of paint would have gone off by the time it had to be taken in. For, really, the smell of paint coming from that doll's house ("Sweet of old Mrs. Hay of course; most sweet and generous!")—but the smell of paint was quite enough to make anyone seriously ill, in Aunt Beryl's opinion. Even before the sacking was taken off. And when it was . . .

There stood the doll's house, a dark, oily, spinach green, picked out with bright yellow. Its two solid little chimneys, glued on to the roof, were painted red and white, and the door, gleaming with yellow varnish, was like a little slab of toffee. Four windows, real windows, were divided into panes by a broad streak of green. There was actually a tiny porch, too, painted yellow, with big lumps of congealed paint hanging along the edge.

But perfect, perfect little house! Who could possibly mind the smell. It was part of the joy, part of the newness.

"Open it quickly, someone!"

The hook at the side was stuck fast. Pat prised it open with his penknife, and the whole house front swung back, and—there you were, gazing at one and the same moment into the drawing-room and dining-room, the kitchen and two bedrooms. That is the way for a house to open! Why don't all houses open like that? How much more exciting than peering through the slit of a door into a mean little hall with a hat-stand and two umbrellas! That is—isn't it?—what you long to know about a house when you put your hand on the knocker. Perhaps it is the way God opens houses at the dead of night when He is taking a quiet turn with an angel. . . .

"Oh-oh!" The Burnell children sounded as though they were in despair. It was too marvellous; it was too much for them. They had never seen anything like it in their lives. All the rooms were papered. There were pictures on the walls, painted on the paper, with gold frames complete. Red carpet covered all the floors except the kitchen; red plush chairs in the drawing-room, green in the dining-room; tables, beds with real bed-clothes, a cradle, a stove, a dresser with tiny plates and one big jug. But what Kezia liked more than anything, what she liked frightfully, was the lamp. It stood in the middle of the dining-room table, an exquisite little amber lamp with a white globe. It was even filled all ready for lighting, though, of course, you couldn't light it. But there was something inside that looked like oil and moved when you shook it.

The father and mother dolls, who sprawled very stiff as though they had fainted in the drawing-room, and their two little children asleep upstairs, were really too big for the doll's house. They didn't look as though they belonged. But the lamp was perfect. It seemed to smile at Kezia, to say, "I live here." The lamp was real.

The Burnell children could hardly walk to school fast enough the next morning. They burned to tell everybody, to describe, to—well—to boast about their doll's house before the school-bell rang.

"I'm to tell," said Isabel, "because I'm the eldest. And you two can join in after. But I'm to tell first."

There was nothing to answer. Isabel was bossy, but she was always right, and Lottie and Kezia knew too well the powers that went with being eldest. They brushed through the thick buttercups at the road edge and said nothing.

"And I'm to choose who's to come and see it first. Mother said I might."

For it had been arranged that while the doll's house stood in the courtyard they might ask the girls at school, two at a time, to come and look. Not to stay to tea, of course, or to come traipsing through the house. But just to stand quietly in the courtyard while Isabel pointed out the beauties, and Lottie and Kezia looked pleased. . . .

But hurry as they might, by the time they had reached the tarred palings of the boys' playground the bell had begun to jangle. They only just had time to whip off their hats and fall into line before the roll was called. Never mind. Isabel tried to make up for it by looking very important and mysterious and by whispering behind her hand to the girls near her, "Got something to tell you at playtime."

Playtime came and Isabel was surrounded. The girls of her class nearly fought to put their arms round her, to walk away with her, to beam flatteringly, to be her special friend. She held quite a court under the huge pine trees at the side of the playground. Nudging, giggling together, the little girls pressed up close. And the only two who stayed outside the ring were the two who were always outside, the little Kelveys. They knew better than to come anywhere near the Burnells.

For the fact was, the school the Burnell children went to was not at all the kind of place their parents would have chosen if there had been any choice. But there was none. It was the only school for miles. And the consequence was all the children of the neighbourhood, the Judge's little girls, the doctor's daughters, the store-keeper's children, the milkman's, were forced to mix together. Not to speak of there being an equal number of rude, rough little boys as well. But the line had to be drawn somewhere. It was drawn at the Kelveys. Many of the children, including the Burnells, were not allowed even to speak to them. They walked past the Kelveys with their heads in the air, and as they set the fashion in all matters of behaviour, the Kelveys were shunned by everybody. Even the teacher had a special voice for them, and a special smile for the other children when Lil Kelvey came up to her desk with a bunch of dreadfully common-looking flowers.

They were the daughters of a spry, hard-working little washerwoman, who went about from house to house by the day. This was awful enough. But where was Mr. Kelvey? Nobody knew for certain. But everybody said he was in prison. So they were the daughters of a washerwoman and a gaolbird. Very nice company for other people's children! And they looked it. Why Mrs. Kelvey made them so conspicuous was hard to understand. The truth was they were dressed in "bits" given to her by the people for whom she worked. Lil, for instance, who was a stout, plain child, with big freckles, came to school in a dress made from a green art-serge tablecloth of the Burnells', with red plush sleeves from the Logans' curtains. Her hat, perched on top of her high forehead, was a grown-up woman's hat, once the property of Miss Lecky, the postmistress. It was turned up at the back and trimmed with a large scarlet quill. What a little guy she looked! It was impossible not to laugh. And her little sister, our Else, wore a long white dress, rather like a nightgown, and a pair of little boy's boots. But whatever our Else wore she would have looked strange. She was a tiny wishbone of a child, with cropped hair and enormous solemn eyes—a little white owl. Nobody had ever seen her smile; she scarcely ever spoke. She went through life holding on to Lil, with a piece of Lil's skirt screwed up in her hand. Where Lil went, our Else followed. In the playground, on the road going to and from school, there was Lil marching in front and our Else holding on behind. Only when she wanted anything, or when she was out of breath, our Else gave Lil a tug, a twitch, and Lil stopped and turned round. The Kelveys never failed to understand each other.

Now they hovered at the edge; you couldn't stop them listening. When the little girls turned round and sneered, Lil, as usual, gave her silly, shamefaced smile, but our Else only looked.

And Isabel's voice, so very proud, went on telling. The carpet made a great sensation, but so did the beds with real bedclothes, and the stove with an oven door.

When she finished Kezia broke in. "You've forgotten the lamp, Isabel."

"Oh yes," said Isabel, "and there's a teeny little lamp, all made of yellow glass, with a white globe that stands on the dining-room table. You couldn't tell it from a real one."

"The lamp's best of all," cried Kezia. She thought Isabel wasn't making half enough of the little lamp. But nobody paid any attention. Isabel was choosing the two who were to come back with them that afternoon and see it. She chose Emmie Cole and Lena Logan. But when the others knew they were all to have a chance, they couldn't be nice enough to Isabel. One by one they put their arms round Isabel's waist and walked her off. They had something to whisper to her, a secret. "Isabel's *my* friend."

Only the little Kelveys moved away forgotten; there was nothing more for them to hear.

Days passed, and as more children saw the doll's house, the fame of it spread. It became the one subject, the rage. The one question was, "Have you seen Burnells' doll's house? Oh, ain't it lovely!" "Haven't you seen it? Oh, I say!"

Even the dinner hour was given up to talking about it. The little girls sat under the pines eating their thick mutton sandwiches and big slabs of johnny cake spread with butter. While always, as near as they could get, sat the Kelveys, our Else holding on to Lil, listening too, while they chewed their jam sandwiches out of a newspaper soaked with large red blobs.

"Mother," said Kezia, "can't I ask the Kelveys just once?"

"Certainly not, Kezia."

"But why not?"

"Run away, Kezia; you know quite well why not."

At last everybody had seen it except them. On that day the subject rather flagged. It was the dinner hour. The children stood together under the pine trees, and suddenly, as they looked at the Kelveys eating out of their paper, always by themselves, always listening, they wanted to be horrid to them. Emmie Cole started the whisper.

"Lil Kelvey's going to be a servant when she grows up."

"O-oh, how awful!" said Isabel Burnell, and she made eyes at Emmie.

7

Emmie swallowed in a very meaning way and nodded to Isabel as she'd seen her mother do on those occasions.

"It's true—it's true—it's true," she said.

Then Lena Logan's little eyes snapped. "Shall I ask her?" she whispered.

"Bet you don't," said Jessie May.

"Pooh, I'm not frightened," said Lena. Suddenly she gave a little squeal and danced in front of the other girls. "Watch! Watch me! Watch me now!" said Lena. And sliding, gliding, dragging one foot, giggling behind her hand, Lena went over to the Kelveys.

Lil looked up from her dinner. She wrapped the rest quickly away. Our Else stopped chewing. What was coming now?

"Is it true you're going to be a servant when you grow up, Lil Kelvey?" shrilled Lena.

Dead silence. But instead of answering, Lil only gave her silly, shamefaced smile. She didn't seem to mind the question at all. What a sell for Lena! The girls began to titter.

Lena couldn't stand that. She put her hands on her hips; she shot forward. "Yah, yer father's in prison!" she hissed spitefully.

This was such a marvellous thing to have said that the little girls rushed away in a body, deeply, deeply excited, wild with joy. Someone found a long rope, and they began skipping. And never did they skip so high, run in and out so fast, or do such daring things as on that morning.

In the afternoon Pat called for the Burnell children with the buggy and they drove home. There were visitors. Isabel and Lottie, who liked visitors, went upstairs to change their pinafores. But Kezia thieved out at the back. Nobody was about; she began to swing on the big white gates of the courtyard. Presently, looking along the road, she saw two little dots. They grew bigger, they were coming towards her. Now she could see that one was in front and one close behind. Now she could see that they were the Kelveys. Kezia stopped swinging. She slipped off the gate as if she was going to run away. Then she hesitated. The Kelveys came nearer, and beside them walked their shadows,

8

very long, stretching right across the road with their heads in the buttercups. Kezia clambered back on the gate; she had made up her mind; she swung out.

"Hullo," she said to the passing Kelveys.

They were so astounded that they stopped. Lil gave her silly smile. Our Else stared.

"You can come and see our doll's house if you want to," said Kezia, and she dragged one toe on the ground. But at that Lil turned red and shook her head quickly.

"Why not?" asked Kezia.

Lil gasped, then she said, "Your ma told our ma you wasn't to speak to us."

"Oh, well," said Kezia. She didn't know what to reply. "It doesn't matter. You can come and see our doll's house all the same. Come on. Nobody's looking."

But Lil shook her head still harder.

"Don't you want to?" asked Kezia.

Suddenly there was a twitch, a tug at Lil's skirt. She turned round. Our Else was looking at her with big, imploring eyes; she was frowning; she wanted to go. For a moment Lil looked at our Else very doubtfully. But then our Else twitched her skirt again. She started forward. Kezia led the way. Like two little stray cats they followed across the courtyard to where the doll's house stood.

"There it is," said Kezia.

There was a pause. Lil breathed loudly, almost snorted; our Else was still as stone.

"I'll open it for you," said Kezia kindly. She undid the hook and they looked inside.

"There's the drawing-room and the dining-room, and that's the—"

"Kezia!"

Oh, what a start they gave!

"Kezia!"

It was Aunt Beryl's voice. They turned round. At the back door stood Aunt Beryl, staring as if she couldn't believe what she saw.

9

"How dare you ask the little Kelveys into the courtyard!" said her cold, furious voice. "You know as well as I do, you're not allowed to talk to them. Run away, children, run away at once. And don't come back again," said Aunt Beryl. And she stepped into the yard and shooed them out as if they were chickens.

"Off you go immediately!" she called, cold and proud.

They did not need telling twice. Burning with shame, shrinking together, Lil huddling along like her mother, our Else dazed, somehow they crossed the big courtyard and squeezed through the white gate.

"Wicked, disobedient little girl!" said Aunt Beryl bitterly to Kezia, and she slammed the doll's house to.

The afternoon had been awful. A letter had come from Willie Brent, a terrifying, threatening letter, saying if she did not meet him that evening in Pulman's Bush, he'd come to the front door and ask the reason why! But now that she had frightened those little rats of Kelveys and given Kezia a good scolding, her heart felt lighter. That ghastly pressure was gone. She went back to the house humming.

When the Kelveys were well out of sight of Burnells', they sat down to rest on a big red drainpipe by the side of the road. Lil's cheeks were still burning; she took off the hat with the quill and held it on her knee. Dreamily they looked over the hay paddocks, past the creek, to the group of wattles where Logan's cows stood waiting to be milked. What were their thoughts?

Presently our Else nudged up close to her sister. But now she had forgotten the cross lady. She put out a finger and stroked her sister's quill; she smiled her rare smile.

"I seen the little lamp," she said softly.

Then both were silent once more.

THE FOG HORN

BY RAY BRADBURY
CHOSEN BY HESTER BURTON

RAY BRADBURY is a splendid writer of science fiction. I like his work because it is both exciting and poetic and because, unlike so much in modern life, it evokes a sense of wonder. *The Fog Horn* moves me particularly because it deals not with man's future among the stars but with earth's primeval past. The pathos of a survivor of that long-dead past seeking affection and an end to loneliness in the familiar coastal waters of the present continues to haunt me long after I have ceased to shiver down the spine.

HESTER BURTON

OUT THERE in the cold water, far from land, we waited every night for the coming of the fog, and it came, and we oiled the brass machinery and lit the fog light up in the stone tower. Feeling like two birds in the grey sky, McDunn and I sent the light touching out, red, then white, then red again, to eye the lonely ships. And if they did not see our light, then there was always our Voice, the great deep cry of our Fog Horn shuddering through the rags of mist to startle the gulls away like packs of scattered cards, and make the waves turn high and foam.

"It's a lonely life, but you're used to it now, aren't you?" asked McDunn.

"Yes," I said. "You're a good talker, thank the Lord."

"Well, it's your turn on land tomorrow," he said, smiling, "to dance the ladies and drink gin."

"What do you think, McDunn, when I leave you out here alone?"

"On the mysteries of the sea." McDunn lit his pipe. It was a quarter past seven of a cold November evening, the heat on, the light switching its tail in two hundred directions, the Fog Horn bumbling in the high throat of the tower. There wasn't a town for a hundred miles down the coast, just a road which came lonely through dead country to the sea, with few cars on it, a stretch of two miles of cold water out to our rock, and rare few ships.

"The mysteries of the sea," said McDunn thoughtfully. "You know, the ocean's the biggest damned snowflake ever? It rolls and swells a thousand shapes and colours, no two alike. Strange. One night, years ago, I was here alone, when all of the fish of the sea surfaced out there. Something made them swim in and lie in the bay, sort of trembling and staring up at the tower light going red, white, red, white across them so I could see their funny eyes. I turned cold. They were like a big peacock's tail, moving out there until midnight. Then, without so much as a sound, they slipped away, the million of them was gone. I kind of think maybe, in some sort of way, they came all those miles to worship. Strange. But think how the tower must look to them, standing seventy feet above the water, the God-light flashing out from it, and the tower declaring itself with a monster voice. They never came back, those fish, but don't you think for a while they thought they were in the Presence?"

I shivered. I looked out at the long grey lawn of the sea stretching away into nothing and nowhere.

"Oh, the sea's full." McDunn puffed his pipe nervously. blinking. He had been nervous all day and hadn't said why. "For all our engines and so-called submarines, it'll be ten thousand centuries before we set foot on the real bottom of the sunken lands, in the fairy kingdoms there, and know *real* terror. Think of it, it's still the year 300,000 Before Christ down under there. While we've paraded around with trumpets, lopping off each other's countries and heads, they have been living beneath the sea twelve miles deep and cold in a time as old as the beard of a comet."

"Yes, it's an old world."

"Come on. I got something special I been saving up to tell you."

We ascended the eighty steps, talking and taking our time. At the top, McDunn switched off the room lights so there'd be no reflection in the plate glass. The great eye of the light was humming, turning easily in its oiled socket. The Fog Horn was blowing steadily, once every fifteen seconds.

"Sounds like an animal, don't it?" McDunn nodded to himself. "A big lonely animal crying in the night. Sitting here on the edge of ten billion years calling out to the Deeps, I'm here, I'm here, I'm here. And the Deeps *do* answer, yes, they do. You been here now for three months, Johnny, so I better prepare you. About this time of year," he said, studying the murk and fog, "something comes to visit the lighthouse."

"The swarms of fish like you said?"

"No, this is something else. I've put off telling you because you might think I'm daft. But tonight's the latest I can put it off, for if my calendar's marked right from last year, tonight's the night it comes. I won't go into detail, you'll have to see it yourself. Just sit down there. If you want, tomorrow you can pack your duffel and take the motorboat in to land and get your car parked there at the dinghy pier on the cape and drive on back to some little inland town and keep your lights burning nights, I won't question or blame you. It's happened three years now, and this is the only time anyone's been here with me to verify it. You wait and watch."

Half an hour passed with only a few whispers between us. When we grew tired waiting, McDunn began describing some of his ideas to me. He had some theories about the Fog Horn itself.

"One day many years ago a man walked along and stood in the sound of the ocean on a cold sunless shore and said, 'We need a voice to call across the water, to warn ships; I'll make one. I'll make a voice like all of time and all of the fog that ever was; I'll make a voice that is like an empty bed beside you all night long, and like an empty house when you open the door, and like trees in autumn with no leaves. A sound like the birds flying south, crying, and a sound like November wind and the sea on the hard, cold shore. I'll make a sound that's so alone that no one can miss it, that whoever hears it will weep in their souls, and hearths will seem warmer, and being inside will seem better to all who hear it in the distant towns. I'll make me a sound and an apparatus and they'll call it a Fog Horn and whoever hears it will know the sadness of eternity and the briefness of life.' "

The Fog Horn blew.

"I made up that story," said McDunn quietly, "to try to explain why this thing keeps coming back to the lighthouse every year. The Fog Horn calls it, I think, and it comes . . ."

"But—" I said.

"Sssst!" said McDunn. "There!" He nodded out to the Deeps.

Something was swimming towards the lighthouse tower.

It was a cold night, as I have said; the high tower was cold, the light coming and going, and the Fog Horn calling and calling through the ravelling mist. You couldn't see far and you couldn't see plain, but there was the deep sea moving on its way about the night earth, flat and quiet, the colour of grey mud, and here were the two of us alone in the high tower, and there, far out at first, was a ripple, followed by a wave, a rising, a bubble, a bit of froth. And then, from the surface of the cold sea came a head, a large head, dark-coloured, with immense eyes, and then a neck. And then—not a body—but more neck and more! The head rose a full forty feet above the water on a slender and beautiful dark neck. Only then did the body, like a little island of black coral and shells and cray-fish, drip up from the subterranean. There was a flicker of tail. In all, from head to tip of tail, I estimated the monster at ninety or a hundred feet.

I don't know what I said. I said something.

"Steady, boy, steady," whispered McDunn.

"It's impossible!" I said.

"No, Johnny, *we're* impossible. *It's* like it always was ten million years ago. *It* hasn't changed. It's *us* and the land that've changed, become impossible. *Us!*"

It swam slowly and with a great dark majesty out in the icy waters, far away. The fog came and went about it, momentarily erasing its shape. One of the monster eyes caught and held and flashed back our immense light, red, white, red, white, like a disc held high and sending a message in primeval code. It was as silent as the fog through which it swam.

"It's a dinosaur of some sort!" I crouched down, holding to the stair rail.

"Yes, one of the tribe."

"But they died out!"

"No, only hid away in the Deeps. Deep, deep down in the deepest Deeps. Isn't *that* a word now, Johnny, a real word, it says so much: the Deeps. There's all the coldness and darkness and deepness in the world in a word like that."

"What'll we do?"

"Do? We got our job, we can't leave. Besides, we're safer here than in any boat trying to get to land. That thing's as big as a destroyer and almost as swift."

"But here, why does it come *here*?"

The next moment I had my answer.

The Fog Horn blew.

And the monster answered.

A cry came across a million years of water and mist. A cry so anguished and alone that it shuddered in my head and my body. The monster cried out at the tower. The Fog Horn blew. The monster roared again. The Fog Horn blew. The monster opened its great toothed mouth and the sound that came from it was the sound of the Fog Horn itself. Lonely and vast and far away. The sound of isolation, a viewless sea, a cold night, apartness. That was the sound.

"Now!" whispered McDunn, "do you know why it comes here?"

I nodded.

"All year long, Johnny, that poor monster there lying far out, a thousand miles at sea, and twenty miles deep maybe, biding its time, perhaps it's a million years old, this one creature. Think of it, waiting a million years; could *you* wait that long? Maybe it's the last of its kind. I sort of think that's true. Anyway, here come men on land and build this lighthouse, five years ago. And set up their Fog Horn and sound it out towards the place where you bury yourself in sleep and sea memories of a world where there were thousands like yourself, but now you're alone, all alone in a world not made for you, a world where you have to hide.

"But the sound of the Fog Horn comes and goes, comes and goes, and you stir from the muddy bottom of the Deeps, and your eyes open like the lenses of two-foot cameras and you move, slow, slow, for you have the ocean sea on your shoulders, heavy. But that Fog Horn comes through a thousand miles of water, faint and familiar, and the furnace in your belly stokes up, and you begin to rise, slow, slow. You feed yourself on great slakes of cod and minnow, on rivers of jellyfish, and you rise slow through the autumn months, through September when the fogs started, through October with more fog and the horn still calling you on, and then, late in November, after pressurising yourself day by day, a few feet higher every hour, you are near the surface and still alive. You've got to go slow; if you surfaced all at once you'd explode. So it takes you all of three months to surface, and then a number of days to swim through the cold waters to the lighthouse. And there you are, out there, in the night, Johnny, the biggest damn monster in creation. And here's the lighthouse calling to you, with a long neck like your neck sticking way up out of the water, and a body like your body, and, most important of all, a voice like your voice. Do you understand now, Johnny, do you understand?"

The Fog Horn blew.

The monster answered.

I saw it all, I knew it all—the million years of waiting alone, for someone to come back who never came back. The million years of isolation at the bottom of the sea, the insanity of time there, while the skies cleared of reptile-birds, the swamps dried on the continental lands, the sloths and sabre-tooths had their day and sank in tar pits, and men ran like white ants upon the hills.

The Fog Horn blew.

"Last year," said McDunn, "that creature swam round and round, round and round, all night. Not coming too near, puzzled, I'd say. Afraid, maybe. And a bit angry after coming all this way. But the next day, unexpectedly, the fog lifted, the sun came out fresh, the sky was blue as a painting. And the monster swam off away from the heat and the silence and didn't come back. I suppose it's been brooding on it for a year now, thinking it over from every which way."

The monster was only a hundred yards off now, it and the Fog Horn crying at each other. As the lights hit them, the monster's eyes were fire and ice, fire and ice.

"That's life for you," said McDunn. "Someone always waiting for someone who never comes home. Always someone loving something more than that thing loves them. And after

18

a while you want to destroy whatever that thing is, so it can't hurt you no more."

The monster was rushing at the lighthouse.

The Fog Horn blew.

"Let's see what happens," said McDunn.

He switched the Fog Horn off.

The ensuing minute of silence was so intense that we could hear our hearts pounding in the glassed area of the tower, could hear the slow greased turn of the light.

The monster stopped and froze. Its great lantern eyes blinked. Its mouth gaped. It gave a sort of rumble, like a volcano. It twitched its head this way and that, as if to seek the sounds now dwindled off into the fog. It peered at the lighthouse. It rumbled again. Then its eyes caught fire. It reared up, threshed the water, and rushed at the tower, its eyes filled with angry torment.

"McDunn!" I cried. "Switch on the horn!"

McDunn fumbled with the switch. But even as he flicked it on the monster was rearing up. I had a glimpse of its gigantic paws, fishskin glittering in webs between the fingerlike projections, clawing at the tower. The huge eye on the right side of its anguished head glittered before me like a cauldron into which I might drop, screaming. The tower shook. The Fog Horn cried; the monster cried. It seized the tower and gnashed at the glass, which shattered in upon us.

McDunn seized my arm. "Downstairs!"

The tower rocked, trembled, and started to give. The Fog Horn and the monster roared. We stumbled and half fell down the stairs. "Quick!"

We reached the bottom as the tower buckled down towards us. We ducked under the stairs into the small stone cellar. There were a thousand concussions as the rocks rained down; the Fog Horn stopped abruptly. The monster crashed upon the tower. The tower fell. We knelt together, McDunn and I, holding tight, while our world exploded.

Then it was over, and there was nothing but darkness and the wash of the sea on the raw stones.

That and the other sound.

"Listen," said McDunn quietly. "Listen."

We waited a moment. And then I began to hear it. First a great vacuumed sucking of air, and then the lament, the bewilderment, the loneliness of the great monster, folded over and upon us, above us, so that the sickening reek of its body filled the air, a stone's thickness away from our cellar. The monster gasped and cried. The tower was gone. The light was gone. The thing that had called to it across a million years was gone. And the monster was opening its mouth and sending out great sounds. The sounds of a Fog Horn, again and again. And ships far at sea, not finding the light, not seeing anything, but passing and hearing late that night, must've thought: There it is, the lonely sound, the Lonesome Bay horn. All's well. We've rounded the cape.

And so it went for the rest of that night.

The sun was hot and yellow the next afternoon when the rescuers came out to dig us from our stoned-under cellar.

"It fell apart, is all," said Mr. McDunn gravely. "We had a few bad knocks from the waves and it just crumbled." He pinched my arm.

There was nothing to see. The ocean was calm, the sky blue. The only thing was a great algaic stink from the green matter that covered the fallen tower stones and the shore rocks. Flies buzzed about. The ocean washed empty on the shore.

The next year they built a new lighthouse, but by that time I had a job in the little town and a wife and a good small warm house that glowed yellow on autumn nights, the doors locked, the chimney puffing smoke. As for McDunn, he was master of the new lighthouse, built to his own specifications, out of steel-reinforced concrete. "Just in case," he said.

The new lighthouse was ready in November. I drove down alone one evening late and parked my car and looked across the grey waters and listened to the new horn sounding, once, twice, three, four times a minute far out there, by itself.

The monster?

It never came back.

"It's gone away," said McDunn. "It's gone back to the Deeps. It's learned you can't love anything too much in this world. It's gone into the deepest Deeps to wait another million years. Ah, the poor thing! Waiting out here, and waiting out there, while man comes and goes on this pitiful little planet. Waiting and waiting."

I sat in my car, listening. I couldn't see the lighthouse or the light standing out in Lonesome Bay. I could only hear the Horn, the Horn, the Horn. It sounded like the monster calling.

I sat there wishing there was something I could say.

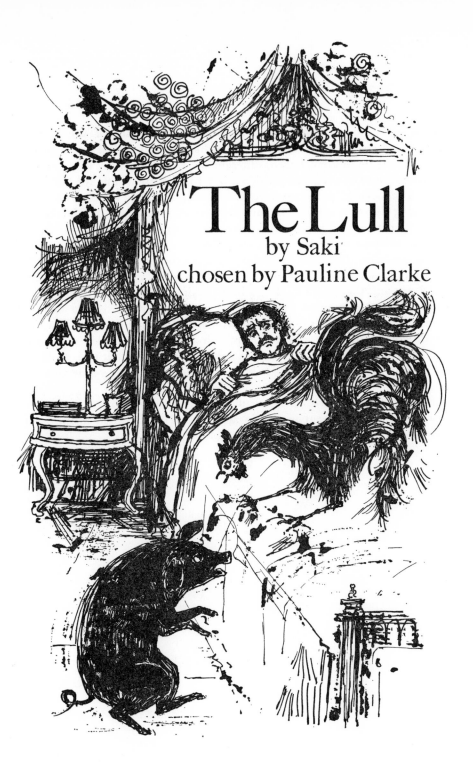

The Lull
by Saki
chosen by Pauline Clarke

GOOD short stories seem somewhat like different kinds of sweets, their flavour and colour, texture and size, hardness or softness all varying, and, if you like them, all delicious in different ways. I will not say that Saki was my favourite of all short-story writers, but I had a great taste for him when I was a schoolgirl: his stories were hard, small, sparkling sweets with acidly refreshing flavours, no softness anywhere, and often a startling jab of surprise. Sometimes a little bitter in the mouth after. Nearly always funny, though amongst them are a few tragedies. They are often built on ideas which are absurdities, or near-impossibilities, or downright lies, like this one: but they are so delicately, so exactly, and so wittily built that they stand up, and they sparkle. If you begin asking, "Could this possibly have happened?" the structure may collapse, as if you breathed on a house of cards. Saki was an exact observer of people, and though he wrote of a time far different from ours, and mostly of rich and leisured circles, his slightly malicious and ironical picture of the weaknesses of human nature is as illuminating and as comical as ever. He had a good line in terrible young girls who play ingenious tricks, like Vera in *The Lull*.

Hector Hugh Munro, as he really was, was born in 1870, and was a newspaper correspondent in Russia and Paris. He was killed in the 1914–1918 war.

PAULINE CLARKE

"I'VE asked Latimer Springfield to spend Sunday with us and stop the night," announced Mrs. Durmot at the breakfast-table.

"I thought he was in the throes of an election," remarked her husband.

"Exactly; the poll is on Wednesday, and the poor man will have worked himself to a shadow by that time. Imagine what electioneering must be like in this awful soaking rain, going along slushy country roads and speaking to damp audiences in draughty schoolrooms, day after day for a fortnight. He'll have to put in an appearance at some place of worship on Sunday morning, and he can come to us immediately afterwards and have a thorough respite from everything connected with politics. I won't let him even think of them. I've had the picture of Cromwell dissolving the Long Parliament taken down from the staircase, and even the portrait of Lord Rosebery's 'Ladas' removed from the smoking-room. And, Vera," added Mrs. Durmot, turning to her sixteen-year-old niece, "be careful what colour ribbon you wear in your hair; not blue or yellow on any account; those are the rival party colours, and emerald green or orange would be almost as bad, with this Home Rule business to the fore."

"On state occasions I always wear a black ribbon in my hair," said Vera with crushing dignity.

Latimer Springfield was a rather cheerless, oldish young man, who went into politics somewhat in the spirit in which other people might go into half mourning. Without being an enthusiast, however, he was a fairly strenuous plodder, and Mrs. Durmot had been resonably near the mark in asserting that he was working at high pressure over this election. The restful lull which his hostess enforced on him was decidedly welcome, and yet the nervous excitement of the contest had too great a hold on him to be totally banished.

"I know he's going to sit up half the night working up points for his final speeches," said Mrs. Durmot regretfully; "however, we've kept politics at arm's length all the afternoon and evening. More than that we cannot do."

"That remains to be seen," said Vera, but she said it to herself.

Latimer had scarcely shut his bedroom door before he was immersed in a sheaf of notes and pamphlets, while a fountain-pen and pocket-book were brought into play for the due marshalling of useful facts and discreet fictions. He had been at work for perhaps thirty-five minutes, and the house was seemingly consecrated to the healthy slumber of country life, when a stifled squealing and scuffling in the passage was followed by a loud tap at his door. Before he had time to answer, a much-encumbered Vera burst into the room with the question: "I say, can I leave these here?"

"These" were a small black pig and a lusty specimen of black-red gamecock.

Latimer was moderately fond of animals, and particularly interested in small livestock rearing from the economic point of view; in fact, one of the pamphlets on which he was at that moment engaged warmly advocated the further development of the pig and poultry industry in our rural districts; but he was pardonably unwilling to share even a commodious bedroom with samples of henroost and sty products.

"Wouldn't they be happier somewhere outside?" he asked, tactfully expressing his own preference in the matter in an apparent solicitude for theirs.

'There is no outside," said Vera impressively, "nothing but a waste of dark, swirling waters. The reservoir at Brinkley has burst."

"I didn't know there was a reservoir at Brinkley," said Latimer.

"Well, there isn't now, it's jolly well all over the place, and as we stand particularly low we're the centre of an inland sea just at present. You see, the river has overflowed its banks as well."

"Good gracious! Have any lives been lost?"

"Heaps, I should say. The second housemaid has already identified three bodies that have floated past the billiard-room window as being the young man she's engaged to. Either she's engaged to a large assortment of the population round here or else she's very careless at identification. Of course it may be the same body coming round again and again in a swirl; I hadn't thought of that."

"But we ought to go out and do rescue work, oughtn't we?" said Latimer, with the instinct of a Parliamentary candidate for getting into the local limelight.

"We can't," said Vera decidedly, "we haven't any boats and we're cut off by a raging torrent from any human habitation. My aunt particularly hoped you would keep to your room and not add to the confusion, but she thought it would be so kind of you if you would take in Hartlepool's Wonder, the gamecock, you know, for the night. You see, there are eight other gamecocks, and they fight like furies if they get together, so we're putting one in each bedroom. The fowl-houses are all flooded out, you know. And then I thought perhaps you wouldn't mind taking in this wee piggie; he's rather a little love, but he has a vile temper. He gets that from his mother—not that I like to say things against her when she's lying dead and drowned in her sty, poor thing. What he really wants is a man's firm hand to keep him in order. I'd try and grapple with him myself, only I've got my chow in my room, you know, and he goes for pigs wherever he finds them."

"Couldn't the pig go in the bathroom?" asked Latimer faintly, wishing he had taken up as determined a stand on the subject of bedroom swine as the chow had.

"The bathroom?" Vera laughed shrilly. "It'll be full of Boy Scouts till morning if the hot water holds out."

"Boy Scouts?"

"Yes, thirty of them came to rescue us while the water was only waist-high; then it rose another three feet or so and we had to rescue them. We're giving them hot baths in batches and drying their clothes in the hot-air cupboard, but, of course, drenched clothes don't dry in a minute, and the corridor and staircase are beginning to look like a bit of coast scenery by Tuke. Two of the boys are wearing your Melton overcoat; I hope you don't mind."

"It's a new overcoat," said Latimer, with every indication of minding dreadfully.

"You'll take every care of Hartlepool's Wonder, won't you?" said Vera. "His mother took three firsts at Birmingham, and he was second in the cockerel class last year at Gloucester. He'll probably roost on the rail at the bottom of your bed. I wonder if he'd feel more at home if some of his wives were up here with him? The hens are all in the pantry, and I think I could pick out Hartlepool Helen; she's his favourite."

Latimer showed a belated firmness on the subject of Hartlepool Helen, and Vera withdrew without pressing the point, having first settled the gamecock on his extemporised perch and taken an affectionate farewell of the pigling. Latimer undressed and got into bed with all due speed, judging that the pig would abate its inquisitorial restlessness once the light was turned out. As a substitute for a cosy, straw-bedded sty the room offered, at first inspection, few attractions, but the disconsolate animal suddenly discovered an appliance in which the most luxuriously contrived piggeries were notably deficient. The sharp edge of the underneath part of the bed was pitched at exactly the right elevation to permit the pigling to scrape himself ecstatically backwards and forwards, with an artistic humping of the back at the crucial moment and an accompanying gurgle of long-drawn delight. The gamecock, who may have fancied that he was being rocked in the branches of a pine-tree, bore the motion with greater fortitude than Latimer was able to command. A series of slaps directed at the pig's body were accepted more as an additional and pleasing irritant than as a criticism of conduct or a hint to desist; evidently something more than a man's firm hand was needed to deal with the case. Latimer slipped out of bed in search of a weapon of dissuasion. There was sufficient light in the room to enable the pig to detect this manœuvre, and the vile temper, inherited from the drowned mother, found full play. Latimer bounded back into bed, and his conqueror, after a few threatening snorts and champings of its jaws, resumed its massage operations with renewed zeal. During the long wakeful hours which ensued Latimer tried to distract his mind from his own immediate troubles by dwelling with decent sympathy on the second housemaid's bereavement, but he found himself more often wondering how many Boy Scouts were sharing his Melton overcoat. The rôle of Saint Martin *malgré lui* was not one which appealed to him.

Towards dawn the pigling fell into a happy slumber, and Latimer might have followed its example, but at about the same time Stupor Hartlepooli gave a rousing crow, clattered down to the floor and forthwith commenced a spirited combat with his reflection in the wardrobe mirror. Remembering that the bird was more or less under his care Latimer performed Hague Tribunal offices by draping a bath-towel over the provocative mirror, but the ensuing peace was local and short-lived. The deflected energies of the gamecock found new outlet in a sudden and sustained attack on the sleeping and temporarily inoffensive pigling, and the duel which followed was desperate and embittered beyond any possibility of effective intervention. The feathered combatant had the advantage of being able, when hard pressed, to take refuge on the bed, and freely availed himself of this circumstance; the pigling never quite succeeded in hurling himself on to the same eminence, but it was not from want of trying.

Neither side could claim any decisive success, and the struggle had been practically fought to a standstill by the time that the maid appeared with the early morning tea.

"Lor, sir," she exclaimed in undisguised astonishment, "do you want those animals in your room?"

Want!

The pigling, as though aware that it might have outstayed its welcome, dashed out at the door, and the gamecock followed it at a more dignified pace.

"If Miss Vera's dog sees that pig—!" exclaimed the maid, and hurried off to avert such a catastrophe.

A cold suspicion was stealing over Latimer's mind; he went to the window and drew up the blind. A light, drizzling rain was falling, but there was not the faintest trace of any inundation.

Some half-hour later he met Vera on the way to the breakfast-room.

"I should not like to think of you as a deliberate liar," he observed coldly, "but one occasionally has to do things one does not like."

"At any rate I kept your mind from dwelling on politics all the night," said Vera.

Which was, of course, perfectly true.

FIRST CONFESSION

BY FRANK O'CONNOR·CHOSEN BY EILÍS DILLON

ONE of the dangers of being a child lies in the need to go through exact rituals, with the risk of bringing disgrace on oneself and one's relations if one fails. Going to a theatre or a hotel, taking tea with crotchety, watchful aunts or grandparents, above all going to church—there is no knowing what may happen, though the minutest explanations may have been given in advance by well-meaning adults.

Not so well-meaning are some of the explanations given by older children, who perhaps feel the need to compensate for what they suffered themselves by teasing the younger ones with imaginary terrors. This is done with a great air of wisdom and certitude, though a moment's reflection should tell the younger child that the older one could not possibly have the necessary advance information.

I remember experiencing a great sense of gratitude to Frank O'Connor when I read *First Confession* for the first time. He recalled so perfectly the helplessness and frustration, the fear of failure and the triumph of success that was all the more sweet for being unexpected, at six or seven years old. Jackie's handling of his first encounter with the notions of good and evil is a success, and he is a better and more independent philosopher afterwards.

EILÍS DILLON

IT WAS a Saturday afternoon in early spring. A small boy whose face looked as though it had been newly scrubbed was being led by the hand by his sister through a crowded street. The little boy showed a marked reluctance to proceed; he affected to be very interested in the shop-windows. Equally, his sister seemed to pay no attention to them. She tried to hurry him; he resisted. When she dragged him he began to bawl. The hatred with which she viewed him was almost diabolical, but when she spoke her words and tone were full of passionate sympathy.

"Ah, sha, God help us!" she intoned into his ear in a whine of commiseration.

"Leave me go!" he said, digging his heels into the pavement. "I don't want to go. I want to go home."

"But, sure, you can't go home, Jackie. You'll have to go. The parish priest will be up to the house with a stick."

"I don't care. I won't go."

"Oh, Sacred Heart, isn't it a terrible pity you weren't a good boy? Oh, Jackie, me heart bleeds for you! I don't know what they'll do to you at all, Jackie, me poor child. And all the trouble you caused your poor old nanny, and the way you wouldn't eat in the same room with her, and the time you kicked her on the shins, and the time you went for me with the bread knife under the table. I don't know will he ever listen to you at all, Jackie. I think meself he might sind you to the bishop. Oh, Jackie, how will you think of all your sins?"

Half stupefied with terror, Jackie allowed himself to be led through the sunny streets to the very gates of the church. It was an old one with two grim iron gates and a long, low, shapeless stone front. At the gates he stuck, but it was already too late. She dragged him behind her across the yard, and the commiserating whine with which she had tried to madden him gave place to a yelp of triumph.

33

"Now you're caught! Now you're caught! And I hope he'll give you the pinitintial psalms! That'll cure you, you suppurating little caffler!"

Jackie gave himself up for lost. Within the old church there was no stained glass; it was cold and dark and desolate, and in the silence, the trees in the yard knocked hollowly at the tall windows. He allowed himself to be led through the vaulted silence, the intense and magical silence which seemed to have frozen within the ancient walls, buttressing them and shouldering the high wooden roof. In the street outside, yet seeming a million miles away, a ballad singer was drawling a ballad.

Nora sat in front of him beside the confession box. There were a few old women before her, and later a thin, sad-looking man with long hair came and sat beside Jackie. In the intense silence of the church that seemed to grow deeper from the plaintive moaning of the ballad singer, he could hear the buzz-buzz-buzz of a woman's voice in the box, and then the husky ba-ba-ba of the priest's. Lastly the soft thud of something that signalled the end of the confession, and out came the woman, head lowered, hands joined, looking neither to right nor left, and tiptoed up to the altar to say her penance.

It seemed only a matter of seconds till Nora rose and with a whispered injunction disappeared from his sight. He was all alone. Alone and the next to be heard and the fear of damnation in his soul. He looked at the sad-faced man. He was gazing at the roof, his hands joined in prayer. A woman in a red blouse and black shawl had taken her place below him. She uncovered her head, fluffed her hair out roughly with her hand, brushed it sharply back, then, bowing, caught it in a knot and pinned it on her neck. Nora emerged. Jackie rose and looked at her with a hatred which was inappropriate to the occasion and the place. Her hands were joined on her stomach, her eyes modestly lowered, and her face had an expression of the most rapt and tender recollection. With death in his heart he crept into the compartment she left open and drew the door shut behind him.

He was in pitch darkness. He could see no priest or anything else. And anything he had heard of confession got all muddled in his mind. He knelt to the right-hand wall and said: "Bless me, father, for I have sinned. This is my first confession." Nothing happened. He repeated it louder. Still it gave no answer. He turned to the opposite wall, genuflected first, then again went and repeated the charm. This time he was certain he would receive a reply, but none came. He repeated the process with the remaining wall without effect. He had the feeling of someone with an unfamiliar machine, of pressing buttons at random. And finally the thought struck him that God knew. God knew about the bad confession he intended to make and had made him deaf and blind so that he could neither hear nor see the priest.

Then as his eyes grew accustomed to the blackness, he perceived something he had not noticed previously: a sort of shelf at about the height of his head. The purpose of this eluded him for a moment. Then he understood. It was for kneeling on.

He had always prided himself upon his power of climbing, but this took it out of him. There was no foothold. He slipped twice before he succeeded in getting his knee on it, and the strain of drawing the rest of his body up was almost more than he was capable of. However, he did at last get his two knees on it, there was just room for those, but his legs hung down uncomfortably and the edge of the shelf bruised his shins. He joined his hands and pressed the last remaining button. "Bless me, father, for I have sinned. This is my first confession."

At the same moment the slide was pushed back and a dim light streamed into the little box. There was an uncomfortable silence, and then an alarmed voice asked, "Who's there?" Jackie found it almost impossible to speak into the grille which was on a level with his knees, but he got a firm grip of the moulding above it, bent his head down and sideways, and as though he were hanging by his feet like a monkey found himself looking almost upside down at the priest. But the priest was looking sideways at him, and Jackie, whose knees were being tortured by this new position, felt it was a queer way to hear confessions.

" 'Tis me, father," he piped, and then, running all his

35

words together in excitement, he rattled off, "Bless me, father, for I have sinned. This is my first confession."

"What?" exclaimed a deep and angry voice, and the sombre soutaned figure stood bolt upright, disappearing almost entirely from Jackie's view. "What does this mean? What are you doing there? Who are you?"

And with the shock Jackie felt his hands lose their grip and his legs their balance. He discovered himself tumbling into space, and, falling, he knocked his head against the door, which shot open and permitted him to thump right into the centre of the aisle. Straight on this came a small, dark-haired priest with a biretta well forward on his head. At the same time Nora came skeltering madly down the church.

"Lord God!" she cried. "The snivelling little caffler! I knew he'd do it! I knew he'd disgrace me!"

Jackie received a clout over the ear which reminded him that for some strange reason he had not yet begun to cry and that people might think he wasn't hurt. Nora slapped him again.

"What's this? What's this?" cried the priest. "Don't attempt to beat the child, you little vixen!"

"I can't do me pinance with him," cried Nora shrilly, cocking a shocked eye on the priest. "He have me driven mad. Stop your crying, you dirty scut! Stop it now or I'll make you cry at the other side of your ugly puss!"

"Run away out of this, you little jade!" growled the priest. He suddenly began to laugh, took out a pocket handkerchief, and wiped Jackie's nose. "You're not hurt, sure you're not. Show us the ould head . . . Ah, 'tis nothing. 'Twill be better before you're twice married . . . So you were coming to confession?"

"I was, father."

"A big fellow like you should have terrible sins. Is it your first?"

" 'Tis, father."

"Oh, my, worse and worse! Here, sit down there and wait till I get rid of these ould ones and we'll have a long chat. Never mind that sister of yours."

36

With a feeling of importance that glowed through his tears, Jackie waited. Nora stuck out her tongue at him, but he didn't even bother to reply. A great feeling of relief was welling up in him. The sense of oppression that had been weighing him down for a week, the knowledge that he was about to make a bad confession, disappeared. Bad confession, indeed! He had made friends, made friends with the priest, and the priest expected, even demanded, terrible sins. Oh, women! Women! It was all women and girls and their silly talk. They had no real knowledge of the world!

And when the time came for him to make his confession he did not beat about the bush. He may have clenched his hands and lowered his eyes, but wouldn't anyone!

"Father," he said huskily, "I made it up to kill me grand-mother."

There was a moment's pause. Jackie did not dare to look up, but he could feel the priest's eyes on him. The priest's voice also sounded a trifle husky.

"Your grandmother?" he asked, but he didn't after all sound very angry.

"Yes, father."

"Does she live with you?"

"She do, father."

"And why do you want to kill her?"

"Oh, God, father, she's a horrible woman!"

"Is she, now?"

"She is, father."

"What way is she horrible?"

Jackie paused to think. It was hard to explain.

"She takes snuff, father."

"Oh, my!"

"And she goes round in her bare feet, father."

"Tut-tut-tut!"

"She's a horrible woman, father," said Jackie with sudden earnestness. "She takes porter. And she ates the potatoes off the table with her hands. And me mother do be out working most days, and since that one came 'tis she gives us our dinner

37

and I can't ate the dinner." He found himself sniffling. "And she gives pinnies to Nora and she doesn't give no pinnies to me because she knows I can't stand her. And me father sides with her, father, and he bates me, and me heart is broken and wan night in bed I made it up the way I'd kill her."

Jackie began to sob again, rubbing his nose with his sleeve, as he remembered his wrongs.

"And what way were you going to kill her?" asked the priest smoothly.

"With a hatchet, father."

"When she was in bed?"

"No, father."

"How, so?"

"When she ates the potatoes and drinks the porter she falls asleep, father."

"And you'd hit her then?"

"Yes, father."

"Wouldn't a knife be better?"

" 'Twould, father, only I'd be afraid of the blood."

"Oh, of course. I never thought of the blood."

"I'd be afraid of that, father. I was near hitting Nora with the bread knife one time she came after me under the table, only I was afraid."

"You're a terrible child," said the priest with awe.

"I am, father," said Jackie non-committally, sniffing back his tears.

"And what would you do with the body?"

"How, father?"

"Wouldn't someone see her and tell?"

"I was going to cut her up with a knife and take away the pieces and bury them. I could get an orange box for threepence and make a cart to take them away."

"My, my," said the priest. "You had it all well planned."

"Ah, I tried that," said Jackie with mounting confidence. "I borrowed a cart and practised it by meself one night after dark."

"And weren't you afraid?"

"Ah, no," said Jackie half heartedly. "Only a bit."

"You have terrible courage," said the priest. "There's a lot of people I want to get rid of, but I'm not like you. I'd never have the courage. And hanging is an awful death."

"Is it?" asked Jackie, responding to the brightness of a new theme.

"Oh, an awful blooming death!"

"Did you ever see a fellow hanged?"

"Dozens of them, and they all died roaring."

"Jay!" said Jackie.

"They do be swinging out of them for hours and the poor fellows lepping and roaring, like bells in a belfry, and then they put lime on them to burn them up. Of course, they pretend they're dead, but sure they don't be dead at all."

"Jay!" said Jackie again.

"So if I were you I'd take my time and think about it. In my opinion 'tisn't worth it, not even to get rid of a grand-mother. I asked dozens of fellows like you that killed their grandmothers about it, and they all said no, 'twasn't worth it . . .'

Nora was waiting in the yard. The sunlight struck down on her across the high wall and its brightness made his eyes dazzle. "Well?" she said. "What did he give you?"

"Three Hail Marys."

"You mustn't have told him anything."

"I told him everything," said Jackie confidently.

"What did you tell him?"

"Things you don't know."

"Bah! He gave you three Hail Marys because you were a cry baby!"

Jackie didn't mind. He felt the world was very good. He began to whistle as well as the hindrance in his jaw permitted.

"What are you sucking?"

"Bull's eyes."

"Was it he gave them to you?"

" 'Twas."

"Almighty God!" said Nora. "Some people have all the luck. I might as well be a sinner like you. There's no use in being good."

39

hISTORY OF ENGLAND

BY JANE AUSTEN
CHOSEN BY LEON GARFIELD

THIS is not a great story; it is not even a story at all. It is just a piece of comedy written by a fourteen-year-old girl to entertain her family. It is dedicated to her sister and at one point, Sir Francis Drake is mentioned only to be compared with the young girl's brother who was a sailor, too.

But this slight piece of work is one of the rarest things in the world. It shows a promise that was most gloriously fulfilled. For here is the young Jane Austen, incorrigibly romantic, outrageously funny and yet with that passionate devotion to a cause that Charlotte Brontë could never find in her. Perhaps this was because Jane Austen possessed what Charlotte herself lacked: the golden ability to laugh at herself. Even her spelling had its comic side.

It is this strange, all-pervading laughter flickering and shifting through her work that, more than anything else, raises her to the summit of the novelist's art. Even on the twentieth reading one is never quite sure of where the centre of her laughter lies. It is everywhere and sometimes the reader looks uneasily over his shoulder, half expecting to see that shrewdly mocking smile directed at *him*.

Of all the great novelists, she is most loved and least known. And of all of them, it is she one would most like to have known.

LEON GARFIELD

THE HISTORY OF ENGLAND FROM THE REIGN OF HENRY THE 4TH TO THE DEATH OF CHARLES THE 1ST

by a partial, prejudiced, and ignorant Historian

N.B. There will be very few dates in this History.

HENRY THE 4TH

HENRY the 4th ascended the throne of England much to his own satisfaction in the year 1399, after having prevailed on his cousin and predecessor Richard the 2nd to resign it to him, and to retire for the rest of his life to Pomfret Castle, where he happened to be murdered. It is to be supposed that Henry was married, since he had certainly four sons, but it is not in my power to inform the reader who was his wife. Be this as it may, he did not live for ever, but falling ill, his son the Prince of Wales came and took away the crown; whereupon the king made a long speech, for which I must refer the reader to Shakespear's plays, and the prince made a still longer. Things being thus settled between them the King died, and was succeeded by his son Henry who had previously beat Sir William Gascoigne.

HENRY THE 5TH

This prince, after he succeeded to the throne grew quite reformed and amiable, forsaking all his dissipated companions, and never thrashing Sir William again. During his reign, Lord Cobham was burnt alive, but I forgot what for. His Majesty then turned his thoughts to France, where he went and fought the famous Battle of Agincourt. He afterwards married the king's daughter Catherine, a very agreable woman by Shakespear's account. In spite of all this however he died, and was succeeded by his son Henry.

HENRY THE 6TH

I cannot say much for this monarch's sense. Nor would I if I could, for he was a Lancastrian. I suppose you know all about the wars between him and the Duke of York who was of the right side; if you do not, you had better read some other history, for I shall not be very diffuse in this, meaning by it only to vent my spleen *against*, and shew my hatred *to* all those people whose parties or principles do not suit with mine, and not to give information. This king married Margaret of Anjou, a woman whose distresses and misfortunes were so great as almost to make me who hate her, pity her. It was in this reign that Joan of Arc lived and made such a *row* amongst the English. They should not have burnt her—but they did. There were several battles between the Yorkists and Lancastrians, in which the former (as they ought) usually conquered. At length they were entirely overcome; the king was murdered—the queen was sent home—and Edward the 4th ascended the throne.

EDWARD THE 4TH

This monarch was famous only for his beauty and his courage, of which the picture we have here given of him, and his un-daunted behaviour in marrying one woman while he was engaged to another, are sufficient proofs. His wife was Elizabeth Woodville, a widow who, poor woman! was afterwards confined in a convent by that monster of iniquity and avarice Henry the 7th. One of Edward's mistresses was Jane Shore, who has had a play written about her, but it is a tragedy and therefore not worth reading. Having performed all these noble actions, his Majesty died, and was succeeded by his son.

EDWARD THE 5TH

This unfortunate prince lived so little a while that nobody had time to draw his picture. He was murdered by his uncle's contrivance, whose name was Richard the 3rd.

RICHARD THE 3RD

The character of this prince has been in general very severely treated by historians, but as he was a *York*, I am rather inclined to suppose him a very respectable man. It has indeed been confidently asserted that he killed his two nephews and his wife, but it has also been declared that he did *not* kill his two nephews, which I am inclined to believe true; and if this is the case, it may also be affirmed that he did not kill his wife, for if Perkin Warbeck was really the Duke of York, why might not Lambert Simnel be the widow of Richard. Whether innocent or guilty, he did not reign long in peace, for Henry Tudor E. of Richmond as great a villain as ever lived, made a great fuss about getting the crown and having killed the king at the battle of Bosworth, he succeeded to it.

HENRY THE 7TH

This monarch soon after his accession married the Princess Elizabeth of York, by which alliance he plainly proved that he thought his own right inferior to hers, tho' he pretended to the contrary. By this marriage he had two sons and two daughters, the elder of which daughters was married to the King of Scotland and had the happiness of being grandmother to one of the first characters in the world. But of *her*, I shall have occasion to speak more at large in future. The youngest Mary, married first the King of France and secondly the D. of Suffolk, by whom she had one daughter, afterwards the mother of Lady Jane Grey, who tho' inferior to her lovely cousin the Queen of Scots, was yet an amiable young woman and famous for reading Greek while other people were hunting. It was in the reign of Henry the 7th that Perkin Warbeck and Lambert Simnel before mentioned made their appearance, the former of whom was set in the stocks, took shelter in Beaulieu Abbey, and was beheaded with the Earl of Warwick, and the latter was taken into the kings kitchen. His Majesty died and was succeeded by his son Henry whose only merit was his not being *quite* so bad as his daughter Elizabeth.

HENRY THE 8TH

It would be an affront to my readers were I to suppose that they were not as well acquainted with the particulars of this king's reign as I am myself. It will therefore be saving *them* the task of reading again what they have read before, and *myself* the trouble of writing what I do not perfectly recollect, by giving only a slight sketch of the principal events which marked his reign. Among these may be ranked Cardinal Wolsey's telling the father Abbott of Leicester Abbey that "he was come to lay his bones among them", the reformation in religion and the king's riding through the streets of London with Anna Bullen. It is however but justice, and my duty to declare that this amiable woman was entirely innocent of the crimes with which she was accused, and of which her beauty, her elegance, and her sprightliness were sufficient proofs, not to mention her solemn protestations of innocence, the weakness of the charges against her, and the king's character; all of which add some confirmation, tho' perhaps but slight ones when in comparison with those before alledged in her favour. Tho' I do not profess giving many dates, yet as I think it proper to give some and shall of course make choice of those which it is most necessary for the reader to know, I think it right to inform him that her letter to the king was dated on the 6th of May. The crimes and cruelties of this prince, were too numerous to be mentioned, (as this history I trust has fully shown) and nothing can be said in his vindication, but that his abolishing religious houses and leaving them to the ruinous depredations of time has been of infinite use to the landscape of England in general, which probably was a principal motive for his doing it, since otherwise why should a man who was of no religion himself be at so much trouble to abolish one which had for ages been established in the kingdom. His Majesty's 5th wife was the Duke of Norfolk's niece who, tho' universally acquitted of the crimes for which she was beheaded, has been by many people supposed to have led an abandoned life before her marriage—of this however I have many doubts, since she was a relation of that noble Duke of Norfolk who was so warm in the Queen of Scotland's cause, and who at last fell a victim to it. The kings last wife contrived to survive him, but with difficulty effected it. He was succeeded by his only son Edward.

EDWARD THE 6TH

As this prince was only nine years old at the time of his father's death he was considered by many people as too young to govern, and the late king happening to be of the same opinion, his mother's brother the Duke of Somerset was chosen Protector of the realm during his minority. This man was on the whole of a very amiable character, and is somewhat of a favourite with me, tho' I would by no means pretend to affirm that he was equal to those first of men Robert Earl of Essex, Delamere, or Gilpin. He was beheaded, of which he might with reason have been proud, had he known that such was the death of Mary Queen of Scotland; but as it was impossible that he should be conscious of what had never happened, it does not appear that he felt particularly delighted with the manner of it. After his decease the Duke of Northumberland had the care of the king and the kingdom, and performed his trust of both so well that the king died and the kingdom was left to his daughter in law the Lady Jane Grey, who has been already mentioned as reading Greek. Whether she really understood that language or whether such a study proceeded only from an excess of vanity for which I believe she was always rather remarkable, it is uncertain. Whatever might be the cause, she preserved the same appearance of knowledge, and contempt of what was generally esteemed pleasure, during the whole of her life, for she declared herself displeased with being appointed queen, and while conducting to the scaffold, she wrote a sentence in Latin and another in Greek on seeing the dead body of her husband accidentally passing that way.

MARY

This woman had the good luck of being advanced to the throne of England, in spite of the superior pretensions, merit and beauty of her cousins Mary Queen of Scotland and Jane Grey. Nor can I pity the kingdom for the misfortunes they experienced during her reign, since they fully deserved them, for having allowed her to succeed her brother—which was a double peice of folly, since they might have foreseen that as she died without children, she would be succeeded by that disgrace to humanity, that pest of society, Elizabeth. Many were the people who fell martyrs to the protestant religion during her reign; I suppose not fewer than a dozen. She married Philip King of Spain who in her sister's reign was famous for building Armadas. She died without issue, and then the dreadful moment came in which the destroyer of all comfort, the deceitful betrayer of trust reposed in her, and the murderess of her cousin succeeded to the throne.

ELIZABETH

It was the peculiar misfortune of this woman to have bad ministers. Since wicked as she herself was, she could not have committed such extensive mischief, had not these vile and abandoned men connived at, and encouraged her in her crimes. I know that it has by many people been asserted and beleived that Lord Burleigh, Sir Francis Walsingham, and the rest of those who filled the chief offices of state were deserving, experienced, and able ministers. But oh! how blinded such writers and such readers must be to true merit, to merit despised, neglected and defamed, if they can persist in such opinions when they reflect that these men, these boasted men were such scandals to their country and their sex as to allow and assist their queen in confining for the space of nineteen years, a *woman* who if the claims of relationship and merit were of no avail, yet as a queen and as one who condescended to place confidence in her, had every reason to expect assistance and protection; and at length in allowing Elizabeth to bring this amiable woman to an untimely, unmerited, and scandalous death. Can any one if he reflects but for a moment on this blot, this everlasting blot upon their understanding and their character, allow any praise to Lord Burleigh or Sir Francis Walsingham? Oh! what must this bewitching princess whose only freind was then the Duke of Norfolk, and whose only ones now Mr. Whitaker, Mrs. Lefroy, Mrs. Knight and myself, who was abandoned by her son, confined by her cousin, abused, reproached and vilified by all, what must not her most noble mind have suffered when informed that Elizabeth had given orders for her death! Yet she bore it with a most unshaken fortitude, firm in her mind; constant in her religion; and prepared herself to meet the cruel fate to which she was doomed, with a magnanimity that would alone proceed from conscious innocence. And yet could you reader have beleived it possible that some hardened and zealous Protestants have even abused her for that steadfastness in the Catholic religion which reflected on her so much credit? But this is a striking proof of *their* narrow souls and prejudiced judgements who accuse her. She was executed in the Great Hall at Fotheringay Castle (sacred place!) on Wednesday the 8th of February 1586—to the everlasting reproach of Elizabeth, her ministers, and of England in general. It may not be unnecessary before I entirely conclude my account of this ill-fated queen, to observe that she had been accused of several crimes during the time of her reigning in Scotland, of which I now most seriously do assure my reader that she was entirely innocent; having never been guilty of anything more than imprudencies into which she was betrayed by the openness of her heart, her youth, and her education. Having I trust by this assurance entirely done away every suspicion and every doubt which might have arisen in the reader's mind, from what other historians have written of her, I shall proceed to mention the remaining events that marked Elizabeth's reign. It was about this time that Sir Francis Drake the first English navigator who sailed round the world, lived, to be the ornament of his country and his profession. Yet great as he was, and justly celebrated as a sailor, I cannot help foreseeing that he will be equalled in this or the next century by one who tho' now but young, already promises to answer all the ardent and sanguine expectations of his relations and friends, amongst whom I may class the amiable lady to whom this work is dedicated, and my no less amiable self.

49

Though of a different profession, and shining in a different sphere of life, yet equally conspicuous in the character of an *Earl*, as Drake was in that of a *sailor*, was Robert Devereux Lord Essex. This unfortunate young man was not unlike in character to that equally unfortunate one *Frederic Delamere*. The simile may be carried still farther, and Elizabeth the torment of Essex may be compared to the Emmeline of Delamere. It would be endless to recount the misfortunes of this noble and gallant Earl. It is sufficient to say that he was beheaded on the 25th of Feb, after having been Lord Lieutenant of Ireland, after having clapped his hand on his sword, and after performing many other services to his country. Elizabeth did not long survive his loss, and died *so* miserable that were it not an injury to the memory of Mary I should pity her.

JAMES THE 1ST

Though this king had some faults, among which and as the most principal, was his allowing his mother's death, yet considered on the whole I cannot help liking him. He married Anne of Denmark, and had several children; fortunately for him his eldest son Prince Henry died before his father or he might have experienced the evils which befell his unfortunate brother.

As I am myself partial to the roman catholic religion, it is with infinite regret that I am obliged to blame the behaviour of any member of it: yet truth being I think very excusable in an historian, I am necessitated to say that in this reign the roman catholics of England did not behave like gentlemen to the protestants. Their behaviour indeed to the Royal Family and both Houses of Parliament might justly be considered by them as very uncivil, and even Sir Henry Percy tho' the best bred man of the party, had none of that general politeness which is so universally pleasing, as his attentions were entirely confined to Lord Mounteagle.

Sir Walter Raleigh flourished in this and the preceeding reign, and is by many people held in great veneration and respect—but as he was an enemy of the noble Essex, I have nothing to say in praise of him, and must refer all those who may wish to be acquainted with the particulars of his life, to Mr. Sheridan's play of the Critic, where they will find many interesting anecdotes as well of him as of his friend Sir Christopher Hatton. His Majesty was of that amiable disposition which inclines to freindship; and in such points was possessed of a keener penetration in discovering merit than many other people. I once heard an excellent sharade on a carpet, of which the subject I am now on reminds me, and as I think it may afford my readers some amusement to *find it out*, I shall here take the liberty of presenting it to them.

Sharade

My first is what my second was to King James the 1st, and you tread on my whole.

The principal favourites of his Majesty were Car, who was afterwards created Earl of Somerset and whose name perhaps may have some share in the above mentioned sharade, and George Villiers afterwards Duke of Buckingham. On his Majesty's death he was succeeded by his son Charles.

CHARLES THE 1ST

This amiable monarch seems born to have suffered misfortunes equal to those of his lovely grandmother; misfortunes which he could not deserve since he was her descendant. Never certainly were there before so many detestable characters at one time in England as in this period of its history; never were amiable men so scarce. The number of them throughout the whole kingdom amounting only to *five*, besides the inhabitants of Oxford who were always loyal to their king and faithful to his interests. The names of his noble five who never forgot the duty of the subject, or swerved from their attachment to his Majesty, were as follows—the king himself, ever stedfast in his own support—Archbishop Laud, Earl of Strafford, Viscount Faulkland and Duke of Ormond, who were scarcely less strenuous or zealous in the cause. While the *villains* of the time would make too long a list to be written or read; I shall therefore

51

content myself with mentioning the leaders of the gang. Cromwell, Fairfax, Hampden, and Pym may be considered as the original causers of all the disturbances, distresses, and civil wars in which England for many years was embroiled. In this reign as well as in that of Elizabeth, I am obliged in spite of my attachment to the Scotch, to consider them as equally guilty with the generality of the English, since they dared to think differently from their sovereign, to forget the adoration which as *Stuarts* it was their duty to pay them, to rebel against, dethrone and imprison the unfortunate Mary; to oppose, to deceive, and to sell the no less unfortunate Charles. The events of this monarch's reign are too numerous for my pen, and indeed the recital of any events (except what I make myself) is uninteresting to me; my principal reason for undertaking the History of England being to prove the innocence of the Queen of Scotland, which I flatter myself with having effectually done, and to abuse Elizabeth, tho' I am rather fearful of having fallen short in the latter part of my scheme. As therefore it is not my intention to give any particular account of the distresses into which this king was involved through the misconduct and cruelty of his parliament, I shall satisfy myself with vindicating him from the reproach of arbitrary and tyrannical government with which he has often been charged. This, I feel, is not difficult to be done, for with one argument I am certain of satisfying every sensible and well disposed person whose opinions have been properly guided by a good education—and this argument is that he was a STUART.

THE TOWER

BY MARGHANITA LASKI

CHOSEN BY ALAN GARNER

IT's impossible to have a "favourite", just as it's impossible for there to be a "best". A story becomes something different with every reader, since the effect it produces is a combination of the written words and of the reader's own personality, which itself changes with the day or the mood. But there are certain stories that present ideas and emotions with a force that is never forgotten. *The Tower* is one of these. It is all the more remarkable for not being perfect. I find the slow beginning, the finicky background of plot, very irritating, but as soon as Caroline arrives at the tower, the author turns relentless, and the result is, simply, the most terrifying story I know.

ALAN GARNER

The road begins to rise in a series of gentle curves, passing through pleasing groves of olives and vines. 5 km. on the left is the fork for Florence. To the right may be seen the Tower of Sacrifice (470 steps) built in 1535 by Niccolo di Ferramano; superstitious fear left the tower intact when, in 1549, the surrounding village was completely destroyed . . .

TRIUMPHANTLY Caroline lifted her finger from the fine italic type. There was nothing to mar the success of this afternoon. Not only had she taken the car out alone for the first time, driving unerringly on the right-hand side of the road, but what she had achieved was not a simple drive but a cultural excursion. She had taken the Italian guide-book Neville was always urging on her, and hesitantly, haltingly, she had managed to piece out enough of the language to choose a route that took in four well-thought-of frescoes, two universally-admired campaniles, and one wooden crucifix in a village church quite a long way from the main road. It was not, after all, such a bad thing that a British Council meeting had kept Neville in Florence. True, he was certain to know all about the campaniles and the frescoes, but there was just a chance that he hadn't discovered the crucifix, and how gratifying if she could, at last, have something of her own to contribute to his constantly accumulating hoard of culture.

But could she add still more? There was at least another hour of daylight, and it wouldn't take more than thirty-five minutes to get back to the flat in Florence. Perhaps there would just be time to add this tower to her dutiful collection? What was it called? She bent to the guide-book again, carefully tracing the text with her finger to be sure she was translating it correctly, word by word.

But this time her moving finger stopped abruptly at the name of Niccolo di Ferramano. There had risen in her mind a picture—no, not a picture, a portrait—of a thin white face

55

with deepset black eyes that stared intently into hers. Why a portrait? she asked, and then she remembered.

It had been about three months ago, just after they were married, when Neville had first brought her to Florence. He himself had already lived there for two years, and during that time had been at least as concerned to accumulate Tuscan culture for himself as to disseminate English culture to the Italians. What more natural than that he should wish to share—perhaps even to show off—his discoveries to his young wife?

Caroline had come out to Italy with the idea that when she had worked through one or two galleries and made a few trips—say to Assisi and Siena—she would have done her duty as a British Council wife, and could then settle down to examining the Florentine shops, which everyone had told her were too marvellous for words. But Neville had been contemptuous of her programme. "You can see the stuff in the galleries at any time," he had said, "but I'd like you to start with the pieces that the ordinary tourist doesn't see," and of course Caroline couldn't possibly let herself be classed as an ordinary tourist. She had been proud to accompany Neville to castles and palaces privately owned to which his work gave him entry, and there to gaze with what she hoped was pleasure on the undiscovered Raphael, the Titian that had hung on the same wall ever since it was painted, the Giotto fresco under which the family that had originally commissioned it still said their prayers.

It had been on one of these pilgrimages that she had seen the face of the young man with the black eyes. They had made a long slow drive over narrowly ill-made roads and at last had come to a castle on the top of a hill. The family was, to Neville's disappointment, away, but the housekeeper remembered him and led them to a long gallery lined with five centuries of family portraits.

Though she could not have admitted it even to herself, Caroline had become almost anaesthetised to Italian art. Dutifully she had followed Neville along the gallery, listening politely while in his light well-bred voice he had told her intimate anecdotes of history, and involuntarily she had let her eyes wander round the room, glancing anywhere but at the particular portrait of Neville's immediate dissertation.

It was thus that her eye was caught by a face on the other side of the room, and forgetting what was due to politeness she caught her husband's arm and demanded, "Neville, who's that girl over there?"

But he was pleased with her. He said, "Ah, I'm glad you picked that one out. It's generally thought to be the best thing in the collection—a Bronzino, of course," and they went over to look at it.

The picture was painted in rich pale colours, a green curtain, a blue dress, a young face with calm brown eyes under plaits of honey-gold hair. Caroline read out the name under the picture—*Giovanna di Ferramano, 1531–1549.* That was the year the village was destroyed, she remembered now, sitting in the car by the roadside, but then she had exclaimed, "Neville, she was only eighteen when she died."

"They married young in those days," Neville commented, and Caroline said in surprise, "Oh, was she married?" It had been the radiantly virginal character of the face that had caught at her inattention.

"Yes, she was married," Neville answered, and added, "Look at the portrait beside her. It's Bronzino again. What do you think of it?"

And this was when Caroline had seen the pale young man. There were no clear light colours in this picture. There was only the whiteness of the face, the blackness of the eyes, the hair, the clothes, and the glint of gold letters on the pile of books on which the young man rested his hand. Underneath this picture was written *Portrait of an Unknown Gentleman.*

"Do you mean he's her husband?" Caroline asked. "Surely they'd know if he was, instead of calling him an Unknown Gentleman?"

"He's Niccolo di Ferramano all right," said Neville. "I've seen another portrait of him somewhere, and it's not a face one would forget, but," he added reluctantly, because he hated to admit ignorance, "there's apparently some queer scandal about him, and though they don't turn his picture out, they won't even mention his name. Last time I was here, the old Count himself took me through the gallery. I asked him about little Giovanna and her husband." He laughed uneasily. "Mind you, my Italian was far from perfect at that time, but it was horribly clear that I shouldn't have asked." "But what did he *say*?" Caroline demanded. "I've tried to remember," said Neville. "For some reason it stuck in my mind. He said either 'She was lost' or 'She was damned', but which word it was I can never be sure. The portrait of Niccolo he just ignored altogether."

"What was wrong with Niccolo, I wonder?" mused Caroline, and Neville answered, "I don't know but I can guess. Do you notice the lettering on those books up there, under his hand? It's all in Hebrew or Arabic. Undoubtedly the unmentionable Niccolo dabbled in Black Magic."

Caroline shivered. "I don't like him," she said. "Let's look at Giovanna again," and they had moved back to the first portrait, and Neville had said casually, "Do you know, she's rather like you."

"I've just got time to look at the tower," Caroline now said aloud, and she put the guide-book back in the pigeon-hole under the dashboard, and drove carefully along the gentle curves until she came to the fork for Florence on the left.

On the top of a little hill to the right stood a tall round tower. There was no other building in sight. In a land where every available piece of ground is cultivated, there was no cultivated ground around this tower. On the left was the fork for Florence: on the right a rough track led up to the top of the hill.

Caroline knew that she wanted to take the fork to the left, to Florence and home and Neville and—said an urgent voice inside her—for safety. This voice so much shocked her that she got out of the car and began to trudge up the dusty track towards the tower.

After all, I may not come this way again, she argued; it seems silly to miss the chance of seeing it when I've already got a reason for being interested. I'm only just going to have a quick look—and she glanced at the setting sun, telling herself that she would indeed have to be quick if she were to get back to Florence before dark.

And now she had climbed the hill and was standing in front of the tower. It was built of narrow red bricks, and only thin slits pierced its surface right up to the top where Caroline could see some kind of narrow platform encircling it. Before her was an arched doorway. I'm just going to have a quick look, she assured herself again, and then she walked in.

She was in an empty room with a low arched ceiling. A narrow stone staircase clung to the wall and circled round the room to disappear through a hole in the ceiling.

"There ought to be a wonderful view at the top," said Caroline firmly to herself, and she laid her hand on the rusty rail and started to climb, and as she climbed, she counted.

"—thirty-nine, forty, forty-one," she said and with the forty-first step she came through the ceiling and saw over her head, far far above, the deep blue evening sky, a small circle of blue framed in a narrowing shaft round which the narrow staircase spiralled. There was no inner wall; only the rusty railing protected the climber on the inside.

"—eighty-three, eighty-four—" counted Caroline. The sky above her was losing its colour and she wondered why the narrow slit windows in the wall had all been so placed that they spiralled round the staircase too high for anyone climbing it to see through them.

"It's getting dark very quickly," said Caroline at the hundred-and-fiftieth step. "I know what the tower is like now. It would be much more sensible to give up and go home."

At the two-hundred-and-sixty-ninth step, her hand, moving foward on the railing, met only empty space. For an interminable second she shivered, pressing back to the hard brick on the other side. Then hesitantly she groped forwards, upwards, and at last her fingers met the rusty rail again, and again she climbed.

But now the breaks in the rail became more and more frequent. Sometimes she had to climb several steps with her left shoulder

59

pressed tightly to the brick wall before her searching hand could find the tenuous rusty comfort again.

At the three-hundred-and-seventy-fifth step, the rail, as her moving hand clutched it, crumpled away under her fingers. "I'd better just go by the wall," she told herself, and now her left hand traced the rough brick as she climbed up and up.

"Four-hundred-and-twenty-two, four-hundred-and-twenty-three," counted Caroline with part of her brain. "I really ought to go down now," said another part, "I wish—oh, I want to do down now—" but she could not. "It would be so silly to give up," she told herself, desperately trying to rationalise what drove her on. "Just because one's afraid—" and then she had to stifle that thought too and there was nothing left in her brain but the steadily mounting tally of the steps.

"—four-hundred-and-seventy!" said Caroline aloud with explosive relief, and then she stopped abruptly because the steps had stopped too. There was nothing ahead but a piece of broken railing barring her way, and the sky, drained now of all its colour, was still some twenty feet above her head.

"But how idiotic," she said to the air. "The whole thing's absolutely pointless," and then the fingers of her left hand, exploring the wall beside her, met not brick but wood.

She turned to see what it was, and then in the wall, level with the top step, was a small wooden door. "So it does go somewhere after all," she said, and she fumbled with the rusty handle. The door pushed open and she stepped through.

She was on a narrow stone platform about a yard wide. It seemed to encircle the tower. The platform sloped downwards away from the tower and its stones were smooth and very shiny —and this was all she noticed before she looked beyond the stones and down.

She was immeasurably, unbelievably high and alone and the ground below was a world away. It was not credible, not possible that she should be so far from the ground. All her being was suddenly absorbed in the single impulse to hurl herself from the sloping platform. "I cannot go down any other way," she said, and then she heard what she said and stepped back, frenziedly clutching the soft rotten wood of the doorway with hands sodden with sweat. There is no other way, said the voice in her brain, there is no other way.

"This is vertigo," said Caroline. "I've only got to close my eyes and keep still for a minute and it will pass off. It's bound to pass off. I've never had it before but I know what it is and it's vertigo." She closed her eyes and kept very still and felt the cold sweat running down her body.

"I should be all right now," she said at last, and carefully she stepped back through the doorway on to the four-hundred-and-seventieth step and pulled the door shut before her. She looked up at the sky, swiftly darkening with night. Then, for the first time, she looked down into the shaft of the tower, down to the narrow unprotected staircase spiralling round and round and round, and disappearing into the dark. She said—she screamed—"I can't go down."

She stood still on the top step, staring downwards, and slowly the last light faded from the tower. She could not move. It was not possible that she should dare to go down, step by step down the unprotected stairs into the dark below. It would be much easier to fall, said the voice in her head, to take one step to the left and fall and it would all be over. You cannot climb down.

She began to cry, shuddering with the pain of her sobs. It could not be true that she had brought herself to this peril, that there could be no safety for her unless she could climb down the menacing stairs. The reality *must* be that she was safe at home with Neville—but this was the reality and here were the stairs; at last she stopped crying and said "Now I shall go down."

"One!" she counted and, her right hand tearing at the brick wall, she moved first one and then the other foot down to the second step. "Two!" she counted, and then she thought of the depth below her and stood still, stupefied with terror. The stone beneath her feet, the brick against her hand were too frail protections for her exposed body. They could not save her from the voice that repeated that it would be easier to fall. Abruptly she sat down on the step.

"Two," she counted again, and spreading both her hands

61

tightly against the step on each side of her, she swung her body off the second step, down on the third. "Three," she counted, then "four" then "five", pressing closer and closer into the wall, away from the empty drop on the other side.

At the twenty-first step she said, "I think I can do it now." She slid her right hand up the rough wall and slowly stood upright. Then with the other hand she reached for the railing it was now too dark to see, but it was not there.

For timeless time she stood there, knowing nothing but fear. "Twenty-one," she said, "twenty-one," over and over again, but she could not step on to the twenty-second stair.

Something brushed her face. She knew it was a bat, not a hand, that touched her but still it was horror beyond conceivable horror, and it was this horror, without any sense of moving from dread to safety, that at last impelled her down the stairs.

"Twenty-three, twenty-four, twenty-five—" she counted, and around her the air was full of whispering skin-stretched wings. If one of them should touch her again, she must fall. "Twenty-six, twenty-seven, twenty-eight—" The skin of her right hand was torn and hot with blood, for she would never lift it from the wall, only press it slowly down and force her rigid legs to move from the knowledge of each step to the peril of the next.

So Caroline came down the dark tower. She could not think. She could know nothing but fear. Only her brain remorselessly recorded the tally. "Five-hundred-and-one," it counted, "five-hundred-and-two—and three—and four—"

The Emperor's New Clothes

BY
Hans Andersen
CHOSEN BY
Janet McNeill

I CHOSE *The Emperor's New Clothes* for three reasons; it's a good plot, it makes you laugh, and though it's an old story it is as fresh as a coat of wet paint.

The plot is exciting and dramatic. Someone, surely, is going to prevent the Emperor from making a fool of himself. (What would you have done if you'd been a member of the Court?) It's interesting to notice that there is only one child in the story, but next to the Emperor he is the most important person in it

I like especially the description of the room where the weavers worked all through that last night. They kept sixteen lights burning, they snipped the air with scissors, they stitched with invisible thread. That would make a splendid scene, if you turned the story into a play.

The ending of the story is surprising. Everyone in the crowd knew that what the child said was true. But the Emperor, because he was an Emperor, decided to go on with the procession. He knew that an Emperor ought to behave with dignity, even in the street in his underclothes. And the train bearers who carried the imaginary train carried it now even more carefully. I think they did it out of respect for their Emperor—it would be a long way back to the Palace for them, but even longer for him.

This is a story you'll remember for years. Like wet paint, it sticks.

JANET MCNEILL

MANY years ago, there was an Emperor, who was so excessively fond of new clothes that he spent all his money in dress. He did not trouble himself in the least about his soldiers; nor did he care to go either to the theatre or the chase, except for the opportunities they afforded him for displaying his new clothes. He had a different suit for each hour of the day; and as of any other king or emperor one is accustomed to say, "He is sitting in council", it was always said of him, "The Emperor is sitting in his wardrobe."

Time passed away merrily in the large town which was his capital; strangers arrived every day at the court. One day two rogues, calling themselves weavers, made their appearance. They gave out that they knew how to weave stuffs of the most beautiful colours and elaborate patterns, the clothes manu-factured from which should have the wonderful property of remaining invisible to every one who was unfit for the office he held, or who was extraordinarily simple in character.

"These must, indeed, be splendid clothes!" thought the Emperor. "Had I such a suit, I might at once find out what men in my realm are unfit for their office, and also be able to distinguish the wise from the foolish! This stuff must be woven for me immediately." And he caused large sums of money to be given to both the weavers, in order that they might begin their work directly.

So the two pretended weavers set up two looms, and affected to work very busily, though in reality they did nothing at all. They asked for the most delicate silk and the purest gold thread; put both into their own knapsacks; and then continued their pretended work at the empty looms until late at night.

"I should like to know how the weavers are getting on with my cloth," said the Emperor to himself, after some little time had elapsed; he was, however, rather embarrassed when he remembered that a simpleton, or one unfit for his office, would

65

be unable to see the manufacture. "To be sure," he thought, "he had nothing to risk in his own person; but yet he would prefer sending somebody else to bring him intelligence about the weavers, and their work, before he troubled himself in the affair." All the people throughout the city had heard of the wonderful property the cloth was to possess; and all were anxious to learn how wise, or how ignorant, their neighbours might prove to be.

"I will send my faithful old Minister to the weavers," said the Emperor at last, after some deliberation; "he will be best able to see how the cloth looks; for he is a man of sense, and no one can be more suitable for his office than he is."

So the honest old Minister went into the hall, where the knaves were working with all their might at their empty looms. "What can be the meaning of this?" thought the old man, opening his eyes very wide; "I cannot discover the least bit of thread on the looms!" However, he did not express his thoughts aloud.

The impostors requested him very courteously to be so good as to come nearer their looms; and then asked him whether the design pleased him, and whether the colours were not very beautiful; at the same time pointing to the empty frames. The poor old Minister looked and looked; he could not discover anything on the looms, for a very good reason, viz. there was nothing there. "What!" thought he again, "is it possible that I am a simpleton? I have never thought so myself; and, at any rate, if I am so, no one must know it. Can it be that I am unfit for my office? No, that must not be said either. I will never confess that I could not see the stuff."

"Well, Sir Minister!" said one of the knaves, still pretending to work, "you do not say whether the stuff pleases you."

"Oh, it is admirable!" replied the old Minister, looking at the loom through his spectacles. "This pattern, and the colours— yes, I will tell the Emperor without delay how very beautiful I think them."

"We shall be much obliged to you," said the impostors, and then they named the different colours and described the

patterns of the pretended stuff. The old Minister listened atten-
tively to their words, in order that he might repeat them to the
Emperor; and then the knaves asked for more silk and gold,
saying that it was necessary to complete what they had begun.
However, they put all that was given them into their knapsacks,
and continued to work with as much apparent diligence as
before at their empty looms.

The Emperor now sent another officer of his court to see
how the men were getting on, and to ascertain whether the
cloth would soon be ready. It was just the same with this
gentleman as with the Minister; he surveyed the looms on all
sides, but could see nothing at all but the empty frames.

"Does not the stuff appear as beautiful to you as it did to my
Lord the Minister?" asked the impostors of the Emperor's
second ambassador; at the same time making the same gestures
as before, and talking of the design and colours which were
not there.

"I certainly am not stupid!" thought the messenger. "It must
be that I am not fit for my good, profitable office! That is very
odd; however, no one shall know anything about it." And
accordingly he praised the stuff he could not see, and declared
that he was delighted with both colours and patterns. "Indeed,
please your Imperial Majesty," said he to his sovereign, when
he returned, "the cloth which the weavers are preparing is
extraordinarily magnificent."

The whole city was talking of the splendid cloth which the
Emperor had ordered to be woven at his own expense.

And now the Emperor himself wished to see the costly
manufacture, whilst it was still on the loom. Accompanied by a
select number of officers of the court, among whom were the
two honest men who had already admired the cloth, he went
to the crafty impostors, who, as soon as they were aware of the
Emperor's approach, went on working more diligently than
ever; although they still did not pass a single thread through the
looms.

"Is not the work absolutely magnificent?" said the two
officers of the crown already mentioned. "If your Majesty will

only be pleased to look at it! What a splendid design! What glorious colours!" and at the same time they pointed to the empty frames; for they imagined that every one but themselves could see this exquisite piece of workmanship.

"How is this?" said the Emperor to himself; "I can see nothing! This is, indeed, a terrible affair! Am I a simpleton? or am I unfit to be an Emperor? that would be the worst thing that could happen. Oh, the cloth is charming!" said he aloud; "it has my entire approbation." And he smiled most graciously, and looked at the empty looms; for on no account would he say that he could not see what two of the officers of his court had praised so much. All his retinue now strained their eyes, hoping to discover something on the looms, but they could see no more than the others; nevertheless they all exclaimed, "Oh! how beautiful!" and advised his Majesty to have some new clothes made from this splendid material for the approaching procession. "Magnificent! charming! excellent!" resounded on all sides; and every one was uncommonly gay. The Emperor shared in the general satisfaction, and presented the impostors with the riband of an order of knighthood to be worn in their buttonholes, and the title of "Gentlemen Weavers".

The rogues sat up the whole of the night before the day on which the procession was to take place, and had sixteen lights burning, so that every one might see how anxious they were to finish the Emperor's new suit. They pretended to roll the cloth off the looms; cut the air with their scissors; and sewed with needles without any thread in them. "See!" cried they at last, "the Emperor's new clothes are ready!"

And now the Emperor, with all the grandees of his court, came to the weavers; and the rogues raised their arms, as if in the act of holding something up, saying, "Here are your Majesty's trousers! here is the scarf! here is the mantle! The whole suit is as light as a cobweb; one might fancy one has nothing at all on, when dressed in it; that, however, is the great virtue of this delicate cloth."

"Yes, indeed!" said all the courtiers, although not one of them could see anything of this exquisite manufacture.

"If your Imperial Majesty will be graciously pleased to take off your clothes, we will fit on the new suit, in front of the looking-glass."

The Emperor was accordingly undressed, and the rogues pretended to array him in his new suit; the Emperor turning round, from side to side, before the looking-glass.

"How splendid his Majesty looks in his new clothes! and how well they fit!" every one cried out. "What a design! What colours! These are, indeed, royal robes!"

"The canopy which is to be borne over your Majesty, in the procession, is waiting," announced the Chief Master of the Ceremonies.

"I am quite ready," answered the Emperor. "Do my new clothes fit well?" asked he, turning himself round again before the looking-glass, in order that he might appear to be examining his handsome suit.

The lords of the bedchamber, who were to carry his Majesty's train, felt about on the ground, as if they were lifting up the ends of the mantle, and pretended to be carrying something; for they would by no means betray anything like simplicity, or unfitness for their office.

So now the Emperor walked under his high canopy in the midst of the procession, through the streets of his capital; and all the people standing by, and those at the windows, cried out, "Oh! how beautiful are our Emperor's new clothes! What a magnificent train there is to the mantle! And how gracefully the scarf hangs!" In short, no one would allow that he could not see these much-admired clothes, because, in doing so, he would have declared himself either a simpleton or unfit for his office. Certainly, none of the Emperor's various suits had ever excited so much admiration as this.

"But the Emperor has nothing at all on!" said a little child. "Listen to the voice of innocence!" exclaimed his father; and what the child had said was whispered from one to another.

"But he has nothing at all on!" at last cried out all the people. The Emperor was vexed, for he knew that the people were right; but he thought "the procession must go on now!" And the lords of the bedchamber took greater pains than ever to appear holding up a train, although, in reality, there was no train to hold.

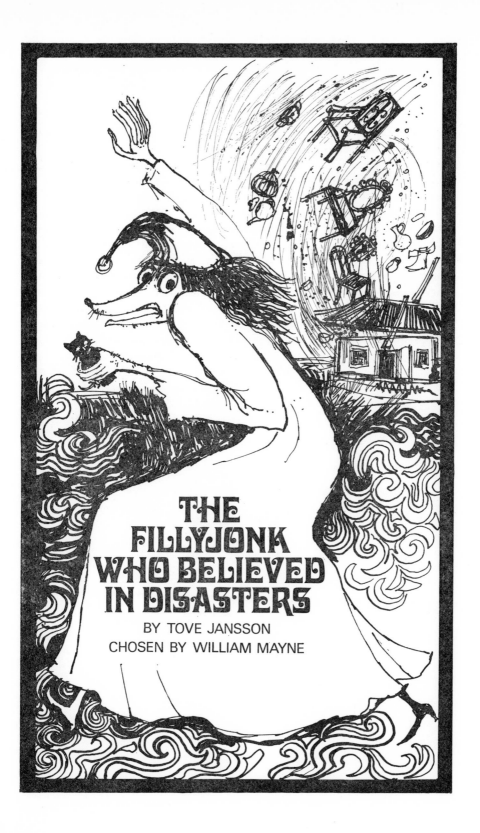

THE FILLYJONK WHO BELIEVED IN DISASTERS

BY TOVE JANSSON

CHOSEN BY WILLIAM MAYNE

I HAVE just moved house. What a great and natural tidying-out I had before the removal men came; how large a funeral fire for the dead things I no longer kept; what a heap of ashes was left to blow away in the wind. Like the fillyjonk in the story I have chosen I welcomed as well as dreaded the storm that was to change either me or my surroundings. I went through the same agonies of premonition and anticipation. I saw my tornado as a black thing, solid, dangerous to me, unavoidable. When it came, and so much rubbish of past life was sucked away and dropped out of sight, the funnel was not black at all, but white, just as it is in the story. And the peace of being delivered from the tyranny of my possessions and all their history was marvellous. My new house will hardly be furnished. Hemulens may come to stay, but they shall sit on the floor with me and my real cats. I often think of this story now, of its sadness, and its finish in peace. I know that sadness of life—we all do—and I know the peace too. I feel that it is possible to go on changing for ever, but only if I don't tie myself down to a shape I already know: there are new shapes I have not learned: the change into each one is accompanied by tornadoes, my own private disasters with happy endings.

WILLIAM MAYNE

ONCE upon a time there was a fillyjonk who was washing her large carpet in the sea. She rubbed it with soap and a brush up to the first blue stripe, and then she waited for a seventh wave to come and wash the soap away.

Then she soaped and rubbed further, to the next blue stripe, and the sun was warming her back, and she stood with her thin legs in the clear water, rubbing and rubbing.

It was a mild and motionless summer day, exactly right for washing carpets. Slow and sleepy swells came rolling in to help her with the rinsing, and around her red cap a few bumble-bees were humming: they took her for a flower!

Don't you pretend, the fillyjonk thought grimly. I know how things are. Everything's always peaceful like this just before a disaster.

She reached the last blue stripe, let the seventh wave rinse it for a moment, and then pulled the whole of the carpet out of the water.

The smooth rock shone redly under the rippling water, reflections of light danced over the fillyjonk's toes and gilded all ten of them.

She stood and mused. A new cap, orange-red perhaps? Or one could embroider reflections of light around the edge of the old one? In gold? But of course it wouldn't look the same because they wouldn't move. And besides, what does one need a new cap for when danger breaks loose? One might just as well perish in the old one. . . .

The fillyjonk pulled her carpet ashore and slapped it down on the rock and sullenly stalked over it to stamp the water from it.

The weather was far too fine, quite unnatural. Something or other had to happen. She knew it. Somewhere below the horizon something black and terrible was lurking—working larger, drawing nearer—faster and faster . . .

73

One doesn't even know what it is, the fillyjonk whispered to herself.

Her heart began to thump and her back felt cold, and she whirled around as if she had an enemy behind her. But the sea was glittering as before, the reflections danced over the floor in playful twists, and the faint summer wind comfortingly stroked her snout.

But it is far from easy to comfort a fillyjonk who is stricken with panic and doesn't know why. With shaking paws she spread her carpet to dry, scrambled together her soap and brush and went rushing homewards to put the tea-kettle on the fire. Gaffsie had promised to drop in at five o'clock.

The fillyjonk lived in a large and not very pretty house. Some-one, who had wanted to get rid of old paint, had painted it dark green on the outside and brown all over the inside. The fillyjonk had rented it unfurnished from a hemulen who had assured her that her grandmother used to live there in the summer, when she was a young girl. And as the fillyjonk was very attached to her kindred and relatives she at once decided that she would honour her grandmother's memory by living in the same house.

The first evening she had sat on her doorstep and wondered about her grandmother who must have been very unlike herself in her youth. How curious that a genuine fillyjonk with a true sense of nature's beauty should have wanted to live on this glum and sandy shore! No garden to grow jam plums in! Not the smallest leafy tree or even bush to start an arbour with. Not even a nice view!

The fillyjonk sighed and looked forlornly at the green evening sea trimming the long beach with its breakers. Green water, white sand, red dried seaweed. An exact setting for disaster; not a single safe spot.

And afterwards, of course, the fillyjonk had found out that it was all a mistake. She had moved into this horrible house on this horrible beach quite unnecessarily. Her grandmother had lived elsewhere. That is life!

But by that time the fillyjonk had written letters to all her

74

relatives about her summer house, and so she didn't think it proper to change her plans.

They might have thought her a little silly.

So the fillyjonk closed her door and tried to make the house cosy inside. This was not easy. The ceilings were so high that they always seemed full of shadows. The windows were large and solemn, and no lace curtains could give them a friendly look. They weren't windows for looking out of, they were windows to look in from—and the fillyjonk did not like this thought.

She tried to arrange cosy corners, but they never became cosy. Her furniture had a lost look. The chairs nestled close to the table, the sofa huddled against the wall, and the lighted patches around the lamps were as dejected as a flash-light in a dark wood.

Like all fillyjonks she owned a lot of knick-knacks. Small mirrors, photographs framed in red velvet and little shells, china kittens and hemulens resting on pieces of crochet work, beautiful maxims embroidered in silk or silver, very small vases and nice mymble-shaped tea-cosies—well, all sorts of things that make life more easy and less dangerous, and large.

But all these beloved things of beauty lost their safety and their meaning in the bleak house by the sea. She moved them from table to sideboard and from sideboard to window-sill, but nowhere did they look right.

There they were again. Just as forlorn.

The fillyjonk stopped at the door and looked at her belongings to comfort herself. But they were just as helpless as she was. She went into the kitchen and laid the soap and scrubbing-brush on the sink. Then she lighted the fire under the tea-kettle and took out her best gold-edged cups. She lifted down the cake-dish, nimbly blew off some crumbs and laid some iced little cakes on top of the others to impress Gaffsie.

Gaffsie never took milk with her tea, but the fillyjonk nevertheless put grandmother's little silver boat on the tray. The sugar lumps she shook out in a tiny plush basket with pearl-crusted handles.

While she set the tea-tray she felt quite calm and was able to shut off all thoughts of disaster.

It was a real pity that no nice flowers were to be found in this unlucky place. All the plants by the shore were cross and prickly little shrubs, and their flowers didn't match her drawing-room. The fillyjonk gave her table vase a displeased nudge and took a step towards the window to look for Gaffsie.

Then she thought hastily: No, no. I won't look for her. I'll wait for her knock. Then I run and answer the door, and we'll both be terribly delighted and sociable and have a good chat. . . . If I look for her perhaps the beach will be quite empty all the way to the lighthouse. Or else I'll see just a tiny little spot coming, and I don't like to watch things that draw nearer and nearer . . . and still worse would it be, wouldn't it, if the little spot started to grow smaller and was going the other way. . . .

The fillyjonk started to tremble. What's come over me, she thought. I mustn't talk about this with Gaffsie. She's really not the person I'd prefer to chat with at all, but then I don't know anybody else hereabouts.

There was a knock on the door. The fillyjonk went rushing out into the hall and was already talking on her way to the door.

" . . . and what splendid weather," she shouted, "and the sea, did you look at the sea . . . how blue today, how friendly it looks, not a ripple! how are you, well, you look really radiant, and so I thought you would . . . But it's all this, of course, living like this, I mean, in the bosom of nature, and everything— it puts everything in order, doesn't it?"

She's more confused than usual, Gaffsie was thinking while she pulled off her gloves (because she was a real lady), and aloud she said:

"Exactly. How right you are, Mrs. Fillyjonk."

They sat down to the table, and the fillyjonk was so happy to have company that she prattled the sheerest nonsense and spilled tea all over the cloth.

Gaffsie said something nice about the cakes and the sugar bowl and everything she could think of, but about the flower vase she said nothing, of course. Gaffsie was a well-brought-up person, and anybody could see that that wild, angry shrub didn't go well with the tea things.

After a while the fillyjonk stopped talking nonsense, and as Gaffsie didn't say anything at all, silence fell.

Then the sun clouded over and the table-cloth suddenly looked grey. The large solemn windows showed a mass of grey clouds, and the ladies could hear a new kind of wind coming in from the sea. Faint and far away, no more than a whisper.

"I saw you've had your carpet out for a wash, Mrs. Fillyjonk," Gaffsie said with great civility.

"Yes, sea-water's said to be the right thing for carpets," the fillyjonk replied. "The colours never run, and there's such a lovely smell. . . ."

I must make Gaffsie understand, she thought. I have to tell somebody that I'm frightened, someone who can answer me: But of course, I quite understand you must be. Or: Really, what on earth is there to be afraid of? A splendid summer day like today. Anything, but something.

"The cakes are my grandma's recipe," said the fillyjonk. And then she leaned forward over the table and whispered:

"This calm is unnatural. It means something terrible is going to happen. Dear Gaffsie, believe me, we are so very small and insignificant, and so are our tea cakes and carpets and all those things, you know, and still they're so important, but always they're threatened by mercilessness. . . ."

"Oh," said Gaffsie, feeling ill at ease.

"Yes, by mercilessness," the fillyjonk continued rather breathlessly. "By something one can't ask anything of, nor argue with, nor understand, and that never tells one anything. Something that one can see drawing near, through a black window-pane, far away on the road, far away to sea, growing and growing but not really showing itself until too late. Mrs. Gaffsie, have you felt it? Tell me that you know what I'm talking about! Please!"

Gaffsie was very red in the face and sat twirling the sugar bowl in her paws and wishing that she had never come.

"There can be very sudden storms at this time of the year," she said at last, cautiously.

The fillyjonk fell silent from disappointment. Gaffsie waited a while, then continued, slightly vexed:

"I hung out my washing last Friday, and believe me, there was such a wind quite suddenly that I found my best pillow-slips by the gate. What washing-material do you use, Mrs. Fillyjonk?"

"I don't remember," the fillyjonk answered, suddenly feeling very tired because Gaffsie didn't even try to understand her. "Would you like some more tea?"

"Thank you, not any more," Gaffsie said. "What a nice visit, only too short. I'm afraid I'll have to start on my way soon."

"Yes," the fillyjonk said, "I see."

Darkness was falling over the sea, and the beach was mumbling to itself. It was a bit too early to light the lamp, but still too dark to be nice. Gaffsie's narrow nose was more wrinkled than usually, and one could see that she didn't feel at ease. But the fillyjonk didn't help her to take her leave, she didn't say a word but sat quite still, only breaking a couple of iced cakes into crumbs.

How painful, Gaffsie thought and smuggled her handbag under her arm. The south-wester slightly raised its voice outside.

"You were talking about wind," the fillyjonk said suddenly. "A wind that carries off your washing. But I'm speaking about cyclones. Typhoons, Gaffsie dear. Tornadoes, whirlwinds, sand-storms. . . . Flood waves that carry houses away. . . . But most of all I'm talking about myself and my fears, even if I know that's not done. I know everything will turn out badly. I think about that all the time. Even while I'm washing my carpet. Do you understand that? Do you feel the same way?"

"Have you tried vinegar," said Gaffsie, staring into her tea-cup. "The colours keep best if you have a little vinegar in the rinsing water."

At this the fillyjonk became angry, which was a most unusual thing. She felt that she had to challenge Gaffsie in some way

78

or other, and she chose the first thing that came to her mind. She pointed a shaking finger at the horrid little shrub in the table vase and cried:

"Look! Isn't it nice? The perfect thing to match my tea-set!"

And Gaffsie was feeling just as tired and cross, so she jumped to her feet and replied:

"Not a bit! It's all too large and prickly and gaudy, it has a brazen look and doesn't belong on a tea-table at all!"

Then the two ladies took leave of each other, and the fillyjonk shut her door and went back to her drawing-room.

She felt miserable and disappointed with her tea party. The small shrub stood on the table, grey and thorny and covered with little dark red flowers. Suddenly it seemed to the fillyjonk that it wasn't the flowers that did not match her tea-set. It was the tea-set that didn't match anything.

She put the vase on the window-sill.

The sea had changed. It was grey all over, but the waves had bared their white teeth and were snapping at the beach. The sky had a ruddy glow, and looked heavy.

The fillyjonk stood in her window for a long time, listening to the rising wind.

Then there was a ring on the telephone.

"Is that Mrs. Fillyjonk?" Gaffsie's voice asked cautiously.

"Of course," said the fillyjonk. "No one else lives here. Did you arrive home all right?"

"Yes, all right," said Gaffsie. "There's quite a wind." She was silent for a while, and then she said in a friendly voice: "Mrs. Fillyjonk? Those terrible things you spoke of. Have they happened often to you?"

"No," said the fillyjonk.

"Just a few times, then?"

"Well, never, really," said the fillyjonk. "It's just how I feel."

"Oh," said Gaffsie. "Well, thank you for inviting me. It was so nice. So nothing has ever happened to you?"

"No," said the fillyjonk. "So kind of you to call me. I hope we'll see more of each other."

"So do I," said Gaffsie and hung up.

79

The fillyjonk sat looking at the telephone for a while. She suddenly felt cold.

My windows are going dark again, she thought. I could hang some blankets against them. I could turn the mirrors face to wall. But she didn't do anything, she sat listening to the wind that had started to howl in the chimney. Not unlike a small homeless animal.

On the south side the hemulen's fishing net had started whacking against the wall, but the fillyjonk didn't dare go out to lift it down.

The house was shivering, very slightly. The wind was coming on in rushes; one could hear a gale getting an extra push on its way in from the sea.

A roof-tile went coasting down the roof and crashed to the ground. The fillyjonk rose and hurried into her bedroom. But it was too large, it didn't feel safe. The pantry. It would be small enough. The fillyjonk took her quilt from the bed and ran down the kitchen passage, kicked open the pantry door and shut it behind her. She panted a bit. Here you heard less of the gale. And here was no window, only a small ventilator grating.

She felt her way in the dark past the sack of potatoes and rolled herself into her quilt, on the floor below the jam shelf.

Slowly her imagination started to picture a gale of its own, very much blacker and wilder than the one that was shaking her house. The breakers grew to great white dragons, a roaring tornado sucked up the sea like a black pillar on the horizon, a gleaming pillar that came rushing towards her, nearer and nearer. . . .

Those storms of her own were the worst ones. And deep down in her heart the fillyjonk was just a little proud of her disasters that belonged to no one else.

Gaffsie is a jackass, she thought. A silly woman with cakes and pillow-slips all over her mind. And she doesn't know a thing about flowers. And least of all about me. Now she's sitting at home thinking that I haven't ever experienced anything. I, who see the end of the world every day, and still I'm going on putting on my clothes, and taking them off again, and eating and washing-up the dishes and receiving visits, just as if nothing ever happened!

The fillyjonk thrust out her nose from the quilt, stared severely out in the dark and said: "I'll show you."

Whatever that meant. Then she snuggled down under her quilt and pressed her paws against her ears.

But outside the gale was steadily rising towards midnight, and by one o'clock it had reached 47 yards per second (or however they measure the big storms).

About two o'clock in the morning the chimney blew down. Half of it fell outside the house and the other half smashed down into the kitchen fireplace. Through the hole in the ceiling one could see the dark night sky and great rushing clouds. And then the gale found its way inside and nothing at all was to be seen except flying ashes, wildly fluttering curtains and table-cloths, and photographs of aunts and uncles whirling through the air. All the fillyjonk's sacred things came to life, rustling, tinkling and clashing everywhere, doors were banging and pictures crashing to the floor.

In the middle of the drawing-room stood the fillyjonk herself, dazed and wild in her fluttering skirt, thinking confusedly: this is it. Now comes the end. At last. Now I don't have to wait any more.

She lifted the telephone receiver to call Gaffsie and tell her . . . well, tell her a few really crushing things. Coolly and triumphantly.

But the telephone wires had blown down.

The fillyjonk could hear nothing but the gale and the rattle of loosening roof-tiles. If I were to go up to the attic the roof would blow off, she thought. And if I go down in the cellar the whole house comes down over me. It's going to do it anyway.

She got hold of a china kitten and pressed it hard in her paw. Then a window blew upon and shattered its pane in small fragments over the floor. A gust of rain spattered the mahogany furniture, and the stately plaster hemulen threw himself from his pedestal and went to pieces.

With a sickening crash her great chandelier fell to the floor. It had belonged to her maternal uncle. All around her the fillyjonk heard her belongings cry and creak. Then she caught a flash of her own pale snout in a fragment of a mirror, and without any further thought she rushed up to the window and jumped out.

She found herself sitting in the sand. She felt warm raindrops on her face, and her dress was fluttering and flapping around her like a sail.

She shut her eyes very tight and knew that she was in the midst of danger, totally helpless.

The gale was blowing, steady and undisturbed. But all the alarming noises had vanished, all the howling and crashing, the thumping, splintering and tearing. The danger had been inside the house, not outside.

The fillyjonk drew a wary breath, smelt the bitter tang of the seaweed, and opened her eyes.

The darkness was no longer as dark as it had been in her drawing-room.

She could see the breakers and the lighthouse's outstretched arm of light that slowly moved through the night, passing her, wandering off over the sand-dunes, losing itself towards the horizon, and returning again. Round and round circled the calm light, keeping an eye on the gale.

I've never been out alone at night before, the fillyjonk thought. If mother knew. . . .

She started to crawl against the wind, down to the beach, to get as far away as possible from the hemulen's house. She still held the china kitten in her left paw, it calmed her to have something to protect. Now she could see that the sea looked almost all blue-white. The wave crests were blown straight off and drifted like smoke over the beach. The smoke tasted of salt.

Behind her something or other was still crashing to pieces, inside the house. But the fillyjonk didn't even turn her head. She had curled up behind a large boulder and was looking wide-eyed into the dark. She wasn't cold any longer. And the strange thing was that she suddenly felt quite safe. It was a very strange feeling, and she found it indescribably nice. But what was there to worry over? The disaster had come at last.

Towards morning the gale was blowing itself out. The fillyjonk hardly noticed it. She was sitting in deep thought about herself and her disasters, and her furniture, and wondering how it all fitted together. As a matter of fact nothing of consequence had happened, except that the chimney had come down.

But she had a feeling that nothing more important had ever happened to her in her life. It had given her quite a shaking-up and turned everything topsy-turvy. The fillyjonk didn't know what she should do to right herself again.

The old kind of fillyjonk was lost, and she wasn't sure that she wanted her back. And what about all the belongings of this old fillyjonk?

All the things that were broken and sooty and cracked and wet? To sit and mend it all, week after week, gluing and patching and looking for lost pieces and fragments. . . .

To wash and iron and paint over and to feel sorry about all the irreparable things, and to know that there would still be cracks everywhere, and that all the things had been in such better shape before. . . . No, no! And to put them all back into place in the dark and bleak rooms and try to find them cosy once more. . . .

No, I won't! cried the fillyjonk and rose on cramped legs. If I try to make everything the same as before, then I'll be the same myself as before. I'll be afraid once more. . . . I can feel that. And the tornadoes will come back to lurk around me, and the typhoons too. . . .

For the first time she looked back at the hemulen's house. It was standing as before. It was filled with broken things. It waited for her to come and take care of them.

No genuine fillyjonk had ever left her old inherited belongings adrift. . . . Mother would have reminded me about duty, the fillyjonk mumbled. It was morning.

The eastern horizon was waiting for sunrise. Small frightened squalls of rain were flying off, and the sky was strewn with clouds that the gale had forgotten to take along with it. A few weak thunderclaps went rolling by.

The weather was uneasy and didn't know its own mind. The fillyjonk hesitated also.

At this moment she caught sight of the tornado.

It didn't look like her own special tornado, which was a gleaming black pillar of water. This was the real thing. It was luminous. It was a whirl of white clouds churning downwards in a large spiral, and it turned to chalk white where it met the water lifting itself upwards out of the sea.

It didn't roar, it didn't rush. It was quite silent and slowly came nearer the shore, slightly swaying on its way. The sun rose, and the tornado turned rose-petal red.

It looked infinitely tall, rotating silently and powerfully around itself, and it drew slowly nearer and nearer. . . .

The fillyjonk was unable to move. She was standing still, quite still, crushing the china kitten in her paw and thinking: Oh, my beautiful, wonderful disaster. . . .

The tornado wandered over the beach, not far from the fillyjonk. The white, majestic pillar passed her, became a pillar of sand, and very quietly lifted the roof off the hemulen's house. The fillyjonk saw it rise in the air and disappear. She saw her furniture go whirling up and disappear. She saw all her knick-knacks fly straight to heaven, tray-cloths, and photo-frames and tea-cosies and grandma's silver cream jug, and the sentences in silk and silver, every single thing! and she thought ecstatically: How very, very wonderful! What can I do, a poor little fillyjonk, against the great powers of nature? What is there to mend and repair now? Nothing! All is washed clean and swept away!

The tornado went solemnly wandering off over the fields, and she saw it taper off, break and disperse. It wasn't needed any more.

The fillyjonk drew a deep breath. Now I'll never be afraid again, she said to herself. Now I'm free. Now I can do anything.

She placed the china kitten on a boulder. It had lost an ear during the night and got a blob of black oil on its nose. It had a new look, slightly impish and cheeky.

The sun rose higher. The fillyjonk went down to the wet sand. There lay her carpet. The sea had decorated it with seaweed and shells, and no carpet had ever been more thoroughly rinsed. The fillyjonk chuckled. She lifted the carpet in both paws and pulled it after her out in the swells.

She dived headlong in a large green swell, she sat on her carpet and surfed on sizzling white foam, she dived again, down and down.

One swell after the other came rolling over her, transparently green, and then the fillyjonk came to the surface again, for a breath, and to look at the sun, spluttering and laughing and shouting and dancing with her carpet in the surf.

Never in her life had she had such fun.

Gaffsie had been shouting and calling for several minutes before the fillyjonk caught sight of her.

"How terrible!" shouted Gaffsie. "Dear, poor little Mrs. Fillyjonk!"

"Good morning!" said the fillyjonk and pulled her carpet to the beach.

"How are you today?"

"I'm beside myself," Gaffsie cried. "What a night! I've thought of you all the time. And I saw it myself! I saw it coming! What a disaster!"

"How do you mean?" asked the fillyjonk innocently.

"How right you were, how very right," said Gaffsie. "You *said* there was a disaster coming. Oh, all your beautiful things! Your beautiful home! I've tried to call you all night, I was so worried, but the line had blown down. . . ."

"That was kind of you," said the fillyjonk and wrenched the water from her cap. "But really quite unnecessary. If you feel worried there's nothing like putting a little vinegar in the rinsing water. Then the colours keep!"

And the fillyjonk sat down in the sand and wept with laughter.

THE TALE OF THE SILVER SAUCER AND THE TRANSPARENT APPLE

From Arthur Ransome's
'Old Peter's Russian Tales'
chosen by
JAMES REEVES

ON my seventh birthday I was given a book which I at once read and went on re-reading for many years. It was Arthur Ransome's OLD PETER'S RUSSIAN TALES. These traditional stories have never ceased to appeal to my deepest imagination. They tell of the wishes and hopes, the foolishness, the wisdom and humour of ordinary people, not only in old Russia but all over Europe—indeed, the whole world, for they appear in many versions wherever stories are handed down from parents to children. So that, in choosing one of these tales, I am in a way repaying a debt contracted long ago, by passing on to younger readers what I was given when a child. It was not easy to make up my mind about which story to take from this wonderful book. I might have taken *The Fool of the World and the Flying Ship*, *Salt*, or *Little Master Misery*—not to mention *The Stolen Turnips*. All these are favourites. But in the end I chose this one because it is the most magical and the most poetic. The apple, some may say, is the very symbol of the imagination itself, offering a vision of the whole world as it spins in the silver saucer; and it is the imagination which is a more precious and satisfying gift than all the robes and necklaces in the world.

JAMES REEVES

THERE was once an old peasant, and he must have had more brains under his hair than ever I had, for he was a merchant, and used to take things every year to sell at the big fair of Nijni Novgorod. Well, I could never do that. I could never be anything better than an old forester.

"Never mind, grandfather," said Maroosia.

God knows best, and He makes some merchants and some foresters, and some good and some bad, all in His own way. Anyhow this one was a merchant, and he had three daughters. They were none of them so bad to look at, but one of them was as pretty as Maroosia. And she was the best of them too. The others put all the hard work on her, while they did nothing but look at themselves in the looking-glass and complain of what they had to eat. They called the pretty one "Little Stupid", because she was so good and did all their work for them. Oh, they were real bad ones, those two. We wouldn't have them in here for a minute.

Well, the time came round for the merchant to pack up and go to the big fair. He called his daughters, and said, "Little pigeons", just as I say to you. "Little pigeons," says he, "what would you like me to bring you from the fair?"

Says the eldest, "I'd like a necklace, but it must be a rich one."

Says the second, "I want a new dress with gold hems."

But the youngest, the good one, Little Stupid, said nothing at all.

"Now little one," says her father, "what is it you want? I must bring something for you too."

Says the little one, "Could I have a silver saucer and a transparent apple? But never mind if there are none."

The old merchant says, "Long hair, short sense," just as I say to Maroosia; but he promised the little pretty one, who was so good that her sisters called her stupid, that if he could get her a silver saucer and a transparent apple she should have them.

Then they all kissed each other, and he cracked his whip, and off he went, with the little bells jingling on the horses' harness.

The three sisters waited till he came back. The two elder ones looked in the looking-glass, and thought how fine they would look in the new necklace and the new dress; but the little pretty one took care of her old mother, and scrubbed and dusted and swept and cooked, and every day the other two said that the soup was burnt or the bread not properly baked.

Then one day there was a jingling of bells and a clattering of horses' hoofs, and the old merchant came driving back from the fair.

The sisters ran out.

"Where is the necklace?" asked the first.

"You haven't forgotten the dress?" asked the second.

But the little one, Little Stupid, helped her old father off with his coat, and asked him if he was tired.

"Well, little one," says the old merchant, "and don't you want your fairing too? I went from one end of the market to the other before I could get what you wanted. I bought the silver saucer from an old Jew, and the transparent apple from a Finnish hag."

"Oh, thank you, father," says the little one.

"And what will you do with them?" says he.

"I shall spin the apple in the saucer," says the little pretty one, and at that the old merchant burst out laughing.

"They don't call you 'Little Stupid' for nothing," says he.

Well, they all had their fairings, and the two elder sisters, the bad ones, they ran off and put on the new dress and the new necklace, and came out and strutted about, preening themselves like herons, now on one leg and now on the other, to see how they looked. But Little Stupid, she just sat herself down beside the stove, and took the transparent apple and set it in the silver saucer, and she laughed softly to herself. And then she began spinning the apple in the saucer.

Round and round the apple spun in the saucer, faster and faster, till you couldn't see the apple at all, nothing but a mist like a little whirlpool in the silver saucer. And the little good one looked at it, and her eyes shone like yours.

Her sisters laughed at her.

"Spinning an apple in a saucer and staring at it, the little stupid," they said, as they strutted about the room, listening to the rustle of the new dress and fingering the bright round stones of the necklace.

But the little pretty one did not mind them. She sat in the corner watching the spinning apple. And as it spun she talked to it.

"Spin, spin, apple in the silver saucer." This is what she said. "Spin so that I may see the world. Let me have a peep at the little father Tzar on his high throne. Let me see the rivers and the ships and the great towns far away."

And as she looked at the little glass whirlpool in the saucer, there was the Tzar, the little father—God preserve him!— sitting on his high throne. Ships sailed on the seas, their white sails swelling in the wind. There was Moscow with its white stone walls and painted churches. Why, there were the market at Nijni Novgorod, and the Arab merchants with their camels, and the Chinese with their blue trousers and bamboo staves. And then there was the great river Volga, with men on the banks towing ships against the stream. Yes, and she saw a sturgeon asleep in a deep pool.

"Oh! oh! oh!" says the little pretty one, as she saw all these things.

And the bad ones, they saw how her eyes shone, and they came and looked over her shoulder, and saw how all the world was there, in the spinning apple and the silver saucer. And the old father came and looked over her shoulder too, and he saw the market at Nijni Novgorod.

"Why, there is the inn where I put up the horses," says he. "You haven't done so badly after all, Little Stupid."

And the little pretty one, Little Stupid, went on staring into the glass whirlpool in the saucer, spinning the apple, and seeing all the world she had never seen before, floating there before her in the saucer, brighter than leaves in sunlight.

The bad ones, the elder sisters, were sick with envy.

"Little Stupid," says the first, "if you will give me your silver saucer and your transparent apple, I will give you my fine new necklace."

"Little Stupid," says the second, "I will give you my new dress with gold hems if you will give me your transparent apple and your silver saucer."

"Oh, I couldn't do that," says the Little Stupid, and she goes on spinning the apple in the saucer and seeing what was happening all over the world.

So the bad ones put their wicked heads together and thought of a plan. And they took their father's axe, and went into the deep forest and hid it under a bush.

The next day they waited till afternoon, when work was done, and the little pretty one was spinning her apple in the saucer. They they said—

"Come along, Little Stupid; we are all going to gather berries in the forest."

"Do you really want me to come too?" says the little one. She would rather have played with her apple and saucer.

But they said, "Why, of course. You don't think we can carry all the berries ourselves!"

So the little one jumped up, and found the baskets, and went with them to the forest. But before she started she ran to her father, who was counting his money, and was not too pleased to be interrupted, for figures go quickly out of your head when you have a lot of them to remember. She asked him to take care of the silver saucer and the transparent apple for fear she would lose them in the forest.

"Very well, little bird," says the old man, and he put the things in a box with a lock and key to it. He was a merchant, you know, and that sort are always careful about things, and go clattering about with a lot of keys at their belt. I've nothing to lock up, and never had, and perhaps it is just as well, for I could never be bothered with keys.

So the little one picks up all three baskets and runs off after the others, the bad ones, with black hearts under their necklaces and new dresses.

They went deep into the forest, picking berries, and the little one picked so fast that she soon had a basket full. She was picking and picking, and did not see what the bad ones were doing. They were fetching the axe.

The little one stood up to straighten her back, which ached after so much stooping, and she saw her two sisters standing in front of her, looking at her cruelly. Their baskets lay on the ground quite empty. They had not picked a berry. The eldest had the axe in her hand.

The little one was frightened.

"What is it, sisters?" says she; "and why do you look at me with cruel eyes? And what is the axe for? You are not going to cut berries with an axe."

"No, Little Stupid," says the first, "we are not going to cut berries with the axe."

"No, Little Stupid," says the second; "the axe is here for something else."

The little one begged them not to frighten her.

Says the first, "Give me your transparent apple."

Says the second, "Give me your silver saucer."

"If you don't give them up at once, we shall kill you." That is what the bad ones said.

The poor little one begged them. "O darling sisters, do not kill me! I haven't got the saucer or the apple with me at all."

"What a lie!" say the bad ones. "You never would leave it behind."

And one caught her by the hair, and the other swung the axe, and between them they killed the little pretty one, who was called Little Stupid because she was so good.

Then they looked for the saucer and the apple, and could not find them. But it was too late now. So they made a hole in the ground, and buried the little one under a birch tree.

When the sun went down the bad ones came home, and they wailed with false voices, and rubbed their eyes to make the tears come. They made their eyes red and their noses too, and they did not look any prettier for that.

"What is the matter with you, little pigeons?" said the old

merchant and his wife. I would not say "little pigeons" to such bad ones. Black-hearted crows is what I would call them.

And they wail and lament aloud—

"We are miserable for ever. Our poor little sister is lost. We looked for her everywhere. We heard the wolves howling. They must have eaten her."

The old mother and father cried like rivers in springtime, because they loved the little pretty one, who was called Little Stupid because she was so good.

But before their tears were dry the bad ones began to ask for the silver saucer and the transparent apple.

"No, no," says the old man; "I shall keep them for ever, in memory of my poor little daughter whom God has taken away."

So the bad ones did not gain by killing their little sister.

"That is one good thing," said Vanya.

"But is that all, grandfather?" said Maroosia.

"Wait a bit, little pigeons. Too much haste set his shoes on fire. You listen, and you will hear what happened," said old Peter. He took a pinch of snuff from a little wooden box, and then he went on with his tale.

Time did not stop with the death of the little girl. Winter came, and the snow with it. Everything was all white, just as it is now. And the wolves came to the doors of the huts, even into the villages, and no one stirred farther than he need. And then the snow melted, and the buds broke on the trees, and the birds began singing, and the sun shone warmer every day. The old people had almost forgotten the little pretty one who lay dead in the forest. The bad ones had not forgotten, because now they had to do the work, and they did not like that at all.

And then one day some lambs strayed away into the forest, and a young shepherd went after them to bring them safely back to their mothers. And as he wandered this way and that through the forest, following their light tracks, he came to a little birch tree, bright with new leaves, waving over a little mound of earth. And there was a reed growing in the mound, and that, you know as well as I, is a strange thing, one reed all by itself under a birch tree in the forest. But it was no stranger than the flowers, for there were flowers round it, some red as the sun at dawn and others blue as the summer sky.

Well, the shepherd looks at the reed, and he looks at those flowers, and he thinks, "I've never seen anything like that before. I'll make a whistle-pipe of that reed, and keep it for a memory till I grow old."

So he did. He cut the reed, and sat himself down on the mound, and carved away at the reed with his knife, and got the pith out of it by pushing a twig through it, and beating it gently till the bark swelled, made holes in it, and there was his whistle-pipe. And then he put it to his lips to see what sort of music he could make on it. But that he never knew, for before his lips touched it the whistle-pipe began playing by itself and reciting in a girl's sweet voice. This is what it sang:

"Play, play, whistle-pipe. Bring happiness to my dear father and to my little mother. I was killed—yes, my life was taken from me in the deep forest for the sake of a silver saucer, for the sake of a transparent apple."

When he heard that the shepherd went back quickly to the village to show it to the people. And all the way the whistle-pipe went on playing and reciting, singing its little song. And every one who heard it said, "What a strange song! But who is it who was killed?"

"I know nothing about it," says the shepherd, and he tells them about the mound and the reed and the flowers, and how he cut the reed and made the whistle-pipe, and how the whistle-pipes does its playing by itself.

And as he was going through the village, with all the people crowding about him, the old merchant, that one who was the father of the two bad ones and of the little pretty one, came along and listened with the rest. And when he heard the words about the silver saucer and the transparent apple, he snatched the whistle-pipe from the shepherd boy. And still it sang:

"Play, play, whistle-pipe! Bring happiness to my dear father and to my little mother. I was killed—yes, for my life was taken from me in the deep forest for the sake of a silver saucer, for the sake of a transparent apple."

95

And the old merchant remembered the little good one, and his tears trickled over his cheeks and down his old beard. Old men love little pigeons, you know. And he said to the shepherd—

"Take me at once to the mound, where you say you cut the reed."

The shepherd led the way, and the old man walked beside him, crying, while the whistle-pipe in his hand went on singing and reciting its little song over and over again.

They came to the mound under the birch tree, and there were the flowers, shining red and blue, and there in the middle of the mound was the stump of the reed which the shepherd had cut.

The whistle-pipe sang on and on.

Well, there and then they dug up the mound, and there was the little girl lying under the dark earth as if she were asleep.

"O God of mine," says the old merchant, "this is my daughter, my little pretty one, whom we called Little Stupid." He began to weep loudly and wring his hands; but the whistle-pipe, playing and reciting, changed its song. This is what it sang:

"My sisters took me into the forest to look for the red berries. In the deep forest they killed poor me for the sake of a silver saucer, for the sake of a transparent apple. Wake me, dear father, from a bitter dream, by fetching water from the well of the Tzar.

How the people scowled at the two sisters! They scowled, they cursed them for the bad ones they were. And the bad ones, the two sisters, wept, and fell on their knees, and confessed everything. They were taken, and their hands were tied, and they were shut up in prison.

"Do not kill them," begged the old merchant, "for then I should have no daughters at all, and when there are no fish in the river we make shift with crays. Besides, let me go to the Tzar and beg water from his well. Perhaps my little daughter will wake up, as the whistle-pipe tells us."

And the whistle-pipe sang again:

"Wake me, wake me, dear father, from a bitter dream, by fetching water from the well of the Tzar. Till then, dear father, a blanket of black earth and the shade of the green birch tree."

96

So they covered the little girl with her blanket of earth, and the shepherd with his dogs watched the mound night and day. He begged for the whistle-pipe to keep him company, poor lad, and all the days and nights he thought of the sweet face of the little pretty one he had seen there under the birch tree.

The old merchant harnessed his horse, as if he were going to the town; and he drove off through the forest, along the roads, till he came to the palace of the Tzar, the little father of all good Russians. And then he left his horse and cart and waited on the steps of the palace.

The Tzar, the little father, with rings on his fingers and a gold crown on his head, came out on the steps in the morning sunshine; and as for the old merchant, he fell on his knees and kissed the feet of the Tzar, and begged—

"O little father, Tzar, give me leave to take water—just a little drop of water—from your holy well."

"And what will you do with it?" says the Tzar.

"I will wake my daughter from a bitter dream," says the old merchant. "She was murdered by her sisters—killed in the deep forest—for the sake of a silver saucer, for the sake of a transparent apple."

"A silver saucer?" says the Tzar—"a transparent apple? Tell me about that."

And the old merchant told the Tzar everything, just as I have told it to you.

And the Tzar, the little father, he gave the old merchant a glass of water from his holy well. "But," says he, "when your daughterkin wakes, bring her to me, and her sisters with her, and also the silver saucer and the transparent apple."

The old man kissed the ground before the Tzar, and took the glass of water and drove home with it, and I can tell you he was careful not to spill a drop. He carried it all the way in one hand as he drove.

He came to the forest and to the flowering mound under the little birch tree, and there was the shepherd watching with his dogs. The old merchant and the shepherd took away the blanket of black earth. Tenderly, tenderly, the shepherd used

97

his fingers, until the little girl, the pretty one, the good one, lay there as sweet as if she were not dead.

Then the merchant scattered the holy water from the glass over the little girl. And his daughterkin blushed as she lay there, and opened her eyes, and passed a hand across them, as if she were waking from a dream. And then she leapt up, crying and laughing, and clung about her old father's neck. And there they stood, the two of them, laughing and crying with joy. And the shepherd could not take his eyes from her, and in his eyes, too, there were tears.

But the old father did not forget what he had promised the Tzar. He set the little pretty one, who had been so good that her wicked sisters had called her Stupid, to sit beside him on the cart. And he brought something from the house in a coffer of wood, and kept it under his coat. And they brought out the two sisters, the bad ones, from their dark prison, and set them in the cart. And the Little Stupid kissed them and cried over them, and wanted to loose their hands, but the old merchant would not let her. And they all drove together till they came to the palace of the Tzar. The shepherd boy could not take his eyes from the little pretty one, and he ran all the way behind the cart.

Well, they came to the palace, and waited on the steps; and the Tzar came out to take the morning air, and he saw the old merchant, and the two sisters with their hands tied, and the little pretty one, as lovely as a spring day. And the Tzar saw her, and could not take his eyes from her. He did not see the shepherd boy, who hid away among the crowd.

Says the great Tzar to his soldiers, pointing to the bad sisters, "These two are to be put to death at sunset. When the sun goes down their heads must come off, for they are not fit to see another day."

Then he turns to the little pretty one, and he says: "Little sweet pigeon, where is your silver saucer, and where is your transparent apple?"

The old merchant took the wooden box from under his coat, and opened it with a key at his belt, and gave it to the little one, and she took out the silver saucer and the transparent apple and gave them to the Tzar.

"O lord Tzar," says she, "O little father, spin the apple in the saucer, and you will see whatever you wish to see—your soldiers, your high hills, your forests, your plains, your rivers, and everything in all Russia."

And the Tzar, the little father, spun the apple in the saucer till it seemed a little whirlpool of white mist, and there he saw glittering towns, and regiments of soldiers marching to war, and ships, and day and night, and the clear stars above the trees. He looked at these things and thought much of them.

Then the little good one threw herself on her knees before him, weeping.

"O little father, Tzar," she says, "take my transparent apple and my silver saucer; only forgive my sisters. Do not kill them because of me. If their heads are cut off when the sun goes down, it would have been better for me to lie under the blanket of black earth in the shade of the birch tree in the forest."

The Tzar was pleased with the kind heart of the little pretty one, and he forgave the bad ones, and their hands were untied, and the little pretty one kissed them, and they kissed her again and said they were sorry.

The old merchant looked up at the sun, and saw how the time was going.

"Well, well," says he, "it's time we were getting ready to go home."

They all fell on their knees before the Tzar and thanked him. But the Tzar could not take his eyes from the little pretty one, and would not let her go.

"Little sweet pigeon," says he, "will you be my Tzaritza, and a kind mother to Holy Russia?"

And the little good one did not know what to say. She blushed and answered, very rightly, "As my father orders, and as my little mother wishes, so shall it be."

The Tzar was pleased with her answer, and he sent a messenger on a galloping horse to ask leave from the little pretty one's old mother. And of course the old mother said that she was more than willing. So that was all right. Then there was a wedding—such a wedding!—and every city in Russia sent a silver plate of bread, and a golden salt-cellar, with their good wishes to the Tzar and Tzaritza.

Only the shepherd boy, when he heard that the little pretty one was to marry the Tzar, turned sadly away and went off into the forest.

"Are you happy, little sweet pigeon?" says the Tzar.

"Oh yes," says the Little Stupid, who was now Tzaritza and mother of Holy Russia; "but there is one thing that would make me happier."

"And what is that?" says the lord Tzar.

"I cannot bear to lose my old father and my little mother and my dear sisters. Let them be with me here in the palace, as they were in my father's house."

The Tzar laughed at the little pretty one, but he agreed, and the little pretty one ran to tell them the good news. She said to her sisters, "Let all be forgotten, and all be forgiven, and may the evil eye fall on the one who first speaks of what has been!"

For a long time the Tzar lived, and the little pretty one the Tzaritza, and they had many children, and were very happy together. And ever since then the Tzars of Russia have kept the silver saucer and the transparent apple, so that, whenever they wish, they can see everything that is going on all over Russia. Perhaps even now the Tzar, the little father—God preserve him!—is spinning the apple in the saucer, and looking at us, and thinking it is time that two little pigeons were in bed.

"Is that the end?" said Vanya.

"That is the end," said old Peter.

"Poor shepherd boy!" said Maroosia.

"I don't know about that," said old Peter. "You see, if he had married the little pretty one, and had to have all the family to live with him, he would have had them in a hut like ours instead of in a great palace, and so he would never have had room to get away from them. And now, little pigeons, who is going to be first into bed?"

SPIT
NOLAN

BY

BILL NAUGHTON

CHOSEN BY

IAN SERRAILLIER

BILL NAUGHTON is best known for his plays for television and the London theatre. But he has also produced some splendid short stories, my favourite collection of which is THE GOALKEEPER'S REVENGE (Harrap 1961, Heinemann Educational Books 1967). The experiences on which they are based obviously derive from his own boyhood—in fact he dedicates the book "To all my old mates who used to gather at the street corner". They are about boys playing football in the schoolyard, making a quick grab in the dockyard when the banana boat is unloading, fishing up to their shins in mud, watching the Flying Pigs and roundabouts and Bumper Cars at the Fairground, arguing and fighting, lying in bed in hospital, or leaving school at fourteen (which used to be the leaving age) to look for a job. The author looks at them with a realistic eye; he neither caricatures nor sentimentalises them. The background too is realistic—the dockyards, back streets, spinning-mills and factory chimneys of an industrial area. The experiences are true to human nature, and the language vivid and compelling. They are wonderful stories for reading aloud.

My favourite among them is *Spit Nolan*. This is about the race between Spit, who made his own trolley and whose delicate health did not prevent him from being the champion rider of Cotton Pocket, and Leslie Duckett the local publican's son, whose trolley was specially made to measure at the Holt Engineering Works. "Five—four—three—two—one—*Off!*" Away they sped, "like two charioteers". It was a thrilling race, but it would have been better if it had never taken place.

IAN SERRAILLIER

S PIT NOLAN was a pal of mine. He was a thin lad with a bony face that was always pale, except for two rosy spots on his cheekbones. He had quick brown eyes, short, wiry hair, rather stooped shoulders, and we all knew that he had only one lung. He had had a disease which in those days couldn't be cured, unless you went away to Switzerland, which Spit certainly couldn't afford. He wasn't sorry for himself in any way, and in fact we envied him, because he never had to go to school.

Spit was the champion trolley-rider of Cotton Pocket; that was the district in which we lived. He had a very good balance, and sharp wits, and he was very brave, so that these qualities, when added to his skill as a rider, meant that no other boy could ever beat Spit on a trolley—and every lad had one.

Our trolleys were simple vehicles for getting a good ride downhill at a fast speed. To make one you had to get a stout piece of wood about five feet in length and eighteen inches wide. Then you needed four wheels, preferably two pairs, large ones for the back and smaller ones for the front. However, since we bought our wheels from the scrapyard, most trolleys had four odd wheels. Now you had to get a poker and put it in the fire until it was red hot, and then burn a hole through the wood at the front. Usually it would take three or four attempts to get the hole bored through. Through this hole you fitted the giant nut-and-bolt, which acted as a swivel for the steering. Fastened to the nut was a strip of wood, on to which the front axle was secured by bent nails. A piece of rope tied to each end of the axle served for steering. Then a knob of margarine had to be slanced out of the kitchen to grease the wheels and bearings. Next you had to paint a name on it: *Invincible* or *Dreadnought*, though it might be a motto: *Death before Dishonour* or *Labour and Wait*. That done, you then stuck your chest out, opened the back gate, and wheeled your trolley out to face the critical eyes of the world.

Spit spent most mornings trying out new speed gadgets on his trolley, or searching Enty's scrapyard for good wheels. Afternoons he would go off and have a spin down Cemetery Brew. This was a very steep road that led to the cemetery, and it was very popular with trolley-drivers as it was the only macadamised hill for miles around, all the others being cobblestones for horse traffic. Spit used to lie in wait for a coal-cart or other horse-drawn vehicle, then he would hitch *Egdam* to the back to take it up the brew. *Egdam* was a name in memory of a girl called Madge, whom he had once met at Southport Sanatorium, where he had spent three happy weeks. Only I knew the meaning of it, for he had reversed the letters of her name to keep his love a secret.

It was the custom for lads to gather at the street corner on summer evenings and, trolleys parked at hand, discuss trolleying, road surfaces, and also show off any new gadgets. Then, when Spit gave the sign, we used to set off for Cemetery Brew. There was scarcely any evening traffic on the roads in those days, so that we could have a good practice before our evening race. Spit, the unbeaten champion, would inspect every trolley and rider, and allow a start which was reckoned on the size of the wheels and the weight of the rider. He was always the last in the line of starters, though no matter how long a start he gave it seemed impossible to beat him. He knew that road like the palm of his hand, every tiny lump or pothole, and he never came a cropper.

Among us he took things easy, but when occasion asked for it he would go all out. Once he had to meet a challenge from Ducker Smith, the champion of the Engine Row gang. On that occasion Spit borrowed a wheel from the baby's pram, removing one nearest the wall, so it wouldn't be missed, and confident he could replace it before his mother took baby out. And after fixing it to his trolley he made that ride on what was called the "belly-down" style—that is, he lay full stretch on his stomach, so as to avoid wind resistance. Although Ducker got away with a flying start he had not that sensitive touch of Spit, and his frequent bumps and swerves lost him valuable inches, so that he lost the race with a good three lengths. Spit arrived home just in time to catch his mother as she was wheeling young Georgie off the doorstep, and if he had not made a dash for it the child would have fallen out as the pram overturned.

It happened that we were gathered at the street corner with our trolleys one evening when Ernie Haddock let out a hiccup of wonder: "Hy, chaps, wot's Leslie got?"

We all turned our eyes on Leslie Duckett, the plump son of the local publican. He approached us on a brand-new trolley, propelled by flicks of his foot on the pavement. From a distance the thing had looked impressive, but now, when it came up among us, we were too dumbfounded to speak. Such a magnificent trolley had never been seen! The riding board was of solid oak, almost two inches thick; four new wheels with pneumatic tyres; a brake, a bell, a lamp, and a spotless steering-cord. In front was a plate on which was the name in bold lettering: *The British Queen*.

"It's called after the pub," remarked Leslie. He tried to edge it away from Spit's trolley, for it made *Egdam* appear horribly insignificant. Voices had been stilled for a minute, but now they broke out:

"Where'd it come from?"

"How much was it?"

"Who made it?"

Leslie tried to look modest. "My dad had it specially made to measure," he said, "by the gaffer of the Holt Engineering Works."

He was a nice lad, and now he wasn't sure whether to feel proud or ashamed. The fact was, nobody had ever had a trolley made by somebody else. Trolleys were swopped and so on, but no lad had ever owned one that had been made by other hands. We went quiet now, for Spit had calmly turned his attention to it, and was examining *The British Queen* with his expert eye. First he tilted it, so that one of the rear wheels was off the ground, and after giving it a flick of the finger he listened intently with his ear close to the hub.

"A beautiful ball-bearing race," he remarked, "it runs like silk." Next he turned his attention to the body. "Grand piece of timber, Leslie—though a trifle on the heavy side. It'll take plenty of pulling up a brew."

"I can pull it," said Leslie, stiffening.

"You might find it a shade *front-heavy*," went on Spit, "which means it'll be hard on the steering unless you keep it well oiled."

"It's well made," said Leslie. "Eh, Spit?"

Spit nodded. "Aye, all the bolts are counter-sunk," he said, "everything chamfered and fluted off to perfection. But—"

"But what?" asked Leslie.

"Do you want me to tell you?" asked Spit.

"Yes, I do," answered Leslie.

"Well, it's got none of *you* in it," said Spit.

"How do you mean?" says Leslie.

"Well, you haven't so much as given it a single tap with a hammer," said Spit. "That trolley will be a stranger to you to your dying day."

"How come," said Leslie, "since I *own* it?"

Spit shook his head. "You don't own it," he said, in a quiet, solemn tone. "You own nothing in this world except those things you have taken a hand in the making of, or else you've earned the money to buy them."

Leslie sat down on *The British Queen* to think this one out. We all sat round, scratching our heads.

"You've forgotten to mention one thing," said Ernie Haddock to Spit, "what about the *speed*?"

"Going down a steep hill," said Spit, "she should hold the road well—an' with wheels like that she should certainly be able to shift some."

"Think she could beat *Egdam*?" ventured Ernie.

"That," said Spit, "remains to be seen."

Ernie gave a shout: "A challenge race! *The British Queen* versus *Egdam*!"

"Not tonight," said Leslie. "I haven't got the proper feel of her yet."

"What about Sunday morning?" I said.

Spit nodded. "As good a time as any."

Leslie agreed. "By then," he said in a challenging tone, "I'll be able to handle her."

Chattering like monkeys, eating bread, carrots, fruit, and bits of toffee, the entire gang of us made our way along the silent Sunday-morning streets for the big race at Cemetery Brew. We were split into two fairly equal sides.

Leslie, in his serge Sunday suit, walked ahead, with Ernie Haddock pulling *The British Queen,* and a bunch of supporters around. They were optimistic, for Leslie had easily outpaced every other trolley during the week, though as yet he had not run against Spit.

Spit was in the middle of the group behind, and I was pulling *Egdam* and keeping the pace easy, for I wanted Spit to keep fresh. He walked in and out among us with an air of imperturbability that, considering the occasion, seemed almost godlike. It inspired a fanatical confidence in us. It was such that Chick Dale, a curly-headed kid with soft skin like a girl's, and a nervous lisp, climbed up on to the spiked railings of the cemetery, and, reaching out with his thin fingers, snatched a yellow rose. He ran in front of Spit and thrust it into a small hole in his jersey.

"I pwesent you with the wose of the winner!" he exclaimed.

"And I've a good mind to present you with a clout on the lug," replied Spit, "for pinching a flower from a cemetery. An' what's more, it's bad luck." Seeing Chick's face, he relented. "On second thoughts, Chick, I'll wear it. Ee, wot a 'eavenly smell!"

Happily we went along, and Spit turned to a couple of lads at the back. "Hy, stop that whistling. Don't forget what day it is—folk want their sleep out."

A faint sweated glow had come over Spit's face when we reached the top of the hill, but he was as majestically calm as ever. Taking the bottle of cold water from his trolley seat, he put it to his lips and rinsed out his mouth in the manner of a boxer.

The two contestants were called together by Ernie.

"No bumpin' or borin'," he said.

They nodded.

"The winner," he said, "is the first who puts the nose of his trolley past the cemetery gates."

They nodded.

"Now, who," he asked, "is to be judge?"

Leslie looked at me. "I've no objection to Bill," he said. "I know he's straight."

I hadn't realised I was, I thought, but by heck I will be!

"Ernie here," said Spit, "can be starter."

With that Leslie and Spit shook hands.

"Fly down to them gates," said Ernie to me. He had his father's pigeon-timing watch in his hand. "I'll be setting 'em off dead on the stroke of ten o'clock."

I hurried down to the gates. I looked back and saw the supporters lining themselves on either side of the road. Leslie was sitting upright on *The British Queen*. Spit was settling himself to ride belly-down. Ernie Haddock, handkerchief raised in the right hand, eye gazing down on the watch in the left, was counting them off—just like when he tossed one of his father's pigeons.

"Five—four—three—two—one—*Off!*"

Spit was away like a shot. That vigorous toe push sent him clean ahead of Leslie. A volley of shouts went up from his supporters, and groans from Leslie's. I saw Spit move straight to the middle of the road camber. Then I ran ahead to take up my position at the winning-post.

When I turned again I was surprised to see that Spit had not increased the lead. In fact, it seemed that Leslie had begun to gain on him. He had settled himself into a crouched position, and those perfect wheels combined with his extra weight were bringing him up with Spit. Not that it seemed possible he could ever catch him. For Spit, lying flat on his trolley, moving with a fine balance, gliding, as it were, over the rough patches, looked to me as though he were a bird that might suddenly open out its wings and fly clean into the air.

The runners along the side could no longer keep up with the trolleys. And now, as they skimmed past the half-way mark, and came to the very steepest part, there was no doubt that Leslie was gaining. Spit had never ridden better; he coaxed *Egdam* over the tricky parts, swayed with her, gave her her head, and guided her. Yet Leslie, clinging grimly to the steering-rope of *The British Queen*, and riding the rougher part of the road, was actually drawing level. Those beautiful ball-bearing wheels, engineer-made, encased in oil, were holding the road, and bringing Leslie along faster than spirit and skill could carry Spit.

Dead level they sped into the final stretch. Spit's slight figure was poised fearlessly on his trolley, drawing the extremes of speed from her. Thundering beside him, anxious but determined, came Leslie. He was actually drawing ahead—and forcing his way to the top of the camber. On they came like two charioteers—Spit delicately edging to the side, to gain inches by the extra downward momentum. I kept my eyes fastened clean across the road as they came belting past the winning-post.

First past was the plate *The British Queen*. I saw that first. Then I saw the heavy rear wheel jog over a pothole and strike Spit's front wheel—sending him in a swerve across the road. Suddenly then, from nowhere, a charabanc came speeding round the wide bend.

Spit was straight in its path. Nothing could avoid the collision. I gave a cry of fear as I saw the heavy solid tyre of the front wheel hit the trolley. Spit was flung up and his back hit the radiator. Then the driver stopped dead.

I got there first. Spit was lying on the macadam road on his side. His face was white and dusty, and coming out between his lips and trickling down his chin was a rivulet of fresh red blood. Scattered all about him were yellow rose petals.

"Not my fault," I heard the driver shouting. "I didn't have a chance. He came straight at me."

The next thing we were surrounded by women who had got out of the charabanc. And then Leslie and all the lads came up.

"Somebody send for an ambulance!" called a woman.

"I'll run an' tell the gatekeeper to telephone," said Ernie Haddock.

"I hadn't a chance," the driver explained to the women.

"A piece of his jersey on the starting-handle there . . ." said someone.

"Don't move him," said the driver to a stout woman who had bent over Spit. "Wait for the ambulance."

"Hush up," she said. She knelt and put a silk scarf under Spit's head. Then she wiped his mouth with her little handkerchief.

He opened his eyes. Glazed they were, as though he couldn't see. A short cough came out of him, then he looked at me and his lips moved.

"Who won?"

"Thee!" blurted out Leslie. "Tha just licked me. Eh, Bill?"

"Aye," I said, "old *Egdam* just pipped *The British Queen*."

Spit's eyes closed again. The women looked at each other. They nearly all had tears in their eyes. Then Spit looked up again, and his wise, knowing look came over his face. After a minute he spoke in a sharp whisper:

"Liars. I can remember seeing Leslie's back wheel hit my front 'un. I didn't win—I lost." He stared upward for a few seconds, then his eyes twitched and shut.

The driver kept repeating how it wasn't his fault, and next thing the ambulance came. Nearly all the women were crying now, and I saw the look that went between the two men who put Spit on a stretcher—but I couldn't believe he was dead. I had to go into the ambulance with the attendant to give him particulars. I went up the step and sat down inside and looked out the little window as the driver slammed the doors. I saw the driver holding Leslie as a witness. Chick Dale was lifting the smashed-up *Egdam* on to the body of *The British Queen*. People with bunches of flowers in their hands stared after us as we drove off. Then I heard the ambulance man asking me Spit's name. Then he touched me on the elbow with his pencil and said:

"Where *did* he live?"

I knew then. That word "did" struck right into me. But for a minute I couldn't answer. I had to think hard, for the way he said it made it suddenly seem as though Spit Nolan had been dead and gone for ages.

A Christmas Tree for Lydia
by Elizabeth Enright
chosen by Noel Streatfeild

ELIZABETH ENRIGHT, who wrote this story, was a friend of mine. She was a very gifted writer, particularly of short stories. As well she wrote books which were liked by children. I don't think she ever wrote specifically for children because, like all the best books children have loved, hers were written to please herself; that children happened to like the result was fine with her. She was in herself a radiant personality though, like Eddy in this story, you could feel she was "one who drinks secretly at a spring of inspiration". Elizabeth Enright died in 1968 and the world is a poorer place without her.

I have not chosen this story because Elizabeth Enright wrote it but because it is a splendid short story and an American story of a special kind. I go so often to America and have so many friends there, I don't like it when Americans are misunderstood. One of the ways in which they are misunderstood is over money; there is often an unexpressed belief that all Americans are rich. There never was greater nonsense of course for, like people anywhere, many Americans have a hard job getting by like the family in this story.

A Christmas Tree for Lydia is, I think, beautiful. It was not written for any particular audience. "Would Jesus care if his birthday was put off for a couple of days?" is a question anyone might ask. And though no one says that what Eddy created was a miracle it was, of course, for what else is inspiration?

NOEL STREATFEILD

LYDIA first learned about Christmas when she was one year old. Draped over her mother's shoulder she drooled and stared, and the lights of the Christmas tree made other lights in her large tranced eyes and in the glaze of spittle on her chin.

When she was two years old she learned about Santa Claus. She paid very little attention to him then, but when she was three she talked about him a lot and they had some difficulty persuading her that he and the infant Jesus were not father and son. By the time she was four she had come to accept him as one of the ordered phenomena that ruled her life, like daytime and nighttime: one seven o'clock for getting up and another seven o'clock for going to bed. Like praise and blame and winter and summer and her brother's right of seniority and her mother's last word. Her father did not exist in her field of magnitudes; he had been killed in Cassino the winter she was born.

"Santa Claus will come," Lydia said, and knew it was as true as saying tomorrow will come. "He will bring a Christmas tree. Big. With lights. With colours."

When she was four, her brother Eddy was nine and had long ago found out the truth concerning the matter. No note of illusion deceived his eye when he passed the street-corner Santas at Christmas time, standing beside their imitation chimneys, ringing their bells; he saw them for what they were. He saw how all their trousers bagged and their sleeves were too long, and how, above the false beards tied loosely on like bibs, their noses ran and their eyes looked out, mortal and melancholy.

"You'd think the kid would catch on," Eddy said to his mother. "Gee, when you notice the differentness of them all."

Lydia believed in every one of them, from the bell-ringers on the street corners to the department-store variety who always asked the same questions and whose hired joviality grew glassy

113

toward evening. She had faith in the monster idol in the store on Fourteenth Street which turned its glaring face from side to side and laughed a huge stony machinery laugh all day long, filling the region with sounds of compulsive derangement. For Lydia, the saint was ubiquitous, ingenious, capable of all, and looking into the different faces of his impersonators she beheld the one good face she had invented for him.

"Eddy, don't you tell her now, will you?" his mother said. "Don't you dare to, now. Remember she's only four."

Sure, let the kid have her fun, thought Eddy, with large scorn and slight compassion. He himself remembered long-ago Christmas Eves when he had listened for bells in the air, and watched the limp shape of his sock hung up over the stove.

"How can he come in through the *stove*, Mum?"

"In houses like this he comes in through the window. Go to sleep now, Eddy, like a good boy."

Eddy went to public school in the daytimes and Lydia went to a day nursery. Her mother called for her every evening on the way home from work. She was a thin dark young woman whose prettiness was often obscured by the ragged shadows of irritation and fatigue. She loved her children, but worry gnawed at her relations with them, sharpening her words and shortening her temper. Coming home in the evening, climbing up the stairs to the flat with one hand pressing the bags of groceries to her chest, and Lydia loitering and babbling, dragging on her other hand, she wished sometimes to let go of everything. To let go of Lydia, perhaps forever; to let go once and for all of the heavy paper grocery bags. It would be a savage happiness, she felt, to see and hear the catsup bottle smashed on the stairs, the eggs broken and leaking, and all the tin cans and potatoes rolling and banging their way downward.

They lived in a two-room flat with linoleum on the floor and a lively corrugated ceiling. In the daytime, from noon on, the rooms were hot with sunshine, but in the morning and at night they were as cold as caves unless the stove was going. The stove and the bathtub and the sink were all in the front room where Eddy slept. Sometimes at night the bathtub would gulp lonesomely, and the leaky tap of the sink had a drip as perfect in tempo as a clock.

Lydia and her mother slept in the back room, a darkish place, painted blue, with a big dim mirror over the bureau, and a window looking on to a shaft. The toilet was by itself in a little cubicle with a window also looking on to the shaft. When the chain was pulled it was as though one had released a river genie; a great storming and rumbling rose upward through the pipes, shaking all the furniture in the flat, then there was a prolonged crashing of waters lasting for minutes, and at last the mighty withdrawal, thundering and wrathful, growing fainter at last, and still fainter, till silence was restored, docile and appeased.

Sometimes when Eddy was alone and the stillness got to be too much for him he went into the water closet and pulled the chain just for the company of the noise.

He was often alone during the first part of his vacation. At noon, wearing his blue and grey Mackinaw and his aviator's helmet with the straps flying, he came stamping up the stairs and into the sun-flooded crowded little flat. Humming and snuffling, he made his lunch: breakfast food, or huge erratic sandwiches filled with curious materials. When he was through he always cleaned up: washed the bowl or dish and swept up the breadcrumbs with his chapped hand. He had learned to be tidy at an early age, and could even make his bed well enough to sleep in it.

In the afternoons and mornings he voyaged forth with Joey Camarda, and others, to the street for contests of skill and wit. Sometimes they went to the upper reaches of the park with its lakes, bridges, battlegrounds and ambushes. Or rainy days they tagged through the museums, shrill and shabby as sparrows, touching the raddled surfaces of meteorites without awe, and tipping back their heads boldly to stare at the furious mask of Tyrannosaurus Rex.

"He isn't real. They made him out of pieces of wood, like," Joey said. "Men with ladders made him."

"He is, too, real," Eddy said. "He walked around and ate and growled and everything. Once he did."

"Naw, he wasn't real. Jeez he *couldn't* be real. You'd believe anything. You'd believe in Santy Claus even."

Christmas and its symbols were more and more in their conversation as the time drew near. They speculated on the subject of possible gifts to themselves. Joey said his uncle was going to give him roller skates and a real Mauser rifle.

"It's one he got when he was in It'ly. What are you going to get, Eddy?"

Eddy said he thought he'd probably get a bike. It was just as likely that he would be given a bike as that he would be given the new moon out of the sky, but having made the statement, he went on to perfect it. He said that it would be a white bike with red trimming and a red piece of glass like a jewel on the back of it, and two raccoon tails floating from the handle bars.

"There's going to be two kinds of bells on the handle bars. One will be kind of a si-reen."

"Will you let me ride on it sometimes, Ed?"

"Sometimes," Eddy said.

That night he rode the bike all around the flat with the raccoon tails lying out on the speed-torn air. The tail-light blazed like a red-hot ruby, and the siren was as terrible as human voice could make it.

"Watch me now, I'm taking a curve," shouted Eddy. "Eee-ow-oooo-eee. Just missed that truck by half an inch!"

Lydia sat safely on the bed in the back room questioning him as he flashed by.

"Is it a plane, Eddy?"

"No."

"Is it a car?"

"No."

"Is it a—is it a train?"

"No. Gosh, it's a bike. Look out now. I got to make that light. Eee-ow-ooo-eee!"

"Eddy, will you please for pity's sake *shut up!*" cried his mother. "I can't hear myself think, even!"

He came to a stop. "Gee, Mum, what are you cross about?"

She didn't look at him; she pushed the potatoes and onions

around the frying pan with a fork. Then she shook salt over them, and spoke from a certain distance.

"Eddy, you kids don't get a tree this year."

"Heck, why not? What did we do? Why not?"

"I can't afford it, that's why!" she cried loudly, angry with him because she was hurting him. Then she lowered her voice. "They don't want me back at the store after Christmas, they told me today. They don't need me any more. I don't dare to get you any presents even but just things you have to have like socks and mittens." She looked at him. "Maybe some candy," she added.

A stinging hot odour arose from the frying pan to join the robust company of cooking smells from other flats on other floors: herring and chili and garlic and pork.

"Gee, Eddy, I'm scared to spend another cent. How do I know I'll get another job?"

"What are you going to tell Lydia? She talks about the Christmas tree all day long."

"She'll have to do without, that's all. Other people have to do without."

"But, gee, she talks about it all day long."

His mother threw down the fork and whirled on him.

"I can't *help* it, can I? My God, what am *I* supposed to do?"

Eddy knew better than to go on with it. He leaned against the sink and thought, and when they ate supper he was kind and forebearing with Lydia who was both hilarious and sloppy. After a while his kindness became preoccupied, like that of one who drinks secretly at a spring of inspiration, and when Lydia had gone to bed he made a suggestion to his mother.

"I have an idea. If we put Christmas off for a few days, maybe a week, I can fix everything."

His mother, as he had expected, said no. It was this response on the part of his mother which was the starting point of all his campaigns, many of them successful. He leaned against the sink and waited.

"What good would it do? And anyway what would Lydia think!" she said.

"Tell her Santa Claus is late. Tell her we made a mistake about the day. She's too dumb to know the difference. Everyone's dumb when they're four."

"And anyway it seems kind of wrong."

"What would Jesus care if we put his birthday off for a couple of days?"

"Oh, Eddy, don't be silly. There won't be any more money than there is now."

"No, but I got an idea. Please, Mum, please. Please."

Eddy knew how to pester nicely. He had a quiet attentive way of looking and looking at one; of following one with his eyes and not saying anything, the request still shimmering all around him like heat-lightning. He waited.

His mother hung up the wet dishtowel and turned the dishpan upside down. She looked into the little mirror above the sink and looked away again. Then she sat down in the rocker and opened the tabloid newspaper.

"Oh, all *right*," she said. "For pity's sake, Eddy. What do you expect, a miracle?"

"Isn't there ever any miracles? Anyway I'm not thinking about a miracle, I'm thinking about something smart," Eddy said.

Christmas came, and for them it was a day like any other, except that their mother was at home. But it was easy to explain to Lydia that this was because her job at the store had ended for good, just as it was easy to explain Lydia's own absence from nursery school by the simple method of rubbing Vick's ointment on her chest. Eddy thought of that one, too.

"Gee, Eddy, I hope you know what you're doing," his mother said.

"I do know," Eddy said.

"You should at least tell *me* what you're going to do."

"It has to be a surprise for you, too," Eddy said, not so much because he wanted to surprise his mother as because he knew if he revealed his plan he would come in contact with a "no" which none of his stratagems could dissolve.

"It will be okay, Mum."

"And when is it to be, if I may ask?"

"On New Year's Day, I guess," Eddy said, and went in search of Joey Camarda whose help he had enlisted.

On New Year's Eve, early, he shut Lydia and his mother into their room.

"No matter what noises you hear, you don't come out, see? Promise."

"But, Eddy, I don't think—"

"You promise."

"Well—" his mother conceded, and that was as good as promising. She went in and shut the door, and before the extraordinary sounds of toil and shuffling commenced in the hall she was lost in the deep sleep of the discouraged: that temporary death which is free from all the images of fear or joy.

At midnight the city woke up and met the New Year with a mighty purring. In the streets people blew horns and shook things that sounded like tin cans full of pebbles. Lydia woke up too and thought that it was Santa Claus.

"I wanna get up, Mum. I wanna see him."

"You lay down this minute or he won't leave a single thing. He doesn't like for people to be awake when he comes," said her mother crossly, clinging to the warm webs of sleep.

But Lydia sat up for a while in her cot, rocking softly to and fro. Through the crack under the door came a fragrance she remembered well from Christmas a year ago, and the Christmas before that.

In the morning it was a long time before Eddy would let them out of their room.

"Eddy, it's cold in here," said his mother.

"I wanna see the tree, I wanna see the tree," chanted Lydia, half singing, half whining. "I wanna see the tree, I wanna see the tree."

"Heck, wait a minute," said Eddy.

"I wanna see the tree, I wanna see the tree," bayed Lydia.

There were sounds of haste and struggle in the next room.

"All right, you can come in now," said Eddy, and opened the door.

They saw a forest.

In a circle, hiding every wall, stood the Christmas trees; spare ones and stout ones, tall ones and short ones, but all tall to Lydia. Some still were hung with threads of silver foil, and here and there among the boughs the ornaments for a single tree had been distributed with justice; calm and bright as planets they turned and burned among the needles. The family stood in a mysterious grove, without bird or breeze, and there was a deep fragrance in the room. It was a smell of health and stillness and tranquillity, and for a minute or two, before she had thought of the dropping needles and the general inconvenience of a forest in the kitchen, Eddy's mother breathed the smell full into her city lungs and felt within herself a lessening of strain.

"Eddy, Eddy, how? How?"

"Me and Joe Camarda," Eddy whispered. "We went all around last night and dragged them out of gutters. We could of filled the whole entire house with them if we wanted to. Last night in here it was like camping out."

It had been like that. He had lain peacefully in his bed under the branches, listening to the occasional snow-flake tinkle of a falling needle, and to the ticking of the leaky tap, hidden now as any forest spring.

"Eddy honey, look at Lydia."

Lydia still looked new from her sleep. She stood in her flannel nightgown with her dark hair rumpled and her eyes full of lights, and her hands clasped in front of her in a composed, elderly way. Naturally a loud exuberant girl, the noise had temporarily been knocked out of her.

"All the Christmas trees," she remarked gently.

"Gee," said Eddy. "Don't get the idea it's going to be this way every year. This is just because he was late, and it's instead of presents."

It was enough for Lydia, anyone could see that. In a way, it was enough for Eddy too. He felt proud, generous and efficient.

He felt successful. With his hands in his pockets he stood looking at his sister.

"All the Christmas trees," Lydia said quietly, and sighed. "All the Christmas trees."

THE MIRACLE
OF
PURUN BHAGAT

BY
RUDYARD KIPLING

CHOSEN BY
ROSEMARY SUTCLIFF

IF you love a story, a picture, a piece of music, or a person for that matter, deeply enough, it becomes extremely difficult to form any judgement of their merit. And so I do not really know how good it is, this story of Sir Purun Dass, K.C.I.E., Prime Minister of an Indian Semi-independent Native State, who laid down all the honour that his world could give him, to take up the begging-bowl, and who became, after his death, the local saint of a little hill village that never knew him for anything other than a wandering holy man.

I only know that for me, Kipling's magnificent word-power, used here with a simplicity and purity he could not always rise to, evokes sights and sounds and smells of a land and a way of life, as though I had known and belonged to them and was homesick for them still.

The Miracle of Purun Bhagat is a simple story, with the simplicity of the very greatest and most deep-running themes, which have no need of surface complexities; and to me it seems beautiful, and true, and oddly luminous; but then, among all the short stories of my acquaintance, it is my best beloved, and so I am really no judge.

ROSEMARY SUTCLIFF

The night we felt the earth would move
  We stole and plucked him by the hand,
Because we loved him with the love
  That knows but cannot understand.

And when the roaring hillside broke
  And all our world fell down in rain,
We saved him, we the Little Folk;
  But lo, he does not come again!

Mourn now, we saved him for the sake
  Of such poor love as wild ones may.
Mourn ye! Our brother will not awake,
  And his own kind drive us away!

Dirge of the Langurs

THERE was once a man in India who was Prime Minister of one of the semi-independent native States in the north-western part of the country. He was a Brahmin, so high-caste that caste ceased to have any particular meaning for him; and his father had been an important official in the gay-coloured tag-rag and bobtail of an old-fashioned Hindu Court. But as Purun Dass grew up he felt that the old order of things was changing, and that if anyone wished to get on in the world he must stand well with the English, and imitate all that the English believed to be good. At the same time a native official must keep his own master's favour. This was a difficult game, but the quiet, close-mouthed young Brahmin, helped by a good English education at a Bombay University, played it coolly, and rose, step by step, to be Prime Minister of the kingdom. That is to say, he held more real power than his master the Maharajah.

When the old king—who was suspicious of the English, their railways and telegraphs—died, Purun Dass stood high with his young successor, who had been tutored by an Englishman; and between them, though he always took care that his master should have the credit, they established schools for little girls, made roads, and started State dispensaries and shows of agricultural implements, and published a yearly blue-book on the "Moral and Material Progress of the State", and the Foreign Office and the Government of India were delighted. Very few native States take up English progress altogether, for they will not believe, as Purun Dass showed he did, that what was good for the Englishman must be twice as good for the Asiatic. The Prime Minister became the honoured friend of Viceroys, and Governors, and Lieutenant-Governors, and medical missionaries, and common missionaries, and hard-riding English officers who came to shoot in the State preserves, as well as of whole hosts of tourists who travelled up and down India in the cold weather, showing how things ought to be managed. In his spare time he would endow scholarships for the study of medicine and manufactures on strictly English lines, and write letters to the *Pioneer*, the greatest Indian daily paper, explaining his master's aims and objects.

At last he went to England on a visit, and had to pay enormous sums to the priests when he came back; for even so high-caste a Brahmin as Purun Dass lost caste by crossing the black sea. In London he met and talked with everyone worth knowing—men whose names go all over the world—and saw a great deal more than he said. He was given honorary degrees by learned universities, and he made speeches and talked of Hindu social reform to English ladies in evening dress, till all London cried, "This is the most fascinating man we have ever met at dinner since cloths were first laid."

When he returned to India there was a blaze of glory, for the Viceroy himself made a special visit to confer upon the Maharajah the Grand Cross of the Star of India—all diamonds and ribbons and enamel; and at the same ceremony, while the cannon boomed, Purun Dass was made a Knight Commander of the Order of the Indian Empire; so that his name stood Sir Purun Dass, K.C.I.E.

That evening, at dinner in the big Viceregal tent, he stood up with the badge and the collar of the Order on his breast, and replying to the toast of his master's health, made a speech few Englishmen could have bettered.

Next month, when the city had returned to its sun-baked quiet, he did a thing no Englishman would have dreamed of doing; for, so far as the world's affairs went, he died. The jewelled order of his knighthood went back to the Indian Government, and a new Prime Minister was appointed to the charge of affairs, and a great game of General Post began in all the subordinate appointments. The priests knew what had happened, and the people guessed; but India is the one place in the world where a man can do as he pleases and nobody asks why; and the fact that Dewan Sir Purun Dass, K.C.I.E., had resigned position, palace, and power, and taken up the begging-bowl and ochre-coloured dress of a Sunnyasi, or holy man, was considered nothing extraordinary. He had been, as the Old Law recommends, twenty years a youth, twenty years a fighter, —though he had never carried a weapon in his life,—and twenty years head of a household. He had used his wealth and his power for what he knew both to be worth; he had taken honour when it came his way; he had seen men and cities far and near, and men and cities had stood up and honoured him. Now he would let those things go, as a man drops the cloak he no longer needs.

Behind him, as he walked through the city gates, an antelope skin and brass-handled crutch under his arm, and a begging-bowl of polished brown *coco-de-mer* in his hand, barefoot, alone, with eyes cast on the ground—behind him they were firing salutes from the bastions in honour of his happy successor. Purun Dass nodded. All that life was ended; and he bore it no more ill-will or good-will than a man bears to a colourless dream of the night. He was a Sunnyasi—a houseless, wandering mendicant, depending on his neighbours for his daily bread; and so long as there is a morsel to divide in India, neither priest nor beggar starves. He had never in his life tasted meat, and very seldom eaten even fish. A five-pound note would have covered his personal expenses for food through any one of the many years in which he had been absolute master of millions of money. Even when he was being lionised in London he had held before him his dream of peace and quiet—the long, white, dusty Indian road, printed all over with bare feet, the incessant, slow-moving traffic, and the sharp-smelling wood smoke curling up under the fig-trees in the twilight, where the wayfarers sit at their evening meal.

When the time came to make that dream true the Prime Minister took the proper steps, and in three days you might more easily have found a bubble in the trough of the long Atlantic seas than Purun Dass among the roving, gathering, separating millions of India.

At night his antelope skin was spread where the darkness overtook him—sometimes in a Sunnyasi monastery by the roadside; sometimes by a mud-pillar shrine of Kala Pir, where the Jogis, who are another misty division of holy men, would receive him as they do those who know what castes and divisions are worth; sometimes on the outskirts of a little Hindu village, where the children would steal up with the food their parents had prepared; and sometimes on the pitch of the bare grazing-grounds, where the flame of his stick fire waked the drowsy camels. It was all one to Purun Dass—or Purun Bhagat, as he called himself now. Earth, people, and food were all one. But unconsciously his feet drew him away northward and eastward; from the south to Rohtak; from Rohtak to Kurnool; from Kurnool to ruined Samanah, and then up-stream along the dried bed of the Gugger river that fills only when the rain falls in the hills, till one day he saw the fire line of the great Himalayas.

Then Purun Bhagat smiled, for he remembered that his mother was of Rajput Brahmin birth, from Kulu way—a Hill-woman, always home-sick for the snows—and that the least touch of Hill blood draws a man in the end back to where he belongs.

"Yonder," said Purun Bhagat, breasting the lower slopes of the Sewaliks, where the cacti stand up like seven-branched candlesticks—"yonder I shall sit down and get knowledge"; and the cool wind of the Himalayas whistled about his ears as he trod the road that led to Simla.

The last time he had come that way it had been in state, with a clattering cavalry escort, to visit the gentlest and most affable of Viceroys; and the two had talked for an hour together about mutual friends in London, and what the Indian common folk really thought of things. This time Purun Bhagat paid no calls, but leaned on the rail of the Mall, watching that glorious view of the Plains spread out forty miles below, till a native Mohammedan policeman told him he was obstructing traffic; and Purun Bhagat salaamed reverently to the Law, because he knew the value of it, and was seeking for a Law of his own. Then he moved on, and slept that night in an empty hut at Chota Simla, which looks like the very last end of the earth, but it was only the beginning of his journey.

He followed the Himalaya-Tibet road, the little ten-foot track that is blasted out of solid rock, or strutted out on timbers over gulfs a thousand feet deep; that dips into warm, wet, shut-in valleys, and climbs out across bare, grassy hill-shoulders where the sun strikes like a burning-glass; or turns through dripping, dark forests where the tree-ferns dress the trunks from head to heel, and the pheasant calls to his mate. And he met Tibetan herdsmen with their dogs and flocks of sheep, each sheep with a little bag of borax on his back; and wandering wood-cutters, and cloaked and blanketed Lamas from Tibet, coming into India on pilgrimage, and envoys of little solitary Hill-states, posting furiously on ring-streaked and piebald ponies, or the cavalcade of a Rajah paying a visit; or else for a long, clear day he would see nothing more than a black bear grunting and rooting below in the valley. When he first started, the roar of the world he had left still rang in his ears, as the roar of a tunnel rings long after the train has passed through; but when he had put the Mutteeanee Pass behind him that was all done, and Purun Bhagat was alone with himself, walking, wondering, and thinking, his eyes on the ground, and his thoughts with the clouds.

One evening he crossed the highest pass he had met till then— it had been a two-days' climb—and came out on a line of snow- peaks that banded all the horizon—mountains from fifteen to twenty thousand feet high, looking almost near enough to hit with a stone, though they were fifty or sixty miles away. The pass was crowned with dense, dark forest—deodar, walnut, wild cherry, wild olive, and wild pear, but mostly deodar, which is the Himalayan cedar; and under the shadow of the deodars stood a deserted shrine to Kali—who is Durga, who is Sitala, who is sometimes worshipped against the smallpox.

Purun Bhagat swept the stone floor clean, smiled at the grinning statue, made himself a little mud fireplace at the back of the shrine, spread his antelope skin on a bed of fresh pine- needles, tucked his *bairagi*—his brass-handled crutch—under his armpit, and sat down to rest.

Immediately below him the hillside fell away, clean and cleared for fifteen hundred feet, where a little village of stone- walled houses, with roofs of beaten earth, clung to the steep tilt. All round it the tiny terraced fields lay out like aprons of patch- work on the knees of the mountain, and cows no bigger than beetles grazed between the smooth stone circles of the threshing- floors. Looking across the valley, the eye was deceived by the size of things, and could not at first realise that what seemed to be low scrub, on the opposite mountain-flank, was in truth a forest of hundred-foot pines. Purun Bhagat saw an eagle swoop across the gigantic hollow, but the great bird dwindled to a dot ere it was half-way over. A few bands of scattered clouds strung up and down the valley, catching on a shoulder of the hills, or rising up and dying out when they were level with the head of the pass. And "Here shall I find peace," said Purun Bhagat.

Now, a Hill-man makes nothing of a few hundred feet up or down, and as soon as the villagers saw the smoke in the deserted shrine, the village priest climbed up the terraced hillside to welcome the stranger.

When he met Purun Bhagat's eyes—the eyes of a man used

to control thousands—he bowed to the earth, took the begging-bowl without a word, and returned to the village, saying, "We have at last a holy man. Never have I seen such a man. He is of the Plains—but pale-coloured—a Brahmin of the Brahmins." Then all the housewives of the village said, "Think you he will stay with us?" and each did her best to cook the most savoury meal for the Bhagat. Hill-food is very simple, but with buckwheat and Indian corn, and rice and red pepper, and little fish out of the stream in the valley, and honey from the flue-like hives built in the stone walls, and dried apricots, and turmeric, and wild ginger, and bannocks of flour, a devout woman can make good things, and it was a full bowl that the priest carried to the Bhagat. Was he going to stay? asked the priest. Would he need a *chela*—a disciple—to beg for him? Had he a blanket against the cold weather? Was the food good?

Purun Bhagat ate, and thanked the giver. It was in his mind to stay. That was sufficient, said the priest. Let the begging-bowl be placed outside the shrine, in the hollow made by those two twisted roots, and daily should the Bhagat be fed; for the village felt honoured that such a man—he looked timidly into the Bhagat's face—should tarry among them.

That day saw the end of Purun Bhagat's wanderings. He had come to the place appointed for him—the silence and the space. After this, time stopped, and he, sitting at the mouth of the shrine, could not tell whether he were alive or dead; a man with control of his limbs, or a part of the hills, and the clouds, and the shifting rain and sunlight. He would repeat a Name softly to himself a hundred hundred times, till, at each repetition, he seemed to move more and more out of his body, sweeping up to the doors of some tremendous discovery; but, just as the door was opening, his body would drag him back, and, with grief, he felt he was locked up again in the flesh and bones of Purun Bhagat.

Every morning the filled begging-bowl was laid silently in the crutch of the roots outside the shrine. Sometimes the priest brought it; sometimes a Ladakhi trader, lodging in the village, and anxious to get merit, trudged up the path; but, more often, it was the woman who had cooked the meal overnight; and she would murmur, hardly above her breath: "Speak for me before the gods, Bhagat. Speak for such a one, the wife of so-and-so!" Now and then some bold child would be allowed the honour, and Purun Bhagat would hear him drop the bowl and run as fast as his little legs could carry him, but the Bhagat never came down to the village. It was laid out like a map at his feet. He could see the evening gatherings, held on the circle of the threshing-floors, because that was the only level ground; could see the wonderful unnamed green of the young rice, the indigo blues of the Indian corn, the dock-like patches of buckwheat, and, in its season, the red bloom of the amaranth, whose tiny seeds, being neither grain nor pulse, make a food that can be lawfully eaten by Hindus in time of fasts.

When the year turned, the roofs of the huts were all little squares of purest gold, for it was on the roofs that they laid out their cobs of the corn to dry. Hiving and harvest, rice-sowing and husking, passed before his eyes, all embroidered down there on the many-sided plots of fields, and he thought of them all, and wondered what they all led to at the long last.

Even in populated India a man cannot a day sit still before the wild things run over him as though he were a rock; and in that wilderness very soon the wild things, who knew Kali's Shrine well, came back to look at the intruder. The *langurs*, the big grey-whiskered monkeys of the Himalayas, were, naturally, the first, for they are alive with curiosity; and when they had upset the begging-bowl, and rolled it round the floor, and tried their teeth on the brass-handled crutch, and made faces at the antelope skin, they decided that the human being who sat so still was harmless. At evening, they would leap down from the pines, and beg with their hands for things to eat, and then swing off in graceful curves. They liked the warmth of the fire, too, and huddled round it till Purun Bhagat had to push them aside to throw on more fuel; and in the morning, as often as not, he would find a furry ape sharing his blanket. All day long, one or other of the tribe would sit by his side, staring out at the snows, crooning and looking unspeakably wise and sorrowful.

After the monkeys came the *barasingh*, that big deer which is like our red deer, but stronger. He wished to rub off the velvet of his horns against the cold stones of Kali's statue, and stamped his feet when he saw the man at the shrine. But Purun Bhagat never moved, and, little by little, the royal stag edged up and nuzzled his shoulder. Purun Bhagat slid one cool hand along the hot antlers, and the touch soothed the fretted beast, who bowed his head, and Purun Bhagat very softly rubbed and ravelled off the velvet. Afterward, the *barasingh* brought his doe and fawn—gentle things that mumbled on the holy man's blanket—or would come alone at night, his eyes green in the fire-flicker, to take his share of fresh walnuts. At last, the musk-deer, the shyest and almost the smallest of the deerlets, came, too, her big rabbity ears erect; even brindled, silent *mushicknabha* must needs find out what the light in the shrine meant, and drop out her moose-like nose into Purun's Bahagat's lap, coming and going with the shadows of the fire. Purun Bhagat called them all "my brothers", and his low call of *"Bhai! Bhai!"* would draw them from the forest at noon if they were within earshot. The Himalayan black bear, moody and suspicious—Sona, who has the V-shaped white mark under his chin—passed that way more than once; and since the Bhagat showed no fear, Sona showed no anger, but watched him, and came closer, and begged a share of the caresses, and a dole of bread or wild berries. Often, in the still dawns, when the Bhagat would climb to the very crest of the pass to watch the red day walking along the peaks of the snows, he would find Sona shuffling and grunting at his heels, thrusting a curious fore-paw under fallen trunks, and bringing it away with a *whoof* of impatience; or his early steps would wake Sona where he lay curled up, and the great brute, rising erect, would think to fight, till he heard the Bhagat's voice and knew his best friend.

Nearly all hermits and holy men who live apart from the big cities have the reputation of being able to work miracles with the wild things, but all the miracle lies in keeping still, in never making a hasty movement, and, for a long time, at least, in never looking directly at a visitor. The villagers saw the outline of the *barasingh* stalking like a shadow through the dark forest behind the shrine; saw the *minaul*, the Himalayan pheasant, blazing in her best colours before Kali's statue; and the *langurs* on their haunches, inside, playing with the walnut shells. Some of the children, too, had heard Sona singing to himself, bear-fashion, behind the fallen rocks, and the Bhagat's reputation as miracle-worker stood firm.

Yet nothing was farther from his mind than miracles. He believed that all things were one big miracle, and when a man knows that much he knows something to go upon. He knew for a certainty that there was nothing great and nothing little in this world: and day and night he strove to think out his way into the heart of things, back to the place whence his soul had come.

So thinking, his untrimmed hair fell down about his shoulders, the stone slab at the side of the antelope skin was dented into a little hole by the foot of his brass-handled crutch, and the place between the tree-trunks, where the begging-bowl rested day after day, sunk and wore into a hollow almost as smooth as the brown shell itself; and each beast knew his exact place at the fire. The fields changed their colours with the seasons; the threshing-floors filled and emptied, and filled again and again; and again and again, when winter came, the *langurs* frisked among the branches feathered with light snow, till the mother-monkeys brought their sad-eyed little babies up from the warmer valleys with the spring. There were few changes in the village. The priest was older, and many of the little children who used to come with the begging-dish sent their own children now; and when you asked of the villagers how long their holy man had lived in Kali's Shrine at the head of the pass, they answered, "Always."

Then came such summer rains as had not been known in the Hills for many seasons. Through three good months the valley was wrapped in cloud and soaking mist—steady, unrelenting downfall, breaking off into thunder-shower after thunder-shower. Kali's Shrine stood above the clouds, for the most part, and there was a whole month in which the Bhagat never caught a glimpse of his village. It was packed away under a white floor

134

of cloud that swayed and shifted and rolled on itself and bulged upward, but never broke from its piers—the streaming flanks of the valley.

All that time he heard nothing but the sound of a million little waters, overhead from the trees, and underfoot along the ground, soaking through the pine-needles, dripping from the tongues of draggled fern, and spouting in newly-torn muddy channels down the slopes. Then the sun came out, and drew forth the good incense of the deodars and the rhododendrons, and that far-off, clean smell which the Hill people call "the smell of the snows". The hot sunshine lasted for a week, and then the rains gathered together for their last downpour, and the water fell in sheets that flayed off the skin of the ground and leaped back in mud. Purun Bhagat heaped his fire high that night, for he was sure his brothers would need warmth; but never a beast came to the shrine, though he called and called till he dropped asleep, wondering what had happened in the woods.

It was in the black heart of the night, the rain drumming like a thousand drums, that he was roused by a plucking at his blanket, and, stretching out, felt the little hand of a *langur*. "It is better here than in the trees," he said sleepily, loosening a fold of blanket; "take it and be warm." The monkey caught his hand and pulled hard. "Is it food, then?" said Purun Bhagat. "Wait awhile, and I will prepare some." As he kneeled to throw fuel on the fire the *langur* ran to the door of the shrine, crooned and ran back again, plucking at the man's knee.

"What is it? What is thy trouble, Brother?" said Purun Bhagat, for the *langur*'s eyes were full of things that he could not tell. "Unless one of thy caste be in a trap—and none set traps here—I will not go into that weather. Look, Brother, even the *barasingh* comes for shelter!"

The deer's antlers clashed as he strode into the shrine, clashed against the grinning statue of Kali. He lowered them in Purun Bhagat's direction and stamped uneasily, hissing through his half-shut nostrils.

"Hai! Hai! Hai!" said the Bhagat, snapping his fingers.

"Is *this* payment for a night's lodging?" But the deer pushed him toward the door, and as he did so Purun Bhagat heard the sound of something opening with a sigh, and saw two slabs of the floor draw away from each other, while the sticky earth below smacked its lips.

"Now I see," said Purun Bhagat. "No blame to my brothers that they did not sit by the fire tonight. The mountain is falling. And yet—why should I go?" His eye fell on the empty begging-bowl, and his face changed. "They have given me good food daily since—since I came, and, if I am not swift, tomorrow there will not be one mouth in the valley. Indeed, I must go and warn them below. Back there, Brother! Let me get to the fire."

The *barasingh* backed unwillingly as Purun Bhagat drove a pine torch deep into the flame, twirling it till it was well lit. "Ah! ye came to warn me," he said, rising. "Better than that we shall do; better than that. Out, now, and lend me thy neck, Brother, for I have but two feet."

He clutched the bristling withers of the *barasingh* with his right hand, held the torch away with his left, and stepped out of the shrine into the desperate night. There was no breath of wind, but the rain nearly drowned the flare as the great deer hurried down the slope, sliding on his haunches. As soon as they were clear of the forest more of the Bhagat's brothers joined them. He heard, though he could not see, the *langurs* pressing about him, and behind them the *uhh! uhh!* of Sona. The rain matted his long white hair into ropes; the water splashed beneath his bare feet, and his yellow robe clung to his frail old body, but he stepped down steadily, leaning against the *barasingh*. He was no longer a holy man, but Sir Purun Dass, K.C.I.E., Prime Minister of no small State, a man accustomed to command, going out to save life. Down the steep, plashy path they poured all together, the Bhagat and his brothers, down and down till the deer's feet clicked and stumbled on the wall of a threshing-floor, and he snorted because he smelt Man. Now they were at the head of the one crooked village street, and the Bhagat beat with his crutch on the barred windows of the blacksmith's house, as his torch blazed up in the shelter of the eaves. "Up and out!" cried Purun Bhagat; and he did not know his own voice, for it was years since he had spoken aloud to a man. "The hill falls! The hill is falling! Up and out, oh, you within!"

"It is our Bhagat," said the blacksmith's wife. "He stands among his beasts. Gather the little ones and give the call."

It ran from house to house, while the beasts, cramped in the narrow way, surged and huddled round the Bhagat, and Sona puffed impatiently.

The people hurried into the street—they were no more than seventy souls all told—and in the glare of the torches they saw their Bhagat holding back the terrified *barasingh*, while the monkeys plucked piteously at his skirts, and Sona sat on his haunches and roared.

"Across the valley and up the next hill!" shouted Purun Bhagat. "Leave none behind! We follow!"

Then the people ran as only Hill folk can run, for they knew that in a landslip you must climb for the highest ground across the valley. They fled, splashing through the little river at the bottom, and panted up the terraced fields on the far side, while the Bhagat and his brethren followed. Up and up the opposite mountain they climbed, calling to each other by name—the roll-call of the village—and at their heels toiled the big *barasingh*, weighted by the failing strength of Purun Bhagat. At last the deer stopped in the shadow of a deep pine-wood, five hundred feet up the hillside. His instinct, that had warned him of the coming slide, told him he would be safe here.

Purun Bhagat dropped fainting by his side, for the chill of the rain and that fierce climb were killing him; but first he called to the scattered torches ahead, "Stay and count your numbers"; then, whispering to the deer as he saw the lights gather in a cluster: "Stay with me, Brother. Stay—till—I—go!"

There was a sigh in the air that grew to a mutter, and a mutter that grew to a roar, and a roar that passed all sense of hearing, and the hillside on which the villagers stood was hit in the darkness, and rocked to the blow. Then a note as steady,

137

deep, and true as the deep C of the organ drowned everything for perhaps five minutes, while the very roots of the pines quivered to it. It died away, and the sound of the rain falling on miles of hard ground and grass changed to the muffled drum of water on soft earth. That told its own tale.

Never a villager—not even the priest—was bold enough to speak to the Bhagat who had saved their lives. They crouched under the pines and waited till the day. When it came they looked across the valley and saw that what had been forest, and terraced field, and track-threaded grazing-ground was one raw, red, fan-shaped smear, with a few trees flung head-down on the scarp. That red ran high up the hill of their refuge, damming back the little river, which had begun to spread into a brick-coloured lake. Of the village, of the road to the shrine, of the shrine itself, and the forest behind, there was no trace. For one mile in width and two thousand feet in sheer depth the mountain-side had come away bodily, planed clean from head to heel.

And the villagers, one by one, crept through the wood to pray before their Bhagat. They saw the *barasingh* standing over him, who fled when they came near, and they heard the *langurs* wailing in the branches, and Sona moaning up the hill; but their Bhagat was dead, sitting cross-legged, his back against a tree, his crutch under his armpit, and his face turned to the north-east.

The priest said: "Behold a miracle after a miracle, for in this very attitude must all Sunnyasis be buried! Therefore where he now is we will build the temple to our holy man."

They built the temple before a year was ended—a little stone-and-earth shrine—and they called the hill the Bhagat's hill, and they worship there with lights and flowers and offerings to this day. But they do not know that the saint of their worship is the late Sir Purun Dass, K.C.I.E., D.C.L., Ph.D., etc., once Prime Minister of the progressive and enlightened State of Mohiniwala, and honorary or corresponding member of more learned and scientific societies than will ever do any good in this world or the next.

The
Glass Peacock
BY ELEANOR FARJEON
CHOSEN BY
MARY TREADGOLD

SOME weeks ago I listened to an ebullient Polish gentleman introducing on the air his personal choice of orchestral record. So immense his enthusiasm, so eager for our enjoyment, before the last notes had died, he was bursting in with a great cry: "Did you like eet, eh? Did that make you oll *'appy?*" In introducing Eleanor Farjeon's *The Glass Peacock*, this small, glowing, entirely magical story about Annar-Mariar, the London slum child, with her generous disposition, earthy practicality, and impartially maternal dealings with every ragged little boy and girl in her alley, I feel much the same. I need to be fidgeting anxiously: " 'as eet made you oll 'appy?" Because it is largely for its capacity to communicate unthinking, unrealised, yet para-doxically piercing and rapturous happiness—yes, even *through*, even *because* of the minute disaster at the last—that I have chosen this story. So rare is happiness.

So rare is contented happiness. Not many very poor people are as accept-ingly happy as Annar-Mariar—happy with that steady rise-and-fall of joy that suggests the up-and-down of the ping-pong ball on the jet of water in the fun-fair shooting-gallery. On Twelfth Night, when Annar-Mariar, after a Christmas of humble window-shopping and no presents, encounters in the dusk of Mellin's Court the mysterious lady bearing the beautiful little shining Christmas tree, the genius of Eleanor Farjeon allows perhaps a hint of the tiny doom to come. For Annar-Mariar's heart moves irre-coverably out towards the spun-glass peacock with the long tail, proudly poised among the lesser but lovely flying glass birds that decorate the foliage of the tree. So this story, in its final count, becomes the story of Annar-Mariar at long last silently asking something for herself.

I will not tell you what happens after the party she gives for the Mellin's Court children to celebrate the tree. I will not reveal the destiny of the spun-glass peacock. I will even refrain from praising the artistry that works by implication, that does not labour its point, going so far almost as to conceal it. I will only tell you that, as Annar-Mariar lies in bed the night after the party, listening in the darkness to the soft falling of the needles from the tree and thinking her own thoughts, Eleanor Farjeon's entirely characteristic benediction falls, like joyful light, across her story, as she sets each of the other lowly, deprived children of Mellin's Court to dreaming . . .

MARY TREADGOLD

ANNAR-MARIAR lived in a queer old alley in one of the queerest and oldest parts of London. Once this part had been a real village all by itself, looking down from its hill upon the field and lanes that divided it from the town. Then gradually the town had climbed the hill, the fields were eaten up by houses, and the lanes suffered that change which turned them into streets. But the hill was so steep, and the ways were so twisty, that even the town couldn't swallow the village when it got to the top. It was too much trouble to make broad roads of all the funny little narrow turnings, so some of them were left much as they were, and one of these was the alley where Annar-Mariar lived. It ran across from one broad road to another, a way for walkers, but not for carts and cars. The two big roads met at a point a little farther on, so there was no need to turn Annar-Mariar's alley into a thoroughfare for traffic, and it remained a paved court, with poor irregular dwellings and a few humble shops on each side. Being paved, and out of the way of motors, it became a natural playground for the children who lived in it; and even from the other alleys nearby children came to play in Mellin's Court. The organ-grinder, making his way from one big road to another, sometimes made it across Mellin's Court. One day, as he was passing, a group of children were clustered round the little sweetstuff shop that sold bright sweets in hap'orths, or even farthings-worths. The shop had an old bow window nearly touching the pavement— it came down about as far as a little girl's skirt, and went up about as high as a man's collar. To enter the shop, you went down three steps into a dim little room. None of the children had any farthings that day except Annar-Mariar, and *she* had a whole penny. Her little brother Willyum was clinging to the hand that held the penny, and telling her all the things he liked best in the jars in the window. He knew his Annar-Mariar, and so did the other children who were not her brothers and sisters.

"I like the lickerish shoe-strings," said Willyum.

"I like the comfits with motters on," said Mabel Baker.

"And I like the pink and white mouses," said Willyum.

"Them bulls' eyes is scrumpchous," observed Doris Goodenough.

"And the chocklit mouses," continued Willyum, "and I like them long stripey sticks, and them chocklit cream bars with pink inside."

"Peardrops," murmured Kitty Farmer.

"And white inside too," said Willyum.

While Annar-Mariar was puzzling and puzzling how to make her penny go round she saw the organ-grinder, and cried, "Oo! an orgin!" The other children turned. "Ply us a chune, mister!" they cried. "Ply us a chune!" The organ-grinder shook his head. "No time today," he said. Annar-Mariar went up to the organ-grinder and smiled at him, plucking his coat.

"Do ply 'em a chune to dance to," she said, and held out her penny. It was Annar-Mariar's nice smile, and not her penny, that won the day. Annar-Mariar was quite an ordinary-looking little girl until she smiled. Then you felt you would do anything for her. This was because Annar-Mariar would always do anything for anybody. It came out in her smile, and got back at her, so to speak, by winning her her own way. All day long Mellin's Court was calling her name. "Annar-Mariar! Johnny's bin and hurted hisself." "Annar-Mariar! Come quick! Bobby and Joan is fighting somethink orful!" "Annar-Mariar, boohoo! I've broke my dolly!" Or it might be an older voice. "Annar-Mariar! jest keep an eye on baby for me while I go round the corner." Yes, everybody knew that Annar-Mariar would always be ready to heal the hurt, and soothe the quarrel, and mend the doll, and mind the baby. She would not only be ready to, but she could *do* it; because everybody did what she wanted them to.

So the organ-grinder refused her penny, and stopped and played three tunes for her smile; and the children got a jolly dance for nothing, and Willyum got a pair of licorice shoe-strings for a farthing. The rest of Annar-Mariar's penny went in Hundreds and Thousands, and every child licked its finger and had a dip. There wasn't a fingerful over for Annar-Mariar, so she tore open the tiny bag and licked it off with her tongue.

After that the organ-grinder made a point of cutting across Mellin's Court on his rounds, stopping outside the Rat-Catcher's where it was at its broadest, to play his tunes; and the children gathered there and danced, and sometimes he got a copper for his kindness, but whether he did or not made no difference. He always came once a week.

Christmas drew near, and the little shops in Mellin's Court began to look happy. The sweetstuff shop had a Fairy Doll in white muslin and tinsel in the middle of the window, and some paper festoons and cheap toys appeared among the glass bottles. At the greengrocer's, a sort of glorified open stall which overflowed into the courtyard, evergreens and pineapples appeared, and on one magic morning Christmas trees. The grocery window at the corner had already blossomed into dates and figs and candied fruits, and blue-and-white jars of ginger; and the big confectioner's in the High Street had in the window, as well as puddings in basins, a Christmas Cake a yard square—a great flat frosted "set piece", covered with robins, windmills, snow babies, and a scarlet Santa Claus with a sled full of tiny toys. This cake would presently be cut up and sold by the pound, and you got the attractions on top "as you came"—oh lucky, lucky buyer-to-be of the Santa Claus sled! The children of Mellin's Court were already choosing their favourite toys and cakes and fruits from the rich windows, and Annar-Mariar and Willyum chose like all the rest. Of course, they never *thought* they could have the Fairy Queen, the Christmas tree, the big box of sugary fruits, or the marvellous cake—but how they *dreamed* they could! As Christmas drew nearer, smaller hopes of what it would actually bring began to take shape in the different homes. Bobby's mother had *told* him he'd better hang his stocking up on Christmas Eve "and see". That meant something. And the Goodenoughs were going to be sent a hamper. And Mabel Baker was going to be taken to the Panto-mime! And the Jacksons were all going to their Granny's in

Lambeth for a party. And this child and that had so much, or so little, in the Sweet Club.

And as Christmas drew nearer, it became plainer and plainer to Annar-Mariar that this year, for one reason or another, Christmas wasn't going to bring her and Willyum anything. And it didn't. Up to the last they got *their* treat from the shop-windows, and did all their shopping there. Annar-Mariar never stinted her Christmas Window-shopping.

"What'll *you* 'ave, Willyum? I'll 'ave the Fairy Queen, I think. Would you like them trains?"

"Ss!" said Willyum. "And I'd like the Fairy Queen."

"Orl right. You 'ave her. I'll 'ave that music box."

At the confectioner's: "Shall we 'ave a big puddin' for us both, or a little puddin' each, Willyum?"

"A big puddin' each," said Willyum.

"Orl right. And them red crackers with the gold bells on, and I'll tell 'em to send the big cake round too, shall I?"

"Ss!" said Willyum, "and I'll 'ave the Farver Crismuss."

"Orl right, ducks. You can."

And at the grocer's Willyum had the biggest box of candied fruits, and at the greengrocer's the biggest pineapple. He agreed, however, to a single tree—the biggest—between them, and under Annar-Mariar's lavish disregard of money there was plenty of everything for them both, and for anybody who cared to "drop in" on Christmas Day.

It came, and passed. The windows began to be emptied of their attractions for another year. Mabel Baker went to the Pantomime, and told them all about it. Annar-Mariar dreamed of it for nights; she thought she was a very lucky girl to have a friend who went to the Panto.

Life went on. The New Year rang itself in. At dusk, on Twelfth Night, Annar-Mariar knelt on the paving-stones in Mellin's Court and renewed a chalk game that had suffered during the day. She happened to be the only child about, a rare occurrence there.

She heard footsteps go by her, but did not look up at once; only, as they passed, she became aware of a tiny tinkling accompaniment in the footsteps. Then she did look up. A lady was going slowly along the alley with something astonishing in her hands.

"Oo!" gasped Annar-Mariar.

The lady stopped. What she was carrying was a Christmas tree, quite a little tree, the eighteenpenny size, but such a *radiant* little tree! It was glittering and twinkling with all the prettiest fantasies in glass that the mind of Christmas had been able to invent, little gas lamps and candlesticks, shining balls of every colour, a scarlet-and-silver Father Christmas, also in glass, chains and festoons of gold and silver beads, stars, and flowers, and long clear drops like icicles; birds, too, in glass, blue and yellow birds, seeming to fly, and one, proudest and loveliest of all, a peacock, shimmering in blue and green and gold, with a crest and long, long tail of fine spun glass, like silk.

"Oo!" gasped Annar-Mariar. "A Christmas tree!"

The lady did an undreamed-of thing. She came straight up to Annar-Mariar and said, "Would you like it?"

Annar-Mariar gazed at her, and very slowly smiled. The lady put the tinkling tree into her hands.

"This," she said, "was for the first little girl that said Oo! and you're the little girl."

Annar-Mariar began to giggle—she simply *couldn't* say "Thank you!" She could only giggle and giggle. Her smile, however, turned her giggling into the loveliest laughter, and seemed to be saying "Thank you" on top of it. The lady laughed, and disappeared from Mellin's Court.

Willyum appeared in her place. "Wot's that?"

"'Ts a Crismuss tree. A lidy give it to me."

Willyum scampered screaming down the alley. "Annar-Mariar's gotter Crismuss tree wot a lidy give 'er!"

The crowd collected. They gathered round the tree, looking, touching, admiring, and the "Oos!" came thick and fast.

"Oo! see ol' Farver Crismuss!"

"Oo! see them birds, like flying, ain't they?"

"Do the lamps reely light, Annar-Mariar?"

"Oo! ain't that flower loverly!"

"Wotcher goin' to do wiv it, Annar?"

"I shall keep it by my bed ternight," said Annar-Mariar, "and termorrer I shall give a party."

Longing glances flew about her.

"Can I come, Annar-Mariar?"

"Can I?"

"Can I?"

"Let *me* come, won't yer, Annar?"

"You can all come," said Annar-Mariar.

That night, that one blissful night, the little tree in all its gleaming beauty shone upon Annar-Mariar's dreams—waking dreams, for she hardly slept at all. She kept looking at it, and feeling it when she couldn't see it, running her finger along the glassy chains, outlining the fragile flowers and stars, stroking the silken tail of the miraculous peacock. Tomorrow night, she knew, her tree would be harvested, but she thought her own particular fruit might be the peacock. If so, he could sit on the tree beside her bed for ever, and every night she could stroke his spun-glass tail.

The morrow came. The party was held after tea. Every child in Mellin's Court took home a treasure. Willyum wanted the Father Christmas, and had him. The other children did not ask for the peacock. Somehow they knew how *much* Annar-Mariar wanted it, and recognised that off *her* tree she should have what she prized most. Little Lily Kensit *did* murmur, when her turn came, "I'd like the peac—" But her big brother clapped his hand over her mouth, and said firmly, "Lil'd like the rose, Annar-Mariar. Look, Lil, it's got a dimond in the middle."

"Oo!" said Lil greedily.

So when the party was over, and the little empty tree was dropping its dried needles on the table, Annar-Mariar was left in possession of the magical bird whose tail she had touched in her dreams.

When she came to put Willyum to bed, he was sobbing bitterly.

"Wot's the matter, ducks?"

"I broke my Farver Crissmuss."

"Oh, Willyum . . . you never."

"Yus, I did." Willyum was inconsolable.

"Don't cry, ducks."

"I want your peacock."

"Orl right. You can. Don't cry."

Annar-Mariar gave Willyum her peacock. He sobbed himself to sleep. clutching it, and in the night he dropped it out of bed. Annar-Mariar heard it "go" as she lay beside her little empty tree. All night long the pungent scent of the Christmas tree was in her nostrils, and the tiny crickle of its dropping needles in her ears.

And in the room of every other child in Mellin's Court some lovely thing was set above its dreams, a bird, or flower, or star of coloured glass; to last perhaps a day, a week, a few months, or a year—or even many years.

All You've Ever Wanted

BY

JOAN AIKEN

CHOSEN BY

GEOFFREY TREASE

I T was easy enough to choose a Joan Aiken short story, not so easy to decide which. But I think *All You've Ever Wanted* must be my selection, though it is only the title-story of a volume full of delightful other things, like *The Ghostly Governess* and *The Lobster's Birthday*, *Dragon Monday* and *Yes, but Today is Tuesday*.

I love these stories for two qualities—their humour and their wildly ingenious fantasy. Humour and fantasy are both difficult to keep up through-out a long book. They are delicate threads that snap if stretched too far. It is just my personal taste, but I like my long books to be solid and real, my short stories gossamer-light.

There are two main sorts of fantasy, the Tolkien kind where everything is weird and strange, and the Joan Aiken or Mary Norton kind where the magic pops up in the midst of our everyday world, as in this story where flowers sprout in the London Underground. It is this second kind I most enjoy.

Joan Aiken comes of a literary family, with the famous Conrad Aiken as father, and a sister and brother who both write novels. She herself has written eleven books for children and six for grown-ups, ranging from THE WIND-SCREEN WEEPERS, science-fiction for adults, to A NECKLACE OF RAIN-DROPS, which is for younger readers.

GEOFFREY TREASE

MATILDA, you will agree, was a most unfortunate child. Not only had she three names each worse than the others—Matilda, Eliza and Agatha—but her father and mother died shortly after she was born, and she was brought up exclusively by her six aunts. These were all energetic women, and so on Monday Matilda was taught Algebra and Arithmetic by her Aunt Aggie, on Tuesday, Biology by her Aunt Beattie, on Wednesday Classics by her Aunt Cissie, on Thursday Dancing and Deportment by her Aunt Dorrie, on Friday Essentials by her Aunt Effie, and on Saturday French by her Aunt Florrie. Friday was the most alarming day, as Matilda never knew beforehand what Aunt Effie would decide on as the day's Essentials—sometimes it was cooking, or revolver practice, or washing, or boiler-making ("For you never know what a girl may need nowadays" as Aunt Effie rightly observed).

So that by Sunday, Matilda was often worn out, and thanked her stars that her seventh aunt, Gertie, had left for foreign parts many years before, and never threatened to come back and teach her Geology or Grammar on the only day when she was able to do as she liked.

However, poor Matilda was not entirely free from her Aunt Gertie, for on her seventh birthday, and each one after it, she received a little poem wishing her well, written on pink paper, decorated with silver flowers, and signed "Gertrude Isabel Jones, to her niece, with much affection". And the terrible disadvantage of the poems, pretty though they were, was that the wishes in them invariably came true. For instance the one on her eighth birthday read:

> *Now you are eight Matilda dear*
> *May shining gifts your place adorn*
> *And each day through the coming year*
> *Awake you with a rosy morn.*

The shining gifts were all very well—they consisted of a torch, a luminous watch, pins, needles, a steel soapbox and a useful little silver brooch which said "Matilda" in case she ever forgot her name—but the rosy morns were a great mistake. As you know, a red sky in the morning is the shepherd's warning, and the fatal result of Aunt Gertie's well-meaning verse was that it rained every day for the entire year.

Another one read:

> *Each morning make another friend*
> *Who'll be with you till light doth end,*
> *Cheery and frolicsome and gay,*
> *To pass the sunny hours away.*

For the rest of her life Matilda was overwhelmed by the number of friends she made in the course of that year—three hundred and sixty-five of them. Every morning she found another of them, anxious to cheer her and frolic with her, and the aunts complained that her lessons were being constantly interrupted. The worst of it was that she did not really like all the friends—some of them were so *very* cheery and frolicsome, and insisted on pillow-fights when she had a toothache, or sometimes twenty-one of them would get together and make her play hockey, which she hated. She was not even consoled by the fact that all her hours were sunny, because she was so busy in passing them away that she had no time to enjoy them.

> *Long miles and weary though you stray*
> *Your friends are never far away,*
> *And every day though you may roam,*
> *Yet night will find you back at home*

was another inconvenient wish. Matilda found herself forced to go for long, tiresome walks in all weathers, and it was no comfort to know that her friends were never far away, for although they often passed her on bicycles or in cars, they never gave her lifts.

However, as she grew older, the poems became less troublesome, and she began to enjoy bluebirds twittering in the garden, and endless vases of roses on her window-sill. Nobody knew where Aunt Gertie lived, and she never put in an address with her birthday greetings. It was therefore impossible to write and thank her for her varied good wishes, or hint that they might have been more carefully worded. But Matilda looked forward to meeting her one day, and thought that she must be a most interesting person.

"You never knew what Gertrude would be up to next," said Aunt Cissie. "She was a thoughtless girl, and got into endless scrapes, but I will say for her, she was very good-hearted."

When Matilda was nineteen she took a job in the Ministry of Alarm and Despondency, a very cheerful place where, instead of typewriter ribbon, they used red tape, and there was a large laundry basket near the main entrance labelled The Usual Channels where all the letters were put which people did not want to answer themselves. Once every three months the letters were re-sorted and dealt out afresh to different people.

Matilda got on very well here and was perfectly happy. She went to see her six aunts on Sundays, and had almost forgotten the seventh by the time that her twentieth birthday had arrived. Her aunt, however, had not forgotten.

On the morning of her birthday Matilda woke very late, and had to rush off to work cramming her letters unopened into her pocket, to be read later on in the morning. She had no time to read them until ten minutes to eleven, but that, she told herself, was as it should be, since, as she had been born at eleven in the morning, her birthday did not really begin till then.

Most of the letters were from her 365 friends, but the usual pink and silver envelope was there, and she opened it with the usual feeling of slight uncertainty.

May all your leisure hours be blest,
Your work prove full of interest,
Your life hold many happy hours
And all your way be strewn with flowers

said the pink and silver slip in her fingers. "From your affectionate Aunt Gertrude."

Matilda was still pondering this when a gong sounded in the passage outside. This was the signal for everyone to leave their work and dash down the passage to a trolley which sold them buns and coffee. Matilda left her letters and dashed with the rest. Sipping her coffee and gossiping with her friends, she had forgotten the poem, when the voice of the Minister of Alarm and Despondency himself came down the corridor.

"What is all this? What does this mean?" he was saying.

The group round the trolley turned to see what he was talking about. And then Matilda flushed scarlet and spilt some of her coffee on the floor. For all along the respectable brown carpeting of the passage were growing flowers in the most riotous profusion—daisies, campanulas, crocuses, mimosa, fox-gloves, tulips and lotuses. In some places the passage looked more like a jungle than anything else. Out of this jungle the little red-faced figure of the Minister fought its way.

"Who did it?" he said. But nobody answered.

Matilda went quietly away from the chattering group and pushed through the vegetation to her room, leaving a trail of buttercups and rhododendrons across the floor to her desk.

"I can't keep this quiet," she thought desperately. And she was quite right. Mr. Willoughby, who presided over the General Gloom Division, noticed almost immediately that when his secretary came into his room, there was something unusual about her.

"Miss Jones," he said, "I don't like to be personal, but have you noticed that wherever you go, you leave a trail of mixed flowers?"

Poor Matilda burst into tears.

"I know, I don't know *what* I shall do about it," she sobbed.

Mr. Willoughby was not used to secretaries who burst into tears, let alone ones who left lobelias, primroses and the rarer forms of cactus behind them when they entered the room.

"It's very pretty," he said. "But not very practical. Already it's almost impossible to get along the passage, and I shudder to think what this room will be like when these have grown a bit higher. I really don't think you can go on with it, Miss Jones."

"You don't think I do it on purpose, do you?" said Matilda sniffing into her handkerchief. "I can't stop it. They just keep on coming."

"In that case I am afraid," replied Mr. Willoughby, "that you will not be able to keep on coming. We really cannot have the Ministry overgrown in this way. I shall be very sorry to lose you, Miss Jones. You have been most efficient. What caused this unfortunate disability, may I ask?"

"It's a kind of spell," Matilda said, shaking the damp out of her handkerchief on to a fine polyanthus.

"But my dear girl," Mr. Willoughby exclaimed testily, "you have a National Magic Insurance card, haven't you? Good heavens—why don't you go to the Public Magician?"

"I never thought of that," she confessed. "I'll go at lunch-time."

Fortunately for Matilda the Public Magician's office lay just across the square from where she worked, so that she did not cause too much disturbance, though the Borough Council could never account for the rare and exotic flowers which suddenly sprang up in the middle of their dusty lawns.

The Public Magician received her briskly, examined her with an occultiscope, and asked her to state particulars of her trouble.

"It's a spell," said Matilda, looking down at a pink Christmas rose growing unseasonably beside her chair.

"In that case we can soon help you. Fill in that form, *if* you please." He pushed a printed slip at her across the table.

It said: "To be filled in by persons suffering from spells, incantations, philtres, Evil Eye, etc."

Matilda filled in name and address of patient, nature of spell, and date, but when she came to name and address of person by whom spell was cast, she paused.

"I don't know her address," she said.

"Then I'm afraid you'll have to find it. Can't do anything without an address," the Public Magician replied.

Matilda went out into the street very disheartened. The Public Magician could do nothing better than advise her to put an advertisement into *The Times* and the *International Sorcerers' Bulletin*, which she accordingly did:

AUNT GERTRUDE PLEASE COMMUNICATE MATILDA MUCH DISTRESSED BY LAST POEM.

While she was in the Post Office sending off her advertisements (and causing a good deal of confusion by the number of forget-me-nots she left about), she wrote and posted her resignation to Mr. Willoughby, and then went sadly to the nearest Underground Station.

"Aintcher left something behind?" a man said to her at the top of the escalator. She looked back at the trail of daffodils across the station entrance and hurried anxiously down the stairs. As she ran round a corner at the bottom angry shouts told her that blooming lilies had interfered with the works and the escalator had stopped.

She tried to hide in the gloom at the far end of the platform, but a furious station official found her.

"Wotcher mean by it?" he said, shaking her elbow. "It'll take three days to put the station right, and look at my platform!"

The stone slabs were split and pushed aside by vast peonies, which kept growing, and threatened to block the line.

"It isn't my fault—really it isn't," poor Matilda stammered.

"The company can sue you for this, you know," he began, when a train came in. Pushing past him, she squeezed into the nearest door.

She began to thank her stars for the escape, but it was too soon. A powerful and penetrating smell of onions rose round her feet where the white flowers of wild garlic had sprung.

When Aunt Gertie finally read the advertisement in a ten-months' old copy of the *International Sorcerers' Bulletin*, she packed her luggage and took the next aeroplane back to England. For she was still just as Aunt Cissie had described her—thoughtless, but very good-hearted.

"Where is the poor child?" she asked Aunt Aggie.

"I should say she was poor," her sister replied tartly. "It's a pity you didn't come home before, instead of making her life a misery for twelve years. You'll find her out in the summerhouse."

Matilda had been living out there ever since she left the Ministry of Alarm and Despondency, because her aunts kindly but firmly, and quite reasonably, said that they could not have the house filled with vegetation.

She had an axe, with which she cut down the worst growths every evening, and for the rest of the time she kept as still as she could, and earned some money by doing odd jobs of typing and sewing.

"My poor dear child," Aunt Gertie said breathlessly. "I had no idea that my little verses would have this sort of effect. What ever shall we do?"

"Please do something," Matilda implored her, sniffing. This time it was not tears, but a cold she had caught from living in perpetual draughts.

"My dear, there isn't anything I can do. It's bound to last till the end of the year—that sort of spell is completely unalterable."

"Well, at least can you stop sending me the verses?" asked Matilda. "I don't want to sound ungrateful. . . ."

"Even that I can't do," her aunt said gloomily. "It's a banker's order at the Magician's Bank. One a year from seven to twenty-one. Oh, dear, and I thought it would be such *fun* for you. At least you only have one more, though."

"Yes, but heaven knows what that'll be." Matilda sneezed despondently and put another sheet of paper into her typewriter. There seemed to be nothing to do but wait. However, they did decide that it might be a good thing to go and see the Public Magician on the morning of Matilda's twenty-first birthday.

Aunt Gertie paid the taxi-driver and tipped him heavily not to grumble about the mass of delphiniums sprouting out of the mat of his cab.

"Good heavens, if it isn't Gertrude Jones!" the Public Magician exclaimed. "Haven't seen you since we were at college together. How are you? Same old irresponsible Gertie?

157

Remember that hospital you endowed with endless beds and the trouble it caused? And the row with the cigarette manufacturers over the extra million boxes of cigarettes for the soldiers?"

When the situation was explained to him he laughed heartily. "Just like you, Gertie. Well-meaning isn't the word."

At eleven promptly, Matilda opened her pink envelope.

Matilda, now you're twenty-one,
May you have every sort of fun;
May you have all you've ever wanted,
And every future wish be granted.

"Every future wish be granted—then I wish Aunt Gertie would lose her power of wishing," cried Matilda; and immediately Aunt Gertie did.

But as Aunt Gertie with her usual thoughtlessness had said, "May you have all you've *ever wanted*" Matilda had quite a lot of rather inconvenient things to dispose of, including a lion cub and a baby hippopotamus.

Our Field

BY MRS. EWING
CHOSEN BY ELFRIDA VIPONT

SOMETIMES an author produces a masterpiece on such a small scale that few people recognise it. Take, for instance, Mrs. Gaskell's COUSIN PHILLIS. Reading COUSIN PHILLIS is like finding the first snowdrops or hearing the first cuckoo in spring; you want to rush off and share the good news. *Our Field* is like that, on an even smaller scale. In almost all Mrs. Ewing's longer books, something lives on in the memory. I seldom smell lilac without thinking of Margery and Eleanor and the crocodile of schoolgirls in SIX TO SIXTEEN, each sniffing the lilac bush in turn, or watch my fantails strutting on the roof without remembering DADDY DARWIN'S DOVECOT. But here, in *Our Field*, everything lives on. It is so true to its period that we accept it, all of a piece, and experience for ourselves the Victorian age in rural England instead of looking at it from the outside, like something in a museum; it is so true to nature that we can see the blackthorn blossom "lying white on the black twigs like snow", and smell the sweet violets under the hedge, and hear the lark singing far above us in the sky; it is so true to childhood in any age that, as Sir Arthur Quiller-Couch said of COUSIN PHILLIS, it is full of "small *recognitions*". As for Perronet, the dog, have we not all known dogs who thought it their duty to "attend" to the birds?—"whenever a bird settled down anywhere, he barked at it, and then it flew away, and he ran barking after it till he lost it. . . . He never caught a bird, and never would let one sit down, if he could see it."

I suppose all this amounts to the reason why I have chosen this story. Yet perhaps it is more than that. Perhaps it is the smell of hawthorn blossom; for me, every word is drenched in it, recalling another field, in another day and age, and in another place, where other children played, and heard the larks singing as they mounted up into the sky, a field to which I shall never dare return, for fear lest it should be there no longer.

ELFRIDA VIPONT

THERE were four of us, and three of us had godfathers and godmothers. Three each. Three times three make nine, and not a fairy godmother in the lot. That was what vexed us.

It was very provoking, because we knew so well what we wanted if we had one, and she had given us three wishes each. Three times three make nine. We could have got all we wanted out of nine wishes, and have provided for Perronet into the bargain. It would not have been any good Perronet having wishes all to himself, because he was only a dog.

We never knew who it was that drowned Perronet, but it was Sandy who saved his life and brought him home. It was when he was coming home from school, and he brought Perronet with him. Perronet was not at all nice to look at when we first saw him, though we were very sorry for him. He was wet all over, and his eyes shut, and you could see his ribs, and he looked quite dark and sticky. But when he dried, he dried a lovely yellow, with two black ears like velvet. People sometimes asked us what kind of dog he was, but we never knew, except that he was the nicest possible kind.

When we had got him, we were afraid we were not going to be allowed to have him. Mother said we could not afford him, because of the tax and his keep. The tax was five shillings, but there wanted nearly a year to the time of paying it. Of course his keep began as soon as he could eat, and that was the very same evening. We were all very miserable, because we were so fond of Perronet—at least, Perronet was not his name then, but he was the same person—and at last it was settled that all three of us would give up sugar, towards saving the expense of his keep, if he might stay. It was hardest for Sandy, because he was particularly fond of sweet things; but then he was particularly fond of Perronet. So we all gave up sugar, and Perronet was allowed to remain.

About the tax, we thought we could save any pennies or half-

161

pennies we got during the year, and it was such a long time to the time for paying, that we should be almost sure to have enough by then. We had not any money at the time, or we should have bought a savings-box; but lots of people save their money in stockings, and we settled that we would. An old stocking would not do, because of the holes, and I had not many good pairs; but we took one of my winter ones to use in the summer, and then we thought we could pour the money into one of my good summer ones when the winter came.

What we most of all wanted a fairy godmother for was about our "homes". There was no kind of play we liked better than playing at houses and new homes. But no matter where we made our "home", it was sure to be disturbed. If it was indoors, and we made a palace under the big table, as soon as ever we had got it nicely divided into rooms according to where the legs came, it was certain to be dinner-time, and people put their feet into it. The nicest house we ever had was in the outhouse; we had it, and kept it quite a secret, for weeks. And then the new load of wood came and covered up everything, our best oyster-shell dinner-service and all.

Anyone can see that it is impossible really to fancy anything when you are constantly interrupted. You can't have any fun out of a railway train stopping at stations, when they take all your carriages to pieces because the chairs are wanted for tea; any more than you can play properly at Grace Darling in a life-boat, when they say the old cradle is too good to be knocked about in that way. It was always the same. If we wanted to play at Thames Tunnel under the beds, we were not allowed; and the day we did Aladdin in the store-closet, old Jane came and would put away the soap, just when Aladdin could not possibly have got the door of the cave open.

It was one day early in May—a very hot day for the time of year, which had made us rather cross—when Sandy came in about four o'clock, smiling more broadly even than usual, and said to Richard and me: "I've got a fairy godmother, and she's given us a field."

Sandy was very fond of eating, especially sweet things. He

used to keep back things from meals to enjoy afterwards, and he almost always had a piece of cake in his pocket. He brought a piece out now, and took a large mouthful, laughing at us with his eyes over the top of it.

"What's the good of a field?" said Richard.

"Splendid houses in it," said Sandy.

"I'm quite tired of fancying homes," said I. "It's no good; we always get turned out."

"It's quite a new place," Sandy continued; "you've never been there," and he took a triumphant bite of the cake.

"How did you get there?" asked Richard.

"The fairy godmother showed me," was Sandy's reply.

There is such a thing as nursery honour. We respected each other's pretendings unless we were very cross, but I didn't disbelieve in his fairy godmother. I only said, "You shouldn't talk with your mouth full," to snub him for making a secret about his field.

Sandy is very good-tempered. He only laughed and said, "Come along. It's much cooler out now. The sun's going down."

He took us along Gipsy Lane. We had been there once or twice, for walks, but not very often, for there was some horrid story about it which rather frightened us. I do not know what it was, but it was a horrid one. Still we had been there, and I knew it quite well. At the end of it there is a stile, by which you go into a field, and at the other end you get over another stile, and find yourself in the high road.

"If this is our field, Sandy," said I, when we got to the first stile, "I'm very sorry, but it really won't do. I know that lots of people come through it. We should never be quiet here."

Sandy laughed. He didn't speak, and he didn't get over the stile; he went through a gate close by it leading into a little sort of bye-lane that was all mud in winter and hard cart-ruts in summer. I had never been up it, but I had seen hay and that sort of thing go in and come out of it.

He went on and we followed him. The ruts were very dis-agreeable to walk on, but presently he led us through a hole in the hedge, and we got into a field. It was a very bare-looking field, and went rather uphill. There was no path, but Sandy walked away up it, and we went after him. There was another hedge at the top, and a stile in it. It had very rough posts, one much longer than the other, and the cross-step was gone, but there were two rails, and we all climbed over. And when we got to the other side, Sandy leaned against the big post and gave a wave with his right hand and said, "This is our field."

It sloped down hill, and the hedges round it were rather high, with awkward branches of blackthorn sticking out here and there without any leaves, and with the blossom lying white on the black twigs like snow. There were cowslips all over the field, but they were thicker at the lower end, which was damp. The great heat of the day was over. The sun shone still, but it shone low down and made such splendid shadows that we all walked about with grey giants at our feet; and it made the bright green of the grass, and the cowslips down below, and the top of the hedge, and Sandy's hair, and everything in the sun and the mist behind the elder bush which was out of the sun, so yellow—so very yellow—that just for a minute I really believed about Sandy's godmother, and thought it was a story come true, and that everything was turning into gold.

But it was only for a minute; of course I know that fairy tales are not true. But it was a lovely field, and when we had put our hands to our eyes, and had a good look at it, I said to Sandy, "I beg your pardon, Sandy, for telling you not to talk with your mouth full. It is the best field I ever heard of."

"Sit down," said Sandy, doing the honours; and we all sat down under the hedge.

"There are violets just behind us," he continued. "Can't you smell them? But whatever you do, don't tell anybody of those, or we shan't keep our field to ourselves for a day. And look here." He had turned over on to his face, and Richard and I did the same, whilst Sandy fumbled among the bleached grass and brown leaves.

"Hyacinths," said Richard, as Sandy displayed the green tops of them.

"As thick as peas," said Sandy. "This bank will be blue in a few weeks; and fiddle-heads everywhere. There will be no end of ferns. May to any extent—it's only in bud yet—and there's a wren's nest in there—" At this point he rolled suddenly over on to his back and looked up.

"A lark," he explained; "there was one singing its head off, this morning. I say, Dick, this will be a good field for a kite, won't it? *But wait a bit.*"

After every fresh thing that Sandy showed us in our field, he always finished by saying, "*Wait a bit*"; and that was because there was always something else better still.

"There's a brook at the bottom there," he said, "with lots of fresh-water shrimps. I wonder whether they would boil red. *But wait a bit.* This hedge, you see, has got a very high bank, and it's worn into kind of ledges. I think we could play at 'shops' there—but *wait a bit.*"

"It's almost *too* good, Sandy dear!" said I, as we crossed the field to the opposite hedge.

"The best is to come," said Sandy. "I've a very good mind not to let it out till tomorrow." And to our distraction he sat down in the middle of the field, put his arms round his knees, as if we were playing at "Honey-pots", and rocked himself backwards and forwards with a face of brimming satisfaction.

Neither Richard nor I would have been so mean as to explore on our own account, when the field was Sandy's discovery, but we tried hard to persuade him to show us everything.

He had the most provoking way of laughing and holding his tongue, and he did that now, besides slowly turning all his pockets inside-out into his hands, and mumbling up the crumbs and odd currants, saying "Guess!" between every mouthful.

But when there was not a crumb left in the seams of his pockets, Sandy turned them back, and jumping up, said— "One can only tell a secret once. It's a hollow oak. Come along!"

He ran and we ran, to the other side of Our Field. I had read of hollow oaks, and seen pictures of them, and once I dreamed of one, with a witch inside, but we had never had one to play in. We were nearly wild with delight. It looked all solid from the field, but when we pushed behind, on the hedge side, there was the door, and I crept in, and it smelt of wood, and delicious damp. There could not be a more perfect castle, and though there were no windows in the sides, the light came in from the top, where the polypody hung over like a fringe. Sandy was quite right. It was the very best thing in Our Field.

Perronet was as fond of the field as we were. What he liked were the little birds. At least, I don't know that he liked them, but they were what he chiefly attended to. I think he knew that it was our field, and thought he was the watch-dog of it, and whenever a bird settled down anywhere, he barked at it, and then it flew away, and he ran barking after it till he lost it; and by that time another had settled down, and then Perronet flew at him, and so on, all up and down the hedge. He never caught a bird, and never would let one sit down, if he could see it.

We had all kinds of games in Our Field. Shops—for there were quantities of things to sell—and sometimes I was a moss-merchant, for there were ten different kinds of moss by the brook, and sometimes I was a jeweller, and sold daisy-chains and pebbles, and coral sets made of holly berries, and oak-apple necklaces; and sometimes I kept a flower-shop, and sold nosegays and wreaths, and umbrellas made of rushes. I liked that kind of shop, because I am fond of arranging flowers, and I always make our birthday wreaths. And sometimes I kept a whole lot of shops, and Richard and Sandy bought my things, and paid for them with money made of elder-pith, sliced into rounds. The first shop I kept was to sell cowslips, and Richard and Sandy lived by the brook, and were wine merchants, and made cowslip wine in a tin mug.

The elder-tree was a beauty. In July the cream-coloured flowers were so sweet, we could hardly sit under it, and in the autumn it was covered with berries; but we were always a little disappointed that they never tasted in the least like elderberry syrup. Richard used to make flutes out of the stalks, and one really did to play tunes on, but it always made Perronet bark.

Richard's every-day cap had a large hole in the top, and when we were in Our Field we always hung it on the top of the tallest of the two stile-posts, to show that we were there; just as the Queen has a flag hung out at Windsor Castle, when she is at home.

We played at castles and houses, and when we were tired of the houses, we pretended to pack up, and went to the seaside for change of air by the brook. Sandy and I took off our shoes and stockings and were bathing-women, and we bathed Perronet; and Richard sat on the bank and was a "tripper", looking at us through a telescope; for when the elder-stems cracked and wouldn't do for flutes, he made them into telescopes. And before we went down to the brook we made jam of hips and haws from the hedge at the top of the field, and put it into acorn cups, and took it with us, that the children might not be short of roly-polies at the seaside.

Whatever we played at we were never disturbed. Birds, and cows, and men and horses ploughing in the distance, do not disturb you at all.

We were very happy that summer: the boys were quite happy, and the only thing that vexed me was thinking of Perronet's tax-money. For months and months went on and we did not save it. Once we got as far as two-pence halfpenny, and then one day Richard came to me and said, "I must have some string for the kite. You might lend me a penny out of Perronet's stocking, till I get some money of my own."

So I did; and the next day Sandy came and said, "You lent Dick one of Perronet's coppers: I'm sure Perronet would lend me one," and then they said it was ridiculous to leave a half-penny there by itself, so we spent it in acid drops.

It worried me so much at last, that I began to dream horrible dreams about Perronet having to go away because we hadn't saved his tax-money. And then I used to wake up and cry, till the pillow was so wet, I had to turn it. The boys never seemed to mind, but then boys don't think about things; so that I was quite surprised when one day I found Sandy alone in our field with Perronet in his arms, crying, and feeding him with cake; and I found he was crying about the tax-money.

I cannot bear to see boys cry. I would much rather cry myself, and I begged Sandy to leave off, for I said I was quite determined to try and think of something.

It certainly was remarkable that the very next day should be the day when we heard about the flower-show.

It was in school—the village school, for mother could not afford to send us anywhere else—and the schoolmaster rapped on his desk and said, "Silence, children!" and that at the agricultural show there was to be a flower-show this year, and that an old gentleman was going to give prizes to the school-children for window-plants and for the best arranged wild flowers. There were to be nosegays and wreaths, and there was to be a first prize of five shillings, and a second prize of half-a-crown, for the best collection of wild flowers with the names put to them.

"The English names," said the schoolmaster; "and there may be—silence, children!—there may be collections of ferns, or grasses, or mosses to compete, too, for the gentleman wishes to encourage a taste for natural history."

And several of the village children said, "What's that?" and I squeezed Sandy's arm, who was sitting next to me, and whispered, "Five shillings!" and the schoolmaster said, "Silence, children!" and I thought I never should have finished my lessons that day for thinking of Perronet's tax-money.

July is not at all a good month for wild flowers; May and June are far better. However, the show was to be in the first week in July.

I said to the boys, "Look here: I'll do a collection of flowers. I know the names, and I can print. It's no good two or three people muddling with arranging flowers; but if you will get me what I want, I shall be very much obliged. If either of you will make another collection, you know there are ten kinds of mosses by the brook; and we have names for them of our own, and they are English. Perhaps they'll do. But everything must come out of Our Field."

The boys agreed, and they were very good. Richard made me a box, rather high at the back. We put sand at the bottom and damped it, and then Feather Moss, lovely clumps of it, and into that I stuck the flowers. They all came out of Our Field. I like to see the grass with flowers, and we had very pretty grasses, and between every bunch of flowers I put a bunch of grass of different kinds. I got all the flowers and all the grasses ready first, and printed the names on pieces of cardboard to stick in with them, and then I arranged them by my eye, and Sandy handed me what I called for, for Richard was busy at the brook making a tray of mosses.

Sandy knew the flowers and the names of them quite as well as I did, of course; we knew everything that lived in Our Field; so when I called, "Ox-eye daisies, cock's-foot grass, labels; meadow-sweet, fox-tail grass, labels; dog-roses, shivering grass, labels" and so on, he gave me the right things, and I had nothing to do but to put the colours that looked best together next to each other, and to make the grass look light, and pull up bits of the moss to show well. And at the very end I put in a label, "All out of Our Field."

I did not like it when it was done; but Richard praised it so much, it cheered me up, and I thought his mosses looked lovely.

The flower-show day was very hot. I did not think it could be hotter anywhere in the world than it was in the field where the show was; but it was hotter in the tent.

We should never have got in at all—for you had to pay at the gate—but they let competitors in free, though not at first. When we got in, there were a lot of grown-up people, and it was very hard work getting along among them, and getting to see the stands with the things on. We kept seeing tickets with "1st Prize" and "2nd Prize", and struggling up; but they were sure to be dahlias in a tray, or fruit that you mightn't eat, or vegetables. The vegetables disappointed us so often, I got to hate them. I don't think I shall ever like very big potatoes (before they are boiled) again, particularly the red ones. It makes me feel sick with heat and anxiety to think of them.

We had struggled slowly all round the tent, and seen all the cucumbers, onions, lettuces, long potatoes, round potatoes, and everything else, when we saw an old gentleman, with spectacles and white hair, standing with two or three ladies. And then we saw three nosegays in jugs, with all the green picked off, and the flowers tied as tightly together as they would go, and then we saw some prettier ones, and then we saw my collection, and it had got a big label in it marked "1st Prize", and next to it came Richard's moss-tray, with the Hair-moss and the Pin-cushion-moss, and the Scale-mosses, and a lot of others with names of our own, and it was marked "2nd Prize". And I gripped one of Sandy's arms just as Richard seized the other, and we both cried, "Perronet is paid for!"

There was two-and-sixpence over. We never had such a feast! It was a picnic tea, and we had it in Our Field. I thought Sandy and Perronet would have died of cake, but they were none the worse.

We were very much frightened at first when the old gentle-man invited himself; but he would come, and he brought a lot of nuts, and he did get inside the oak, though it is really too small for him.

I don't think there ever was anybody so kind. If he were not a man, I should really and truly believe in Sandy's fairy god-mother.

Of course I don't really believe in fairies. I am not so young as that. And I know that Our Field does not exactly belong to us.

I wonder to whom it does belong? Richard says he believes it belongs to the gentleman who lives at the big red house among the trees. But he must be wrong; for we see that gentleman at church every Sunday, but we never saw him in Our Field.

And I don't believe anybody could have such a field of their very own, and never come to see it, from one end of summer to the other.

The Maltese Cat
by Rudyard Kipling

chosen by Barbara Willard

TALKING animals are rather out of fashion, but the conversation between the Maltese Cat and his colleagues seems perfectly reasonable. Anyway, horses have such a way of nudging one another, of moving their lips close to a neighbouring ear, that communication is obvious. Kipling had every excuse, therefore, to translate horse-talk into the only language with which he and you and I are comfortably familiar.

This is a story, as simple as simple, which contains almost every desirable ingredient. It has excitement, suspense, humour, courage, generosity. You need not know how to play polo to enjoy the game described here. If you feel intolerant of the days of Empire, you can still appreciate Kipling's evocation of this very graceful manifestation of those times. How hot and bright it is on the Umballa polo ground, with the uniforms and the parasols and the excited ponies. "It was a glorious sight, and the come-and-go of the little quick hoofs, and the incessant salutations of ponies that had met before on other polo grounds or racecourses, were enough to drive a four-footed thing wild."

I commend to you especially the final two paragraphs—I think they are pretty well perfect. But don't read them first! Just *begin at the beginning and go on until you come to the end*.

BARBARA WILLARD

THEY had good reason to be proud, and better reason to be afraid, all twelve of them; for, though they had fought their way, game by game, up the teams entered for the polo tournament, they were meeting the Archangels that afternoon in the final match; and the Archangels' men were playing with half-a-dozen ponies apiece. As the game was divided into six quarters of eight minutes each, that meant a fresh pony after every halt. The Skidars' team, even supposing there were no accidents, could only supply one pony for every other change; and two to one is heavy odds. Again, as Shiraz, the grey Syrian, pointed out, they were meeting the pink and pick of the polo ponies of Upper India; ponies that had cost from a thousand rupees each, while they themselves were a cheap lot gathered, often from country carts, by their masters who belonged to a poor but honest native infantry regiment.

"Money means pace and weight," said Shiraz, rubbing his black silk nose dolefully along his neat-fitting boot, "and by the maxims of the game as I know it—"

"Ah, but we aren't playing the maxims," said the Maltese Cat. "We're playing the game, and we've the great advantage of knowing the game. Just think a stride, Shiraz. We've pulled up from bottom to second place in two weeks against all those fellows on the ground here; and that's because we play with our heads as well as with our feet."

"It makes me feel undersized and unhappy all the same," said Kittiwynk, a mouse-coloured mare with a red browband and the cleanest pair of legs that ever an aged pony owned. "They've twice our size, these others."

Kittiwynk looked at the gathering and sighed. The hard, dusty Umballa polo-ground was lined with thousands of soldiers, black and white, not counting hundreds and hundreds of carriages, and drags, and dog-carts, and ladies with brilliant-coloured parasols, and officers in uniform and out of it, and crowds of natives behind them; and orderlies on camels who had halted to watch the game, instead of carrying letters up and down the station, and native horse-dealers running about on thin-eared Biluchi mares, looking for a chance to sell a few first-class polo ponies. Then there were the ponies of thirty teams that had entered for the Upper India Free For All Cup— nearly every pony of worth and dignity from Mhow to Peshawar, from Allahabad to Multan; prize ponies, Arabs, Syrian, Barb, countrybred, Deccanee, Waziri, and Kabul ponies of every colour and shape and temper that you could imagine. Some of them were in mat-roofed stables close to the polo-ground, but most were under saddle while their masters, who had been defeated in the earlier games, trotted in and out and told each other exactly how the game should be played.

It was a glorious sight, and the come-and-go of the little quick hoofs, and the incessant salutations of ponies that had met before on other polo-grounds or race-courses, were enough to drive a four-footed thing wild.

But the Skidars' team were careful not to know their neighbours, though half the ponies on the ground were anxious to scrape acquaintance with the little fellows that had come from the North, and, so far, had swept the board.

"Let's see," said a soft, golden-coloured Arab, who had been playing very badly the day before, to the Maltese Cat, "didn't we meet in Abdul Rahman's stable in Bombay four seasons ago? I won the Paikpattan Cup next season, you may remember."

"Not me," said the Maltese Cat politely. "I was at Malta then, pulling a vegetable cart. I don't race. I play the game."

"O-oh!" said the Arab, cocking his tail and swaggering off.

"Keep yourselves to yourselves," said the Maltese Cat to his companions. "We don't want to rub noses with all those goose-rumped half-breeds of Upper India. When we've won this cup they'll give their shoes to know us."

"*We* shan't win the cup," said Shiraz. "How do you feel?"

"Stale as last night's feed when a musk-rat has run over it," said Polaris, a rather heavy-shouldered grey, and the rest of the team agreed with him.

"The sooner you forget that the better," said the Maltese Cat cheerfully. "They've finished tiffin in the big tent. We shall be wanted now. If your saddles are not comfy, kick. If your bits aren't easy, rear, and let the *saises* know whether your boots are tight."

Each pony had his *sais*, his groom, who lived and ate and slept with the pony, and had betted a great deal more than he could afford on the result of the game. There was no chance of anything going wrong, and, to make sure, each *sais* was shampooing the legs of his pony to the last minute. Behind the *saises* sat as many of the Skidars' regiment as had leave to attend the match—about half the native officers, and a hundred or two dark, black-bearded men with the regimental pipers nervously fingering the big be-ribboned bagpipes. The Skidars were what they call a Pioneer regiment; and the bagpipes made the national music of half the men. The native officers held bundles of polo-sticks, long cane-handled mallets, and as the grandstand filled after lunch they arranged themselves by ones and twos at different points round the ground, so that if a stick were broken the player would not have far to ride for a new one. An impatient British cavalry band struck up "If you want to know the time, ask a p'leeceman!" and the two umpires in light dust-coats danced out on two little excited ponies. The four players of the Archangels' team followed and the sight of their beautiful mounts made Shiraz groan again.

"Wait till we know," said the Maltese Cat. "Two of 'em are playing in blinkers, and that means they can't see to get out of the way of their own side, or they *may* shy at the umpires' ponies. They've *all* got white web reins that are sure to stretch or slip!"

"And," said Kittiwynk, dancing to take the stiffness out of her, "they carry their whips in their hands instead of on their wrists. Hah!"

"True enough. No man can manage his stick and his reins, and his whip that way," said the Maltese Cat. "I've fallen over every square yard of the Malta ground, and *I* ought to know." He quivered his little flea-bitten withers just to show how

175

satisfied he felt; but his heart was not so light. Ever since he
had drifted into India on a troopship, taken, with an old rifle,
as part payment for a racing debt, the Maltese Cat had played
and preached polo to the Skidars' team on the Skidars' stony
polo-ground. Now a polo pony is like a poet. If he is born with
a love for the game he can be made. The Maltese Cat knew
that bamboos grew solely in order that polo-balls might be
turned from their roots, that grain was given to ponies to keep
them in hard condition, and that ponies were shod to prevent
them slipping on a turn. But, besides all these things, he knew
every trick and device of the finest game of the world, and for
two seasons he had been teaching the others all he knew or
guessed.

"Remember," he said for the hundredth time as the riders
came up, "we *must* play together, and you *must* play with your
heads. Whatever happens, follow the ball. Who goes out first?"

Kittiwynk, Shiraz, Polaris, and a short high little bay fellow
with tremendous hocks and no withers worth speaking of (he
was called Corks) were being girthed up, and the soldiers in the
background stared with all their eyes.

"I want you men to keep quiet," said Lutyens, the captain
of the team, "and especially *not* to blow your pipes."

"Not if we win, Captain Sahib?" asked a piper.

"If we win, you can do what you please," said Lutyens, with
a smile, as he slipped the loop of his stick over his wrist, and
wheeled to canter to his place. The Archangels' ponies were a
little bit above themselves on account of the many-coloured crowd
so close to the ground. Their riders were excellent players, but
they were a team of crack players instead of a crack team; and
that made all the difference in the world. They honestly meant
to play together, but it is very hard for four men, each the
best of the team he is picked from, to remember that in polo
no brilliancy of hitting or riding makes up for playing alone.
Their captain shouted his orders to them by name, and it is a
curious thing that if you call his name aloud in public after an
Englishman you make him hot and fretty. Lutyens said nothing
to his men because it had all been said before. He pulled up

Shiraz, for he was playing "back", to guard the goal. Powell on Polaris was half-back, and Macnamara and Hughes on Corks and Kittiwynk were forwards. The tough bamboo-root ball was put into the middle of the ground one hundred and fifty yards from the ends, and Hughes crossed sticks, heads-up, with the captain of the Archangels, who saw fit to play forward, and that is a place from which you cannot easily control the team. The little click as the cane-shafts met was heard all over the ground, and then Hughes made some sort of quick wrist-stroke that just dribbled the ball a few yards. Kittiwynk knew that stroke of old, and followed as a cat follows a mouse. While the captain of the Archangels was wrenching his pony round Hughes struck with all his strength, and next instant Kittiwynk was away. Corks followed close behind her, their little feet pattering like rain-drops on glass.

"Pull out to the left," said Kittiwynk between her teeth, "it's coming our way, Corks!"

The back and half-back of the Archangels were tearing down on her just as she was within reach of the ball. Hughes leaned forward with a loose rein, and cut it away to the left almost under Kittiwynk's feet, and it hopped and skipped off to Corks, who saw that, if he were not quick, it would run beyond the boundaries. That long bouncing drive gave the Archangels time to wheel and send three men across the ground to head off Corks. Kittiwynk stayed where she was, for she knew the game. Corks was on the ball half a fraction of a second before the others came up, and Macnamara, with a back-handed stroke, sent it back across the ground to Hughes, who saw the way clear to the Archangels' goal, and smacked the ball in before anyone quite knew what had happened.

"That's luck," said Corks, as they changed ends. "A goal in three minutes for three hits and no riding to speak of."

"Don't know," said Polaris. "We've made 'em angry too soon. Shouldn't wonder if they try to rush us off our feet next time."

"Keep the ball hanging then," said Shiraz. "That wears out every pony that isn't used to it."

Next time there was no easy galloping across the ground. All the Archangels closed up as one man, but there they stayed, for Corks, Kittiwynk, and Polaris were somewhere on the top of the ball, marking time among the rattling sticks, while Shiraz circled about outside, waiting for a chance.

"*We* can do this all day," said Polaris, ramming his quarters into the side of another pony. "Where do you think you're shoving to?"

"I'll—I'll be driven in an *ekka* if I know," was the gasping reply, "and I'd give a week's feed to get my blinkers off. I can't see anything."

"The dust is rather bad. Whew! That was one for my off hock. Where's the ball, Corks?"

"Under my tail. At least a man's looking for it there. This is beautiful. They can't use their sticks, and it's driving 'em wild. Give old blinkers a push and he'll go over!"

"Here, don't touch me! I can't see. I'll—I'll back out, I think," said the pony in blinkers, who knew that if you can't see all round your head you cannot prop yourself against a shock.

Corks was watching the ball where it lay in the dust close to his near fore with Macnamara's shortened stick tap-tapping it from time to time. Kittiwynk was edging her way out of the scrimmage, whisking her stump of a tail with nervous excitement.

"Ho! They've got it," she snorted. "Let me out!" and she galloped like a rifle-bullet just behind a tall lanky pony of the Archangels, whose rider was swinging up his stick for a stroke.

"Not today, thank you," said Hughes, as the blow slid off his raised stick, and Kittiwynk laid her shoulder to the tall pony's quarters, and shoved him aside just as Lutyens on Shiraz sent the ball where it had come from, and the tall pony went skating and slipping away to the left. Kittiwynk, seeing that Polaris had joined Corks in the chase for the ball up the ground, dropped into Polaris's place, and then time was called.

The Skidars' ponies wasted no time in kicking or fuming. They knew each minute's rest meant so much gain, and trotted off to the rails and their *saises*, who began to scrape and blanket and rub them at once.

"Whew!" said Corks, stiffening up to get all the tickle out of the big vulcanite scraper. "If we were playing pony for pony we'd bend those Archangels double in half an hour. But they'll bring out fresh ones and fresh ones, and fresh ones after that—you see."

"Who cares?" said Polaris. "We've drawn first blood. Is my hock swelling?"

"Looks puffy," said Corks. "You must have had rather a wipe. Don't let it stiffen. You'll be wanted again in half an hour."

"What's the game like?" said the Maltese Cat.

"Ground's like your shoe, except where they've put too much water on it," said Kittiwynk. "Then it's slippery. Don't play in the centre. There's a bog there. I don't know how their next four are going to behave, but we kept the ball hanging and made 'em lather for nothing. Who goes out? Two Arabs and a couple of countrybreds! That's bad. What a comfort it is to wash your mouth out!"

Kitty was talking with a neck of a leather-covered soda-water bottle between her teeth and trying to look over her withers at the same time. This gave her a very coquettish air.

"What's bad?" said Gray Dawn, giving to the girth and admiring his well-set shoulders.

"You Arabs can't gallop fast enough to keep yourselves warm —that's what Kitty means," said Polaris, limping to show that his hock needed attention. "Are you playing 'back', Gray Dawn?"

"Looks like it," said Gray Dawn, as Lutyens swung himself up. Powell mounted the Rabbit, a plain bay countrybred much like Corks, but with mulish ears. Macnamara took Faiz Ullah, a handy short-backed little red Arab with a long tail, and Hughes mounted Benami, an old and sullen brown beast, who stood over in front more than a polo pony should.

"Benami looks like business," said Shiraz. "How's your temper, Ben?" The old campaigner hobbled off without answering, and the Maltese Cat looked at the new Archangel ponies prancing about on the ground. They were four beautiful blacks, and they saddled big enough and strong enough to eat the Skidars' team and gallop away with the meal inside them.

"Blinkers again," said the Maltese Cat. "Good enough!"

"They're chargers—cavalry chargers!" said Kittiwynk indignantly. "*They'll* never see thirteen three again."

"They've all been fairly measured and they've all got their certificates," said the Maltese Cat, "or they wouldn't be here. We must take things as they come along, and keep our eyes on the ball."

The game began, but this time the Skidars were penned to their own end of the ground, and the watching ponies did not approve of that.

"Faiz Ullah is shirking, as usual," said Polaris, with a scornful grunt.

"Faiz Ullah is eating whip," said Corks. They could hear the leather-thonged polo quirt lacing the little fellow's well-rounded barrel. Then the Rabbit's shrill neigh came across the ground. "I can't do all the work," he cried.

"Play the game, don't talk," the Maltese Cat whickered; and all the ponies wriggled with excitement, and the soldiers and the grooms gripped the railings and shouted. A black pony with blinkers had singled out old Benami, and was interfering with him in every possible way. They could see Benami shaking his head up and down and flapping his underlip.

"There'll be a fall in a minute," said Polaris. "Benami is getting stuffy."

The game flickered up and down between goal-post and goal-post, and the black ponies were getting more confident as they felt they had the legs of the others. The ball was hit out of a little scrimmage, and Benami and the Rabbit followed it; Faiz Ullah only too glad to be quiet for an instant.

The blinkered black pony came up like a hawk, with two of his own side behind him, and Benami's eye glittered as he raced. The question was which pony should make way for the other; each rider was perfectly willing to risk a fall in a good cause. The black who had been driven nearly crazy by his blinkers trusted to his weight and his temper; but Benami knew how to apply his weight and how to keep his temper. They met, and there was a cloud of dust. The black was lying on his side with all the breath knocked out of his body. The Rabbit was a hundred yards up the ground with the ball, and Benami was sitting down. He had slid nearly ten yards, but he had had his revenge, and sat cracking his nostrils till the black pony rose.

"That's what you get for interfering. Do you want any more?" said Benami, and he plunged into the game. Nothing was done because Faiz Ullah would not gallop, though Macnamara beat him whenever he could spare a second. The fall of the black pony had impressed his companions tremendously, and so the Archangels could not profit by Faiz Ullah's bad behaviour.

But as the Maltese Cat said, when time was called and the four came back blowing and dripping, Faiz Ullah ought to have been kicked all round Umballa. If he did not behave better next time, the Maltese Cat promised to pull out his Arab tail by the root and eat it.

There was no time to talk, for the third four were ordered out.

The third quarter of a game is generally the hottest, for each side thinks that the others must be pumped; and most of the winning play in a game is made about that time.

Lutyens took over the Maltese Cat with a pat and a hug, for Lutyens valued him more than anything else in the world. Powell had Shikast, a little grey rat with no pedigree and no manners outside polo; Macnamara mounted Bamboo, the largest of the team, and Hughes took Who's Who, *alias* The Animal. He was supposed to have Australian blood in his veins, but he looked like a clothes horse, and you could whack him on the legs with an iron crow-bar without hurting him.

They went out to meet the very flower of the Archangels' team, and when Who's Who saw their elegantly booted legs and their beautiful satiny skins he grinned a grin through his light, well-worn bridle.

"My word!" said Who's Who. "We must give 'em a little football. Those gentlemen need a rubbing down."

"No biting," said the Maltese Cat warningly, for once or twice in his career Who's Who had been known to forget himself in that way.

"Who said anything about biting? I'm not playing tiddly-winks. I'm playing the game."

The Archangels came down like a wolf on the fold, for they were tired of football and they wanted polo. They got it more and more. Just after the game began, Lutyens hit a ball that was coming towards him rapidly, and it rose in the air, as a ball sometimes will, with the whirr of a frightened partridge. Shikast heard, but could not see it for the minute, though he looked everywhere and up into the air as the Maltese Cat had taught him. When he saw it ahead and overhead, he went forward with Powell as fast as he could put foot to ground. It was then that Powell, a quiet and level-headed man as a rule, became inspired and played a stroke that sometimes comes off successfully on a quiet afternoon of long practice. He took his stick in both hands, and standing up in his stirrups, swiped at the ball in the air, Munipore fashion. There was one second of paralysed astonishment, and then all four sides of the ground went up in a yell of applause and delight as the ball flew true (you could see the amazed Archangels ducking in their saddles to get out of the line of flight, and looking at it with open mouths), and the regimental pipes of the Skidars squealed from the railings as long as the piper had breath.

Shikast heard the stroke; but he heard the head of the stick fly off at the same time. Nine hundred and ninety-nine ponies out of a thousand would have gone tearing on after the ball with a useless player pulling at their heads, but Powell knew him and he knew Powell; and the instant he felt Powell's right leg shift a trifle on the saddle-flap he headed to the boundary, where a native officer was frantically waving a new stick. Before the shouts had ended Powell was armed again.

Once before in his life the Maltese Cat had heard that very same stroke played off his own back, and had profited by the confusion it made. This time he acted on experience, and leaving Bamboo to guard the goal in case of accidents, came through the others like a flash, head and tail low, Lutyens standing up to ease him—swept on and on before the other side knew what was the matter, and nearly pitched on his head between the Archangels' goal-post as Lutyens tipped the ball in after a straight scurry of a hundred and fifty yards. If there was one thing more than another upon which the Maltese Cat prided himself it was on this quick, streaking kind of run half across the ground. He did not believe in taking balls round the field unless you were clearly over-matched. After this they gave the Archangels five minutes' football, and an expensive fast pony hates football because it rumples his temper.

Who's Who showed himself even better than Polaris in this game. He did not permit any wriggling away, but bored joyfully into the scrimmage as if he had his nose in a feed-box, and were looking for something nice. Little Shikast jumped on the ball the minute it got clear, and every time an Archangel pony followed it he found Shikast standing over it asking what was the matter.

"If we can live through this quarter," said the Maltese Cat, "I shan't care. Don't take it out of yourselves. Let them do the lathering."

So the ponies, as their riders explained afterwards, "shut up". The Archangels kept them tied fast in front of their goal, but it cost the Archangels' ponies all that was left of their tempers; and ponies began to kick, and men began to repeat compliments, and they chopped at the legs of Who's Who, and he set his teeth and stayed where he was, and the dust stood up like a tree over the scrimmage till that hot quarter ended.

They found the ponies very excited and confident when they went to their *saises*; and the Maltese Cat had to warn them that the worst of the game was coming.

"Now *we* are all going in for the second time," said he, "and *they* are trotting out fresh ponies. You'll think you can gallop, but you'll find you can't; and then you'll be sorry."

"But two goals to nothing is a halter-long lead," said Kittiwynk prancing.

"How long does it take to get a goal?" the Maltese Cat

183

answered. "For pity sake, don't run away with the notion that the game is half-won just because we happen to be in luck now. They'll ride you into the grandstand if they can; you must *not* give 'em a chance. Follow the ball."

"Football, as usual?" said Polaris. "My hock's half as big as a nose-bag."

"Don't let them have a look at the ball if you can help it. Now leave me alone, I must get all the rest I can before the last quarter."

He hung down his head and let all his muscles go slack; Shikast, Bamboo, and Who's Who copying his example.

"Better not watch the game," he said. "We aren't playing, and we shall only take it out of ourselves if we grow anxious. Look at the ground and pretend it's fly-time."

They did their best, but it was hard advice to follow. The hoofs were drumming and the sticks were rattling all up and down the ground, and yells of applause from the English troops told that the Archangels were pressing the Skidars hard. The native soldiers behind the ponies groaned and grunted, and said things in undertones, and presently they heard a long-drawn shout and a clatter of hurrahs!

"One to the Archangels," said Shikast, without raising his head. "Time's nearly up. Oh, my sire and dam!"

"Faiz Ullah," said the Maltese Cat, "if you don't play to the last nail in your shoes this time, I'll kick you on the ground before all the other ponies."

"I'll do my best when my time comes," said the little Arab sturdily.

The *saises* looked at each other gravely as they rubbed their ponies' legs. This was the first time when long purses began to tell, and everybody knew it. Kittiwynk and the others came back with the sweat dripping over their hoofs and their tails telling sad stories.

"They're better than we are," said Shiraz. "I knew how it would be."

"Shut your big head," said the Maltese Cat; "we've one goal to the good yet."

"Yes, but it's two Arabs and two countrybreds to play now," said Corks. "Faiz Ullah, remember!" He spoke in a biting voice.

As Lutyens mounted Gray Dawn he looked at his men, and they did not look pretty. They were covered with dust and sweat in streaks. Their yellow boots were almost black, their wrists were red and lumpy, and their eyes seemed two inches deep in their heads, but the expression in the eyes was satisfactory.

"Did you take anything at tiffin?" said Lutyens, and the team shook their heads. They were too dry to talk.

"All right. The Archangels did. They are worse pumped than we are."

"They've got the better ponies," said Powell. "I shan't be sorry when this business is over."

That fifth quarter was a sad one in every way. Faiz Ullah played like a little red demon; and the Rabbit seemed to be everywhere at once, and Benami rode straight at anything and everything that came in his way, while the umpires on their ponies wheeled like gulls outside the shifting game. But the Archangels had the better mounts—they had kept their racers till late in the game—and never allowed the Skidars to play football. They hit the ball up and down the width of the ground till Benami and the rest were outpaced. Then they went forward, and time and again Lutyens and Gray Dawn were just, and only just, able to send the ball away with a long splitting back-hander. Gray Dawn forgot that he was an Arab; and turned from gray to blue as he galloped. Indeed, he forgot too well, for he did not keep his eyes on the ground as an Arab should, but stuck out his nose and scuttled for the dear honour of the game. They had watered the ground once or twice between the quarters, and a careless water-man had emptied the last of his skinful all in one place near the Skidars' goal. It was close to the end of play, and for the tenth time Gray Dawn was bolting after a ball when his near hind foot slipped on the greasy mud and he rolled over and over, pitching Lutyens just clear of the goal-post; and the triumphant Archangels made their goal. Then time was called—two goals all;

but Lutyens had to be helped up, and Gray Dawn rose with his near hind leg strained somewhere.

"What's the damage?" said Powell, his arm round Lutyens.

"Collar-bone, of course," said Lutyens between his teeth. It was the third time he had broken it in two years, and it hurt him.

Powell and the others whistled. "Game's up," said Hughes.

"Hold on. We've five good minutes yet, and it isn't my right hand," said Lutyens. "We'll stick it out."

"I say," said the captain of the Archangels, trotting up. "Are you hurt, Lutyens? We'll wait if you care to put in a substitute. I wish—I mean—the fact is, you fellows deserve this game if any team does. Wish we could give you a man or some of our ponies—or something."

"You're awfully good, but we'll play it to a finish, I think."

The captain of the Archangels stared for a little. "That's not half bad," he said, and went back to his own side, while Lutyens borrowed a scarf from one of his native officers and made a sling of it. Then an Archangel galloped up with a big bath-sponge and advised Lutyens to put it under his arm-pit to ease his shoulder, and between them they tied up his left arm scientifically, and one of the native officers leaped forward with four long glasses that fizzed and bubbled.

The team looked at Lutyens piteously, and he nodded. It was the last quarter, and nothing would matter after that. They drank out the dark golden drink, and wiped their moustaches, and things looked more hopeful.

The Maltese Cat had put his nose into the front of Lutyens' shirt, and was trying to say how sorry he was.

"He knows," said Lutyens, proudly. "The beggar knows. I've played him without a bridle before now—for fun."

"It's no fun now," said Powell. "But we haven't a decent substitute."

"No," said Lutyens. "It's the last quarter, and we've got to make our goal and win. I'll trust the Cat."

"If you fall this time you'll suffer a little," said Macnamara.

"I'll trust the Cat," said Lutyens.

"You hear that?" said the Maltese Cat proudly to the others.

"It's worth while playing polo for ten years to have that said of you. Now then, my sons, come along. We'll kick up a little bit, just to show the Archangels *this* team haven't suffered."

And, sure enough, as they went on to the ground the Maltese Cat, after satisfying himself that Lutyens was home in the saddle, kicked out three or four times, and Lutyens laughed. The reins were caught up anyhow in the tips of his strapped hand, and he never pretended to reply on them. He knew the Cat would answer to the least pressure of the leg, and by way of showing off—for his shoulder hurt him very much—he bent the little fellow in a close figure-of-eight in and out between the goal-posts. There was a roar from the native officers and men, who dearly loved a piece of *dugabashi* (horse-trick work), as they called it, and the pipes very quietly and scornfully droned out the first bars of a common bazaar tune called "Freshly Fresh and Newly New", just as a warning to the other regiments that the Skidars were fit. All the natives laughed.

"And now," said the Cat, as they took their place, "remember that this is the last quarter, and follow the ball!"

"Don't need to be told," said Who's Who.

"Let me go on. All those people on all four sides will begin to crowd in—just as they did at Malta. You'll hear people calling out, and moving forward and being pushed back, and that is going to make the Archangel ponies very unhappy. But if a ball is struck to the boundary, you go after it, and let the people get out of your way. I went over the pole of a four-in-hand once, and picked a game out of the dust by it. Back me up when I run, and follow the ball."

There was a sort of an all-round sound of sympathy and wonder as the last quarter opened, and then there began exactly what the Maltese Cat had foreseen. People crowded in close to the boundaries, and the Archangels' ponies kept looking sideways at the narrowing space. If you know how a man feels to be cramped at tennis—not because he wants to run out of the court, but because he likes to know that he can at a pinch— you will guess how ponies must feel when they are playing in a box of human beings.

"I'll bend some of those men if I can get away," said Who's Who, as he rocketed behind the ball; and Bamboo nodded without speaking. They were playing the last ounce in them, and the Maltese Cat had left the goal undefended to join them. Lutyens gave him every order that he could to bring him back, but this was the first time in his career that the little wise gray had ever played polo on his own responsibility, and he was going to make the most of it.

"What are you doing here?" said Hughes, as the Cat crossed in front of him and rode off an Archangel.

"The Cat's in charge—mind the goal!" shouted Lutyens, and bowing forward hit the ball full, and followed on, forcing the Archangels towards their own goal.

"No football," said the Cat. "Keep the ball by the boundaries and cramp 'em. Play open order and drive 'em to the boundaries."

Across and across the ground in big diagonals flew the ball, and whenever it came to a flying rush and a stroke close to the boundaries the Archangel ponies moved stiffly. They did not care to go headlong at a wall of men and carriages, though if the ground had been open they could have turned on a sixpence.

"Wriggle her up the sides," said the Cat. "Keep her close to the crowd. They hate the carriages. Shikast, keep her up this side."

Shikast with Powell lay left and right behind the uneasy scuffle of an open scrimmage, and every time the ball was hit away Shikast galloped on it at such an angle that Powell was forced to hit it towards the boundary; and when the crowd had been driven away from that side, Lutyens would send the ball over to the other, and Shikast would slide desperately after it till his friends came down to help. It was billiards, and no football, this time—billiards in a corner pocket; and the cues were not well chalked.

"If they get us out in the middle of the ground they'll walk away from us. Dribble her along the sides," cried the Cat.

So they dribbled all along the boundary, where a pony could not come on their right-hand side; and the Archangels were furious, and the umpires had to neglect the game to shout at the people to get back, and several blundering mounted police-men tried to restore order, all close to the scrimmage, and the nerves of the Archangels' ponies stretched and broke like cobwebs.

Five or six times an Archangel hit the ball up into the middle of the ground, and each time the watchful Shikast gave Powell his chance to send it back, and after each return, when the dust had settled, men could see that the Skidars had gained a few yards.

Every now and again there were shouts of " 'Side. Off side!" from the spectators; but the teams were too busy to care, and the umpires had all they could do to keep their maddened ponies clear of the scuffle.

At last Lutyens missed a short easy stroke, and the Skidars had to fly back helter-skelter to protect their own goal, Shikast leading. Powell stopped the ball with a back-hander when it was not fifty yards from the goal-posts, and Shikast spun round with a wrench that nearly hoisted Powell out of his saddle.

"Now's our last chance," said the Cat, wheeling like a cockchafer on a pin. "We've got to ride it out. Come along."

Lutyens felt the little chap take a deep breath, and, as it were, crouch under his rider. The ball was hopping towards the right-hand boundary, an Archangel riding for it with both spurs and a whip; but neither spur nor whip would made his pony stretch himself as he neared the crowd. The Maltese Cat glided under his very nose, picking up his hind legs sharp, for there was not a foot to spare between his quarters and the other pony's bit. It was as neat an exhibition as fancy figure-skating. Lutyens hit with all the strength he had left, but the stick slipped a little in his hand, and the ball flew off to the left instead of keeping close to the boundary. Who's Who was far across the ground, thinking hard as he galloped. He repeated, stride for stride, the Cat's manœuvres with another Archangel pony, nipping the ball away from under his bridle, and clearing his opponent by half a fraction of an inch, for Who's Who was clumsy behind. Then he drove away towards the right as the

189

Maltese Cat came up from the left; and Bamboo held a middle
course exactly between them. The three were making a sort of
Government-broad-arrow-shaped attack; and there was only
the Archangels' back to guard the goal; but immediately behind
them were three Archangels racing all they knew, and mixed
up with them was Powell, sending Shikast along on what he
felt was their last hope. It takes a very good man to stand up
to the rush of seven crazy ponies in the last quarters of a cup
game, when men are riding with their necks for sale, and the
ponies are delirious. The Archangels' back missed his stroke,
and pulled aside just in time to let the rush go by. Bamboo and
Who's Who shortened stride to give the Maltese Cat room, and
Lutyens got the goal with a clean, smooth, smacking stroke
that was heard all over the field. But there was no stopping the
ponies. They poured through the goal-posts in one mixed mob,
winners and losers together, for the pace had been terrific. The
Maltese Cat knew by experience what would happen, and, to
save Lutyens, turned to the right with one last effort that
strained a back-sinew beyond hope of repair. As he did so he
heard the right-hand goal-post crack as a pony cannoned into
it—crack, splinter, and fall like a mast. It had been sawed
three parts through in case of accidents, but it upset the pony
nevertheless, and he blundered into another, who blundered
into the left-hand post, and then there was confusion and dust
and wood. Bamboo was lying on the ground, seeing stars; an
Archangel pony rolled beside him, breathless and angry;
Shikast had sat down dog-fashion to avoid falling over the others,
and was sliding along on his little bobtail in a cloud of dust;
and Powell was sitting on the ground, hammering with his
stick and trying to cheer. All the others were shouting at the
top of what was left of their voices, and the men who had been
split were shouting too. As soon as the people saw no one was
hurt, ten thousand native and English shouted and clapped and
yelled, and before anyone could stop them the pipers of the
Skidars broke on to the ground, with all the native officers and
men behind them, and marched up and down, playing a wild
northern tune called "Zakhme Bagān", and through the

insolent blaring of the pipes and high-pitched native yells you could hear the Archangels' band hammering, "For they are all jolly good fellows", and then reproachfully to the losing team, "Ooh, Kafoozalum! Kafoozalum! Kafoozalum!"

Besides all these things and many more, there was a Commander-in-Chief, and an Inspector General of Cavalry, and the principal veterinary officer in all India, standing on the top of a regimental coach, yelling like school-boys; and brigadiers and colonels and commissioners, and hundreds of pretty ladies joined the chorus. But the Maltese Cat stood with his head down, wondering how many legs were left to him; and Lutyens watched the men and ponies pick themselves out of the wreck of the two goal-posts, and he patted the Cat very tenderly.

"I say," said the captain of the Archangels, spitting a pebble out of his mouth, "will you take three thousand for that pony—as he stands?"

"No, thank you. I've an idea he's saved my life," said Lutyens, getting off and lying down at full length. Both teams were on the ground too, waving their boots in the air, and coughing and drawing deep breaths, as the *saises* ran up to take away the ponies, and an officious water-carrier sprinkled the players with dirty water till they sat up.

"My Aunt!" said Powell, rubbing his back and looking at the stumps of the goal-posts, "that was a game!"

They played it over again, every stroke of it, that night at the big dinner, when the Free-for-All Cup was filled and passed down the table, and emptied and filled again, and everybody made most eloquent speeches. About two in the morning, when there might have been some singing, a wise little, plain little, gray little head looked in through the open door.

"Hurrah! Bring him in," said the Archangels; and his *sais*, who was very happy indeed, patted the Maltese Cat on the flank, and he limped in to the blaze of light and the glittering uniforms, looking for Lutyens. He was used to messes, and men's bedrooms, and places where ponies are not usually encouraged, and in his youth had jumped on and off a mess-table for a bet. So he behaved himself very politely, and ate bread dipped in salt, and was petted all round the table, moving gingerly; and they drank his health, because he had done more to win the Cup than any man or horse on the ground.

That was glory and honour enough for the rest of his days, and the Maltese Cat did not complain much when his veterinary surgeon said that he would be no good for polo any more. When Lutyens married, his wife did not allow him to play, so he was forced to be an umpire; and his pony on these occasions was a flea-bitten gray with a neat polo-tail, lame all round, but desperately quick on his feet, and, as everybody knew, Past Pluperfect Prestissimo Player of the Game.

ITS WALLS WERE AS OF JASPER

BY KENNETH GRAHAME
CHOSEN BY URSULA MORAY WILLIAMS

KENNETH GRAHAME's two-volumed saga, A GOLDEN AGE and DREAM DAYS, was given to my twin sister and myself when we were too young to appreciate them; in fact we resented his intrusion upon a world that we felt was not his province, and for a long while the books bored us.

But we could never completely reject them, and throughout the whole of my reading childhood I read and re-read them with a growing affection, until they seemed to be the chronicle of a family that was almost our own kith and kin.

These children with their company of Olympian aunts and uncles, the despots of their daily lives, had much in common with ourselves, since we too lived in a world of our own in which the grown-ups played no part. Unlike Edward and his brothers and sisters we dearly loved our despots, but between them and ourselves a great gulf was fixed, filled with uncomprehension on our part and a mild compassion that their days, unlike our own, could be so sterile and lacking in interest. But not for one moment would we have offered them the freedom of our private kingdoms, so, ignoring them fondly, we continued in the pattern of our many-splendoured existence that slowly cemented our attachment to Kenneth Grahame's children and made them our allies.

Re-reading *Its Walls Were as of Jasper* I can feel again the hearth-rug hard beneath my stomach, as my twin sister and I turned over the pages of our picture books (Willebeek Le Mair, now published in quarter size with faded blocks but still available! Edmund Dulac, Arthur Rackham, and endless Kate Greenaways, supplied by loving aunts!), allotting the characters in much the same manner as did Charlotte and the rest: "This is me!" . . . "That is you!" as we lived the adventures far beyond the point at which the artist finished.

Kenneth Grahame knew how we felt about it all, and although while we were still in Arcady his descriptions seemed invasive and rather tedious, later, when fewer and fewer pictures crept into the books we read, and we groped our way uncertainly towards that adult world which still we half despised . . . only then did we realise the full import of his gift to us, as he rendered back, untarnished, the fading citadels whose walls were, and will always remain, as of jasper.

URSULA MORAY WILLIAMS

IN THE long winter evenings, when we had the picture-books out on the floor, and sprawled together over them, with elbows deep in the hearthrug, the first business to be gone through was the process of allotment. All the characters in the pictures had to be assigned and dealt out among us, according to seniority, as far as they would go. When once that had been satisfactorily completed, the story was allowed to proceed; and thereafter, in addition to the excitement of the plot, one always possessed a personal interest in some particular member of the cast, whose successes or rebuffs one took as so much private gain or loss.

For Edward this was satisfactory enough. Claiming his right of the eldest, he would annex the hero in the very frontispiece; and for the rest of the story his career, if chequered at intervals, was sure of heroic episodes and a glorious close. But his juniors, who had to put up with characters of a clay more mixed—nay, sometimes with undiluted villainy—were hard put to it on occasion to defend their other selves (as it was strict etiquette to do) from ignominy perhaps only too justly merited.

Edward was indeed a hopeless grabber. In the "Buffalo-book", for instance (so named from the subject of its principal picture, though indeed it dealt with varied slaughter in every zone), Edward was the stalwart, bearded figure, with yellow leggings and a powder-horn, who undauntedly discharged the fatal bullet into the shoulder of the great bull bison, charging home to within a yard of his muzzle. To me was allotted the subsidiary character of the friend who had succeeded in bringing down a cow; while Harold had to be content to hold Edward's spare rifle in the background, with evident signs of uneasiness. Farther on, again, where the magnificent chamois sprang rigid into mid-air, Edward, crouched dizzily against the precipice-face, was the sportsman from whose weapon a puff of white smoke was floating away. A bare-kneed guide was all that fell to my share, while poor Harold had to take the boy with the haversack, or abandon, for this occasion at least, all Alpine ambitions.

Of course the girls fared badly in this book, and it was not surprising that they preferred the "Pilgrim's Progress" (for instance), where women had a fair show, and there was generally enough of 'em to go round; or a good fairy story, wherein princesses met with a healthy appreciation. But indeed we were all best pleased with a picture wherein the characters just fitted us, in number, sex, and qualifications; and this, to us, stood for artistic merit.

All the Christmas numbers, in their gilt frames on the nursery-wall, had been gone through and allotted long ago; and in these, sooner or later, each one of us got a chance to figure in some satisfactory and brightly coloured situation. Few of the other pictures about the house afforded equal facilities. They were generally wanting in figures, and even when these were present they lacked dramatic interest. In this picture that I have to speak about, although the characters had a stupid way of not doing anything, and apparently not wanting to do anything, there was at least a sufficiency of them; so in due course they were allotted, too.

In itself the picture, which—in its ebony and tortoise-shell frame—hung in a corner of the dining-room, had hitherto possessed no special interest for us, and would probably never have been dealt with at all but for a revolt of the girls against a succession of books on sport, in which the illustrator seemed to have forgotten that there were such things as women in the world. Selina accordingly made for it one rainy morning, and announced that she was the lady seated in the centre, whose gown of rich, flowered brocade fell in such straight, severe lines to her feet, whose cloak of dark blue was held by a jewelled clasp, and whose long, fair hair was crowned with a diadem of gold and pearl. Well, we had no objection to that; it seemed fair enough, especially to Edward, who promptly proceeded to "grab" the armour-man who stood leaning on his shield at the lady's right hand. A dainty and delicate armour-man this! And

I confess, though I knew it was all right and fair and orderly, I felt a slight pang when he passed out of my reach into Edward's possession. His armour was just the sort I wanted myself— scalloped and fluted and shimmering and spotless; and, though he was but a boy by his beardless face and golden hair, the shattered spear-shaft in his grasp proclaimed him a genuine fighter and fresh from some such agreeable work. Yes, I grudged Edward the armour-man, and when he said I could have the fellow on the other side, I hung back and said I'd think about it.

This fellow had no armour nor weapons, but wore a plain jerkin with a leather pouch—a mere civilian—and with one hand he pointed to a wound in his thigh. I didn't care about him, and when Harold eagerly put in his claim, I gave way and let him have the man. The cause of Harold's anxiety only came out later. It was the wound he coveted, it seemed. He wanted to have a big, sore wound of his very own, and go about and show it to people, and excite their envy or win their respect. Charlotte was only too pleased to take the child-angel seated at the lady's feet, grappling with a musical instrument much too big for her. Charlotte wanted wings badly, and, next to those, a guitar or a banjo. The angel, besides, wore an amber necklace, which took her fancy immensely.

This left the picture allotted, with the exception of two or three more angels, who peeped or perched behind the main figures with a certain subdued drollery in their faces, as if the thing had gone on long enough, and it was now time to upset something or kick up a row of some sort. We knew these good folk to be saints and angels, because we had been told they were; otherwise we should never have guessed it. Angels, as we knew them in our Sunday books, were vapid, colourless, uninteresting characters, with straight up-and-down sort of figures, white nightgowns, white wings, and the same straight yellow hair parted in the middle. They were serious, even melancholy, and we had no desire to have any traffic with them. These bright bejewelled little persons, however, piquant of face and radiant of feather, were evidently hatched from quite a different egg, and we felt we might have interests in common with them. Short-nosed, shock-headed, with mouths that went up at the corners and with an evident disregard for all their fine clothes, they would be the best of good company, we felt sure, if only we could manage to get at them. One doubt alone disturbed my mind. In games requiring agility, those wings of theirs would give them a tremendous pull. Could they be trusted to play fair? I asked Selina, who replied scornfully that angels *always* played fair. But I went back and had another look at the brown-faced one peeping over the back of the lady's chair, and still I had my doubts.

When Edward went off to school a great deal of adjustment and re-allotment took place, and all the heroes of illustrated literature were at my call, did I choose to possess them. In this particular case, however, I made no haste to seize upon the armour-man. Perhaps it was because I wanted a *fresh* saint of my own, not a stale saint that Edward had been for so long a time. Perhaps it was rather that, ever since I had elected to be saintless, I had got into the habit of strolling off into the background, and amusing myself with what I found there.

A very fascinating background it was, and held a great deal, though so tiny. Meadow-land came first, set with flowers, blue and red, like gems. Then a white road ran, with wilful, un-called-for loops, up a steep, conical hill, crowned with towers, bastioned walls, and belfries; and down the road the little knights came riding, two and two. The hill on one side descended to water, tranquil, far-reaching, and blue; and a very curly ship lay at anchor, with one mast having an odd sort of crow's-nest at the top of it.

There was plenty to do in this pleasant land. The annoying thing about it was, one could never penetrate beyond a certain point. I might wander up that road as often as I liked, I was bound to be brought up at the gateway, the funny galleried, top-heavy gateway, of the little walled town. Inside, doubtless, there were high jinks going on; but the password was denied to me. I could get on board a boat and row up as far as the curly ship, but around the headland I might not go. On the other side, of a surety, the shipping lay thick. The merchants walked on the quay, and the sailors sang as they swung out the corded bales. But as for me, I must stay down in the meadow, and imagine it all as best I could.

Once I broached the subject to Charlotte, and found, to my surprise, that she had had the same joys and encountered the same disappointments in this delectable country. She, too, had walked up that road and flattened her nose against that port-cullis; and she pointed out something that I had overlooked— to wit, that if you rowed off in a boat to the curly ship, and got hold of a rope, and clambered aboard of her, and swarmed up the mast, and got into the crow's-nest, you could just see over the headland, and take in at your ease the life and bustle of the port. She proceeded to describe all the fun that was going on there, at such length and with so much particularity that I looked at her suspiciously. "Why, you talk as if you'd been in that crow's-nest yourself! " I said. Charlotte answered nothing, but pursed her mouth up and nodded violently for some minutes; and I could get nothing more out of her. I felt rather hurt. Evidently she had managed, somehow or other, to get up into that crow's-nest. Charlotte had got ahead of me on this occasion.

It was necessary, no doubt, that grown-up people should dress themselves up and go forth to pay calls. I don't mean that we saw any sense in the practice. It would have been much more reasonable to stay at home in your old clothes and play. But we recognised that these folk had to do many unaccountable things, and after all it was *their* life and not ours, and we were not in a position to criticise. Besides, they had many habits more objectionable than this one, which to us generally meant a free and untrammelled afternoon, wherein to play the devil in our own way. The case was different, however, when the press-gang was abroad, when prayers and excuses were alike disregarded, and we were forced into the service, like native levies impelled toward the foe less by the inherent righteousness of the cause than by the indisputable rifles of their white allies. This was unpardonable and altogether detestable. Still, the thing happened, now and again; and when it did, there was no arguing about it. The order was for the front, and we just had to shut up and march.

Selina, to be sure, had a sneaking fondness for dressing up and paying calls, though she pretended to dislike it, just to keep on the soft side of public opinion. So I thought it extremely mean in her to have the earache on that particular afternoon when Aunt Eliza ordered the pony-carriage and went on the war-path. I was ordered also, in the same breath as the pony-carriage; and, as we eventually trundled off, it seemed to me that the utter waste of that afternoon, for which I had planned so much, could never be made up nor atoned for in all the tremendous stretch of years that still lay before me.

The house that we were bound for on this occasion was a "big house"; a generic title applied by us to the class of residence that had a long carriage-drive through rhododendrons; and a portico propped by fluted pillars; and a grave butler who bolted back swing-doors, and came down steps, and pretended to have entirely forgotten his familiar intercourse with you at less serious moments; and a big hall, where no boots or shoes or upper garments were allowed to lie about frankly and easily, as with us; and where, finally, people were apt to sit about dressed up as if they were going on to a party.

The lady who received us was effusive to Aunt Eliza and hollowly gracious to me. In ten seconds they had their heads together and were hard at it talking *clothes*. I was left high and dry on a straight-backed chair, longing to kick the legs of it, yet not daring. For a time I was content to stare; there was lots to stare at, high and low and around. Then the inevitable fidgets came on, and scratching one's legs mitigated slightly, but did not entirely disperse them. My two warders were still deep in clothes; I slipped off my chair and edged cautiously around the room, exploring, examining, recording.

Many strange, fine things lay along my route—pictures and gimcracks on the walls, trinkets and globular old watches and snuff-boxes on the tables; and I took good care to finger everything within reach thoroughly and conscientiously. Some articles, in addition, I smelt. At last in my orbit I happened on an open

door, half concealed by the folds of a curtain. I glanced carefully around. They were still deep in clothes, both talking
together, and I slipped through.

This was altogether a more sensible sort of room that I had
got into; for the walls were honestly upholstered with books,
though these for the most part glimmered provoking through
the glass doors of their tall cases. I read their titles longingly,
breathing on every accessible pane of glass, for I dared not
attempt to open the doors, with the enemy encamped so near.
In the window, though, on a high sort of desk, there lay, all by
itself, a most promising-looking book, gorgeously bound. I
raised the leaves by one corner, and like scent from a pot-pourri
jar there floated out a brief vision of blues and reds, telling of
pictures, and pictures all highly coloured! Here was the right
sort of thing at last, and my afternoon would not be entirely
wasted. I inclined an ear to the door by which I had entered. Like
the brimming tide of a full-fed river the grand, eternal, inex-
haustible clothes-problem bubbled and eddied and surged
along. It seemed safe enough. I slid the book off its desk with
some difficulty, for it was very fine and large, and staggered
with it to the hearthrug—the only fit and proper place for
books of quality, such as this.

They were excellent hearthrugs in that house; soft and wide,
with the thickest of pile, and one's knees sank into them most
comfortably. When I got the book open there was a difficulty
at first in making the great stiff pages lie down. Most fortunately
the coal-scuttle was actually at my elbow, and it was easy to
find a flat bit of coal to lay on the refractory page. Really, it was
just as if everything had been arranged for me. This was not
such a bad sort of house after all.

The beginnings of the thing were gay borders—scrolls and
strap-work and diapered backgrounds, a maze of colour, with
small misshapen figures clambering cheerily up and down everywhere. But first I eagerly scanned what text there was in the
middle, in order to get a hint of what it was all about. Of
course I was not going to waste any time in reading. A clue, a
sign-board, a finger-post was all I required. To my dismay and

disgust it was all in a stupid foreign language! Really, the perversity of some people made one at times almost despair of the whole race. However, the pictures remained; pictures never lied, never shuffled nor evaded; and as for the story, I could invent it myself.

Over the page I went, shifting the bit of coal to a new position; and, as the scheme of the picture disengaged itself from out the medley of colour that met my delighted eyes, first there was a warm sense of familiarity, then a dawning recognition, and then—O then! along with blissful certainty came the imperious need to clasp my stomach with both hands, in order to repress the shout of rapture that struggled to escape—it was my own little city!

I knew it well enough, I recognised it at once, though I had never been quite so near it before. Here was the familiar gateway, to the left that strange, slender tower with its grim, square head shot far above the walls; to the right, outside the town, the hill—as of old—broke steeply down to the sea. But today everything was bigger and fresher and clearer, the walls seemed newly hewn, gay carpets were hung out over them, fair ladies and long-haired children peeped and crowded on the battlements. Better still, the portcullis was up—I could even catch a glimpse of the sunlit square within—and a dainty company was trooping through the gate on horseback, two and two. Their horses, in trappings that swept the ground, were gay as themselves; and *they* were the gayest crew, for dress and bearing, I had ever yet beheld. It could mean nothing else but a wedding, I thought, this holiday attire, this festal and solemn entry; and, wedding or whatever it was, I meant to be there. This time I would not be balked by any grim portcullis; this time I would slip in with the rest of the crowd, find out just what my little town was like, within those exasperating walls that had so long confronted me, and, moreover, have my share of the fun that was evidently going on inside. Confident, yet breathless with expectation, I turned the page.

Joy! At last I was in it, at last I was on the right side of those provoking walls; and, needless to say, I looked about me with much curiosity. A public place, clearly, though not such as I was used to. The houses at the back stood on a sort of colonnade, beneath which the people jostled and crowded. The upper stories were all painted with wonderful pictures. Above the straight line of the roofs the deep blue of a cloudless sky stretched from side to side. Lords and ladies thronged the foreground, while on a dais in the centre a gallant gentleman, just alighted off his horse, stooped to the fingers of a girl as bravely dressed out as Selina's lady between the saints; and round about stood venerable personages, robed in the most variegated clothing. There were boys, too, in plenty, with tiny red caps on their thick hair; and their shirts had bunched up and worked out at the waist, just as my own did so often, after chasing anybody; and each boy of them wore an odd pair of stockings, one blue and the other red. This system of attire went straight to my heart. I had tried the same thing so often, and had met with so much discouragement; and here, at last, was my justification, painted deliberately in a grown-up book! I looked about for my saint-friends—the armour-man and the other fellow—but they were not to be seen. Evidently they were unable to get off duty, even for a wedding, and still stood on guard in that green meadow down below. I was disappointed, too, that not an angel was visible. One or two of them, surely, could easily have been spared for an hour, to run up and see the show; and they would have been thoroughly at home here, in the midst of all the colour and the movement and the fun.

But it was time to get on, for clearly the interest was only just beginning. Over went the next page, and there we were, the whole crowd of us, assembled in a noble church. It was not easy to make out exactly what was going on; but in the throng I was delighted to recognise my angels at last, happy and very much at home. They had managed to get leave off, evidently, and must have run up the hill and scampered breathlessly through the gate; and perhaps they cried a little when they found the square empty, and thought the fun must be all over. Two of them had got hold of a great wax candle apiece, as much as they could stagger under, and were tittering sideways at each other as the grease ran bountifully over their clothes. A third had strolled in among the company, and was chatting to a young gentleman, with whom she appeared to be on the best of terms. Decidedly, this was the right breed of angel for us. None of your sick-bed or night-nursery business for them!

Well, no doubt they were now being married, He and She, just as always happened. And then, of course, they were going to live happily ever after; and *that* was the part I wanted to get to. Storybooks were so stupid, always stopping at the point where they became really nice; but this picture-story was only in its first chapters, and at last I was to have a chance of knowing *how* people lived happily ever after. We would all go home together, He and She and the angels, and I; and the armour-man would be invited to come and stay. And then the story would really begin, at the point where those other ones always left off. I turned the page, and found myself free of the dim and splendid church and once more in the open country.

This was all right; this was just as it should be. The sky was a fleckless blue, the flags danced in the breeze, and our merry bridal party, with jest and laughter, jogged down to the water-side. I was through the town by this time, and out on the other side of the hill, where I had always wanted to be; and, sure enough, there was the harbour, all thick with curly ships. Most of them were piled high with wedding-presents—bales of silk, and gold and silver plate, and comfortable-looking bags suggesting bullion; and the gayest ship of all lay close up to the carpeted landing-stage. Already the bride was stepping daintily down the gangway, her ladies following primly, one by one; a few minutes more and we should all be aboard, the hawsers would splash in the water, the sails would fill and strain. From the deck I should see the little walled town recede and sink and grow dim, while every plunge of our bows brought us nearer to the happy island—it was an island we were bound for, I knew well! Already I could see the island-people waving hands on the crowded quay, whence the little houses ran up the hill to the castle, crowning all with its towers and battlements. Once more we should ride together, a merry procession, clattering up the steep street and through the grim gateway; and then we should have arrived, then we should all dine together, then we should have reached home! And then—

Ow! Ow! Ow!

Bitter it is to stumble out of an opalescent dream into the cold daylight: cruel to lose in a second a sea voyage, an island, and a castle that was to be practically your own; but cruellest and bitterest of all to know, in addition to your loss, that the fingers of an angry aunt have you tight by the scruff of your neck. My beautiful book was gone too—ravished from my grasp by the dressy lady, who joined in the outburst of denunciation as heartily as if she had been a relative—and naught was left me but to blubber dismally, awakened of a sudden to the harshness of real things and the unnumbered hostilities of the actual world. I cared little for their reproaches, their abuse; but I sorrowed heartily for my lost ship, my vanished island, my uneaten dinner, and for the knowledge that, if I wanted any angels to play with, I must henceforth put up with the anaemic nightgowned nonentities that hovered over the bed of the Sunday-school child in the pages of the *Sabbath Improver*.

I was led ignominiously out of the house, in a pulpy, watery state, while the butler handled his swing-doors with a stony, impassive countenance, intended for the deception of the very elect, though it did not deceive me. I knew well enough that next time he was off duty, and strolled around our way, we should meet in our kitchen as man to man, and I would punch him and ask him riddles, and he would teach me tricks with corks and bits of string. So his unsympathetic manner did not add to my depression.

I maintained a diplomatic blubber long after we had been packed into our pony-carriage and the lodge-gate had clicked behind us, because it served as a sort of armour-plating against heckling and argument and abuse, and I was thinking hard and wanted to be let alone. And the thoughts that I was thinking were two. First I thought, "I've got ahead of Charlotte *this* time!"

And next I thought, "When I've grown up big, and have

money of my own, and a full-sized walking-stick, I will set out early one morning, and never stop till I get to that little walled town."

There ought to be no real difficulty in the task. It only meant asking here and asking there, and people were very obliging, and I could describe every stick and stone of it.

As for the island which I had never even seen, that was not so easy. Yet I felt confident that somehow, at some time, sooner or later, I was destined to arrive.

The Choosers

GILLIAN AVERY was born in Redhill, Surrey, in 1926, and her education at Dunottar School in Reigate was followed by two years with the *Surrey Mirror*, for whom she worked as a Junior Reporter. Between the years 1950 and 1954, she was employed as assistant illustrations editor on the *Oxford Junior Encyclopaedia*, during which time she married A. O. J. Cockshut, then a research Fellow of Balliol College, now a Fellow of Hertford College, Oxford. It was largely through her husband that Miss Avery developed the deep interest in Victorian life which reflects itself in all her work. Her first children's book, THE WARDEN'S NIECE, published in 1957, was set in Victorian Oxford, and was followed by other children's novels with Victorian settings. In addition to compiling a number of anthologies of Victorian stories for children, Miss Avery has written a short biographical study of the well-known 19th-century writer Mrs. Ewing, and in 1967 she became editor of "Gollancz Revivals"—a series of reprints of Victorian children's classics. Gillian Avery has one daughter, and lives in Oxford.

The youngest daughter of a country doctor, HESTER BURTON spent her childhood in Beccles, Suffolk. She was educated at Headington School, Oxford, and read English at St. Anne's College, Oxford. After her marriage to R. W. B. Burton, Fellow and Tutor in Classics at Oriel College, Oxford, Mrs. Burton taught English Literature at a girls' school for nine years, and worked as assistant editor in the revision of the *Oxford Junior Encyclopaedia*, besides editing such works as COLERIDGE AND THE WORDSWORTHS and TENNYSON for Oxford University Press. Her first book for children, THE GREAT GALE, was published in 1960, followed by three historical novels, for one of which, TIME OF TRIAL, Mrs. Burton was awarded the Carnegie Medal in 1963; her recent novel, IN SPITE OF ALL TERROR, is one of the very few children's books to have for its setting the Second World War. In 1969, THOMAS, a Quaker story, was published. Mrs. Burton and her husband live in a 17th-century mill house in a village just outside Oxford, and have three grown-up daughters.

PAULINE CLARKE took a degree in English at Somerville College, Oxford. Her first children's book, THE PEKINESE PRINCESS, was illustrated by her friend Cecil Leslie, whose home on the north Norfolk coast Pauline Clarke shared for years and who was to illustrate most of her later books. Because she has always liked writing not only different kinds of stories, but also stories for different ages of children, her books have both historical and contemporary settings, and she won the 1962 Carnegie Medal with a fantasy, THE TWELVE AND THE GENII (THE RETURN OF THE TWELVES), which in 1968 was awarded a Deutscher Jugendbuchpreis in its German edition. She has written a number of books for children under the name Helen Clare, the best-known being the "Five Dolls" stories. Her own favourite of her books is TOROLV THE FATHERLESS, a story of the Anglo-Saxons. Since her recent marriage to a don who teaches Anglo-Saxon history, Pauline Clarke has moved from Blakeney to live in Cambridge.

EILÍS DILLON was born in 1920 in Galway, the daughter of a Professor of Chemistry at the University, and her family lived for a time in a neighbouring village where the common language spoken was Irish. It was during this period that she gained an early insight into the mind of the western people of Ireland, and they and their country have remained her favourite background for stories both for children and adults. Although she studied music intensively when young in the hope of becoming a professional 'cellist, soon after her marriage to Cormac Ó Cuilleanáin—later to become Professor of University College, Cork, and subsequently Warden—Eilís Dillon settled down to writing regularly. She is the author of seven adult novels, many full-length children's stories as well as numerous shorter works, and a play which was put on at the Abbey Theatre in Dublin. In 1968 she translated from Irish the long 18th-century classic poem, LAMENT FOR ARTHUR O'LEARY, and over the years she has made three tours of the United States of America lecturing at Universities and Colleges on Irish poetry and Anglo-Irish literature. Eilís Dillon and her husband have recently returned to Dublin after a six-year stay in Rome, an experience which inspired the author to write several stories with Italian settings. They have two grown-up daughters and a son.

LEON GARFIELD was born in 1921 in Brighton, Sussex. He trained at first to be an artist, and then spent five years in the army in which he studied Biochemistry, and returned to work in a London laboratory, fitting his writing around the edges of his day. JACK HOLBORN, published in 1964, was Leon Garfield's first novel for young readers and in it he introduced the style reminiscent of 18th-century writing, which he has made so uniquely and powerfully his own. JACK HOLBORN was awarded the Gold Medal of the Boys' Clubs of America. Subsequent books followed: DEVIL-IN-THE-FOG (1966), which was the first winner of the *Guardian* Award; SMITH (1967) for which he was awarded the Arts Council Prize for the best book for older children for the period 1966–8; BLACK JACK (1968) and MR. CORBETT'S GHOST (1969). Most of his books are set in the 18th century, a period he has studied intensively and can evoke with complete conviction, peopling it with memorably full-blooded characters. DEVIL-IN-THE-FOG and SMITH were made into successful television films for children, and a full-colour film about Leon Garfield himself has been made by Penguin Books. Leon Garfield lives in Highgate, London, with his wife and daughter.

ALAN GARNER was born in Cheshire and educated at Alderley Edge Primary School, the Grammar School, Manchester, and Magdalen College, Oxford. In his early years, his formal education was interrupted by periods of illness, but he later went on to become a notable athlete. After a spell in the Royal Artillery he turned seriously to writing and his first book, THE WEIRDSTONE OF BRISINGAMEN, was published in 1960. This was followed by THE MOON OF GOMRATH (1963), ELIDOR (1965), and THE OWL SERVICE (1967), which was awarded both the Carnegie Medal and the *Guardian* Award for that year. Recognised as a landmark in writing for young people, THE OWL SERVICE has been filmed in colour by Granada Television, with a script by Alan Garner himself. Two books with photographs by Roger Hill bear witness to Alan Garner's passion for the Cheshire countryside and his abiding interest in its folklore and customs: these are THE OLD MAN OF MOW (1967), and HOLLY FROM THE BONGS (1966), the latter a Nativity play with music by William Mayne which was first performed by local children in the stable of a village inn. THE HAMISH HAMILTON BOOK OF GOBLINS (1969) is further evidence of Alan Garner's deep interest in the world of the supernatural and its effect on everyday lives.

Alan Garner lives in an inaccessible and beautiful fourteenth-century manor house, literally in the middle of a Cheshire field, which is overlooked by the giant Jodrell Bank telescope.

JANET McNEILL's early childhood was spent in Dublin where she was born in 1907 and lived until her family moved briefly to Birkenhead, Cheshire, in 1913. After gaining an M.A. degree in Classics at St. Andrews University in Scotland, she returned to Ireland, married a civil engineer, Robert Alexander, and settled in County Antrim for thirty-one years. Janet

McNeill's writing career has been long and varied: one-act plays for student productions while at University, stage and radio plays, magazine articles, several adult novels and numerous books for children of all ages, including three collections of short stories, most of them with Irish settings, TOM'S TOWER—a fantasy—and the 'Specs McCann' stories. Her two most recent children's novels, THE BATTLE OF ST. GEORGE WITHOUT and its sequel, GOODBYE DOVE SQUARE, were both inspired by her new surroundings in Bristol where she and her husband moved five years ago to be nearer their four grown-up children. Besides writing, Janet McNeill's interests lie with the theatre, and in gardening.

WILLIAM MAYNE was born in 1928. The Choir School in Canterbury, where he was educated, has formed the setting for several of his earlier books, including A SWARM IN MAY and CHORISTERS' CAKE. Since his first book for children was published in 1953, Mr. Mayne's output has been prodigious and in recent years he has widened his range to write for all ages of children, and has also edited a number of anthologies of folk- and fairy-tales, two of which were compiled in collaboration with the late Eleanor Farjeon. William Mayne has a great fondness for the Wensleydale countryside, having lived there for much of his life, and his story THE GRASS ROPE, for which he was awarded the Carnegie Medal in 1958, takes place in the Yorkshire Dales, as do many of his books. He has a great interest in the past, and a "quest" for a long-lost or long-forgotten object is often a feature of his plots. His other interests include music, his two black cats, cars (especially old Bentleys) and numerous mechanical devices. The new house to which he refers in his introductory note will be his third home in the old Yorkshire village of Thornton Rust "where," he says, "my aim in life is to make time to look at things, hear them, sometimes write about them, and now and then even think about them."

Born in 1909, JAMES REEVES was educated at Stowe and Cambridge, and has since lived mainly in the country, his strong feeling for the English landscape having influenced much of his work. He spent many years teaching in schools, but since 1952 has devoted himself entirely to writing and broadcasting. He has published several books of poems, the best known being THE WANDERING MOON and THE BLACKBIRD IN THE LILAC; stories, including MULBRIDGE MANOR, PIGEONS AND PRINCESSES and THE COLD FLAME; picture books, including THE TROJAN HORSE and RHYMING WILL: many plays, and a number of anthologies of verse and prose, notably

A GOLDEN LAND and THE MERRY-GO-ROUND. Mr. Reeves lives in Lewes, Sussex, where his interests outside writing include gardening, listening to music—to folk-song, in particular—poetry, education, and everything that interests young readers. He has three children.

IAN SERRAILLIER was born in London and educated at Brighton College and St. Edmund Hall, Oxford. For much of his life he has been a school-master, teaching in public and grammar schools, but since 1961 he has devoted most of his time to the writing of fiction and non-fiction, poems, retellings of ancient legends for children, and educational programmes for television. Many of his books have been translated into foreign languages and his poems, too, have been broadcast all over the world. The best known of his novels, THE SILVER SWORD, was serialised in a BBC children's television programme and, like THE IVORY HORN, his retelling of the Roland legend, was a runner-up for the Carnegie Medal. Ian Serraillier is the founder and co-editor—with his wife—of Heinemann's New Windmill Series of widely varied fiction, travel and biography for older readers, and he also takes part in broadcasts in the BBC schools programmes from time to time. He loves mountains, hills and the sea, and lives and works in an old flint cottage near Chichester in Sussex. Mr. Serraillier and his wife have three daughters and a son.

NOEL STREATFEILD was born in 1897 at Frant in Sussex, the daughter of a country vicar (who later became Suffragan Bishop of Lewes). She is the great-great-grandchild of the 19th-century prison reformer, Elizabeth Fry. Having decided on an acting career at an early age, Miss Streatfeild trained at the Academy of Dramatic Art and remained on the stage for nine years, appearing in plays, a revue and one pantomime. She was thus well-equipped with authentic background material for the many stories featuring theatrical families with which she initially made her name as a children's writer. Some of her best-known titles are BALLET SHOES, THE CIRCUS IS COMING (Carnegie Medal Winner for 1938) and WHITE BOOTS. In 1954 came the publication in book form of Miss Streatfeild's THE BELL FAMILY, which had been serialised on the BBC during the previous six years; it was also adapted for television. Apart from her extensive number of family stories for children of all ages, Noel Streatfeild has written several adult novels as well as two autobiographies recounting her own childhood experiences: A VICARAGE FAMILY and AWAY FROM THE VICARAGE. Today she is still writing busily away from her London home in Belgravia.

ROSEMARY SUTCLIFF was born at West Clandon, Surrey. Her father was a naval officer, and she and her mother accompanied him around the world until his retirement, when the family settled in North Devon. Owing to an illness developed in early childhood, she was taught by her mother until the age of nine, and it was during this time that she first became familiar with the history of the Roman Empire, ancient legends and fairy-tales, and the work of Kipling, all of which were to influence much of her later writing. After leaving school when she was fourteen, Rosemary Sutcliff trained as a painter at the Bideford School of Art, subsequently becoming a professional miniaturist whose work was exhibited at the Royal Academy. It was not until she was in her mid-twenties that Miss Sutcliff transferred her talents from painting to writing, having found this medium the more satisfying and enjoyable of the two. Her first book, THE CHRONICLES OF ROBIN HOOD, appeared in 1950, to be followed by more than twenty historical stories for children, many of which were set during the Roman occupation of Britain and include such titles as THE EAGLE OF THE NINTH, THE LANTERN BEARERS (Carnegie Medal Winner for 1959) and THE BRIDGE BUILDERS. She has also written a critical survey of Rudyard Kipling, a re-telling of the Anglo-Saxon poem BEOWULF, and THE HIGH DEEDS OF FINN MAC COOL— a collection of legendary tales about the great Irish hero. Miss Sutcliff now lives and writes in a country cottage near Arundel in Sussex.

MARY TREADGOLD was born in London and educated at St. Paul's School and Bedford College, London. Although she started writing between the ages of six and twelve, her first book to be published, WE COULDN'T LEAVE DINAH, was written when her school and university days were over, in an air-raid shelter during the London Blitz—"to take my mind off the falling bombs", she says. "Nobody was more surprised than I when the book was awarded the Carnegie Medal!" (1941). After the war Miss Tread-gold wrote a sequel to the earlier book, NO PONIES, and spent some years as Literary Editor of the BBC Overseas Book Review Programme. Her later titles include THE POLLY HARRIS, two further pony books, THE HERON RIDE and RETURN TO THE HERON, and several stories for younger children which have either Victorian or contemporary working-class backgrounds. Miss Treadgold now lives in Chelsea, London, where she spends a con-siderable amount of time in writing.

Born in Nottingham in 1909, GEOFFREY TREASE was educated at Notting-ham High School and Queen's College, Oxford. At twenty-four he wrote his first book for young people, BOWS AGAINST THE BARONS, which was followed by many other junior historical novels, including CUE FOR TREASON, THE HILLS OF VARNA and THE WHITE NIGHTS OF ST. PETERSBURG. Meanwhile, in 1949, he began his sequence of five "Bannermere" stories depicting modern teenagers in a day-school setting, going on to write THE MAYTHORN STORY and CHANGE AT MAYTHORN laid in the West Midland countryside where he has made his home, on the Malvern (or "Maythorn") Hills. Altogether, Mr. Trease has written more than sixty books, including adult novels and historical works such as THE GRAND TOUR and THE ITALIAN STORY, biographies for teenagers, such as BYRON: A POET DANGEROUS TO KNOW, and a history of the modern world, THIS IS YOUR CENTURY, which won the *New York Herald Tribune* award for the best book in the 12-to-16 age group. His work appears in sixteen languages and is the subject of a study, entitled GEOFFREY TREASE, by Margaret Meek.

ELFRIDA VIPONT was born in Manchester in 1902, and educated at Manchester High School for Girls and the Mount School, York. After further studies in History and Music, she became a professional singer, free-lance writer and lecturer. In 1926 she married a research technologist, R. P. Foulds. During the Second World War she served as Headmistress of the Quaker Evacuation School at Yealand Manor. Since then Miss Vipont has written more than thirty books, and was awarded the Carnegie Medal in 1950 for LARK ON THE WING, the second of five family stories following the musical career of Kit Haverard, which are perhaps the best known of all her works. In addition to writing, Miss Vipont devotes much of her time to serving on Quaker committees; she has also travelled in the United States, Canada, Australia and New Zealand lecturing to young people and giving talks on radio and television. She now lives in the small Lancashire village of Yealand Conyers, where she is an active participant in community affairs and is frequently visited by her very large family which includes four daughters and thirteen grandchildren.

BARBARA WILLARD started writing stories at the age of seven, and soon after leaving school she completed her first novel. Following the family tradition she went on the stage for some years but from this she retired, disappointed, to re-write the earlier novel and eventually to have it published. She wrote several more novels, worked in the story departments of various film companies, reviewed and wrote articles and short stories for magazines. During the last ten years—which she considers to be the most pleasant period of her life—Barbara Willard has been writing mainly for children. Her books for older readers have included THE BATTLE OF WEDNESDAY WEEK, THE FAMILY TOWER, THE TOPPLING TOWERS, and THE GROVE OF GREEN HOLLY; THE PENNY PONY, A DOG AND A HALF and SURPRISE ISLAND are just three of the many stories she has written for younger children. Barbara Willard now lives at Nutley in Sussex where she is an enthusiastic gardener, keeps cats and dogs, enjoys driving, cooking—and eating—and remains passionately interested in the theatre.

Since the publication of her first book in 1932, URSULA MORAY WILLIAMS has written more than fifty children's stories, many of which have been illustrated either by herself or by her twin sister, Barbara Arrason, and several of which have been made into plays and acted as far afield as Japan. Her ADVENTURES OF THE LITTLE WOODEN HORSE has been in print since 1938, and is now regarded as a children's classic.

Born in 1911, married to an aircraft engineer, Ursula Moray Williams has four sons and several grandchildren, and lives in Beckford, Gloucestershire, where she is a Justice of the Peace and governor of several local schools. Outside the field of children's books, her chief interests lie in her home—she is a very keen gardener—and in village life.

The Chosen Authors

JOAN AIKEN, the daughter of Conrad Aiken, was born in 1924 and now lives in Arundel, Sussex. She received the *Guardian* Award for children's fiction in 1968.

HANS CHRISTIAN ANDERSEN was born at Odense in Denmark in 1805 and died in 1875. *The Emperor's New Clothes* is one of the best known of all his classic fairy tales.

JANE AUSTEN was born in 1775 and died in 1817. She lived for some time in the village of Chawton where her house can still be visited. *The History of England* is one of her "juvenilia", written at the age of fourteen.

RAY BRADBURY, the distinguished American science fiction writer, was born in 1920. *The Fog Horn* is from his collection of stories entitled THE GOLDEN APPLES OF THE SUN. Ray Bradbury lives in Los Angeles.

ELIZABETH ENRIGHT was born in 1909 and died in 1968. She lived in New York City. In 1939 she was awarded the Newbery Medal for *Thimble Summer*.

JULIANA HORATIA EWING, the daughter of the Victorian writer Mrs. Gatty, was born in 1841 and died in 1885. She was a regular contributor to the popular Victorian children's paper *Aunt Judy's Magazine*. Her best-known books are DADDY DARWIN'S DOVECOT and JACKANAPES.

ELEANOR FARJEON was born in 1881 and died in 1965. She lived for many years in Hampstead, London, where one of the alleys was the model for Mellin's Court. *The Glass Peacock* is taken from THE LITTLE BOOKROOM which won the Carnegie Medal in 1955 and the first Hans Christian Andersen Award in 1956.

KENNETH GRAHAME was born in 1859 and died in 1932. He was for many years Secretary of the Bank of England, and lived in Berkshire beside the

215

River Thames, the inspiration for his greatly loved book THE WIND IN THE WILLOWS. *Its Walls Were as of Jasper* comes from DREAM DAYS.

TOVE JANSSON, the Finnish writer, was born in 1914. The story is taken from TALES FROM MOOMIN VALLEY. Tove Jansson won the Hans Christian Andersen Award in 1966, and her *Moomin* books have been translated into many languages.

RUDYARD KIPLING was born in India in 1865 and died in 1936. His last home was Bateman's, a farm house in Sussex, now in the care of the National Trust and open to visitors. *The Miracle of Purun Bhagat* is from THE SECOND JUNGLE BOOK and *The Maltese Cat* from THE DAY'S WORK.

MARGHANITA LASKI, distinguished novelist, critic, and broadcaster, was born in 1915 and lives in London.

KATHERINE MANSFIELD was born in New Zealand in 1883, lived much of her short life in England, and died in France in 1923. *The Doll's House* is taken from THE COLLECTED STORIES OF KATHERINE MANSFIELD.

BILL NAUGHTON is widely known as a playwright for stage and television. He was born in Ireland in 1910 and lives in London.

FRANK O'CONNOR was born in Ireland in 1903 and died in 1967. He was at one time a Director of the famous Abbey Theatre in Dublin.

ARTHUR RANSOME was born in 1884 and died in 1967. He is known the world over for the twelve books in the *Swallows and Amazons* sequence, one of which, PIGEON POST, was awarded the first Carnegie Medal in 1936. Arthur Ransome lived in the English Lake District, where many of the books are set. *The Tale of the Silver Saucer and the Transparent Apple* is from OLD PETER'S RUSSIAN TALES.

SAKI (Hector Hugh Munro) was a Scottish short story writer who was born in 1870, and was killed in action (1916) during the First World War.

216

Barbara Willard

Gillian Avery

Alan Garner

Ursu

Pauline Clarke

Cynnie Vipont

Geoff

Janet McNeill

Rosemary Sutcliff